Thank you.
To all the family and friends who have supported me
through this journey, thank you.

This is a work of fiction. Names, characters, places, and incidents are either the product of the author's imagination or are used fictitiously, and any resemblance to actual persons living or dead, business establishments, events, or locales, is entirely coincidental.

Husband of Convenience: Kaya and Paul Book 1
Conrad Chronicles Book 1

COPYRIGHT © 2021 by Emelia Publishers LLC and C.K. Mackenzie

All rights reserved. No part of this book may be used or reproduced in any manner whatsoever without written permission of the author except in the case of brief quotations embodied in critical articles or reviews.

Contact Information: ckmackenzieauthor@gmail.com

Cover Art by Lynn Andreozzi

Publishing History
First Edition, 2021
Digital ISBN 979-8-9850526-0-2

Published in the United States of America

Chapter One

Cairo, Egypt
September 1784

The deafening quiet echoed around Kaya, and she strained to hear any sound other than her breath. A call or song from Derya, sounds from the kitchens. She closed her eyes, as if that might enhance her hearing, and strived to catch even the faintest whisper. The familiarity of life, the echoes of companionship she'd taken for granted.

Only the pounding of her heart resonated.

Eyes squeezed tight, Kaya tried to remember what not being alone sounded like. She moved her legs just to hear noise. Her linen dress slid across the tile floor, echoing like a hawk's call.

Throat closed, grief choking her, Kaya pressed her palms to the floor. She needed the reminder—she still lived.

No more tears. Kaya had cried enough since learning of Derya's death. The empty ache for the woman who raised her burned her throat. Each grain of sand dug into her palms, scratched against her skin with no relief. Her grandfather's lessons had not prepared her for this *emptiness*.

None of her fighting skills, her learning, practicing, studying—nothing kept the horrible, stabbing pain at bay.

Kaya sat in silence in the late September heat. The drought dried the winds as well as the rains, leaving the air thick and heavy. The last of the sun's rays barely peeked through the locked shutters.

Always locked. Hiding her inside this too quiet house.

It closed around her, cutting off her air. Gasping, Kaya tore her gaze from the fading sunlight and the outside world she never knew. Instead, she stared at the gold-encrusted lattice around the door, barely visible but so familiar despite the dimness.

The barrier between her and the world. Derya hadn't lived with barriers—she enjoyed life outside this house.

Angry heat flushed Kaya's cheeks and spread down her chest. Mortified, remorseful, she swallowed the rush of bitter resentment.

Derya deserved better.

"You can't go, my child."

Kaya's gaze jerked from the door to her grandfather, sneaky and silent, even in his retirement. General Tahir ibn Zanki ibn al-Nafis stood tall and proud and adamant in the decorated room. Stubborn old man. Her grandfather may have been a brilliant strategist, commanding the Egyptian forces, but when it came to her, his desire to keep her safe blinded him.

"No one will know who I am." Kaya's insistence was faint, barely audible over the roaring in her ears. In the stifling antechamber of the main room, she stood and straightened her shoulders, glaring at her grandfather. "No one *knows* who I am, that I even exist."

"Kaya—"

"Please, Gidd." Kaya begged for the first time since childhood.

She'd long stopped asking the impossible; he never yielded to her pleas. Today, however, wasn't about seeing *en-Nīl* or sneaking into one of the dinners he hosted for foreign emissaries. She needed this chance, needed to say goodbye.

"Derya meant everything to me. She has no one else in Cairo." Kaya swallowed and willed the tears away. "She's my family. Who will cleanse her?"

"She would not want you exposing yourself during her funeral," Tahir snapped. He took her hand, rough and calloused around hers, and patted her knuckles gently, soft and understanding despite his words. He said nothing of Derya's funeral rites. "Kaya, my child, I know how you feel about her. But Derya wouldn't want you endangering yourself simply to see her grave."

Resentful laughter burned her throat, and her fingers clenched around his. Kaya held back the mocking words that wanted to burst free. Derya died in a riot, trying to buy what little food remained in the drought-stricken city.

Even the great beys of Egypt were not immune to famine. Unlike so many in Cairo, Kaya couldn't flee to Istanbul or one of the outlying provinces.

"I must leave now, Kaya. Abdul waits for me with the horses." He kissed her forehead and stepped back. "Please stay inside. I'll return before supper. Then we'll talk."

Gidd guided her down the hall to the rear doors, his progress slow with the pronounced limp in his left leg. Her only solace, the gardens, were nothing more than an extension of her prison. Kaya breathed in deeply the stale, dry air but only found decay, hopelessness, death.

She choked.

She pulled her hand from Tahir's and sat in a chair by the table where she and Derya used to eat. *Used to eat.* In a moment of weakness, she rested her forehead in her hand and closed her eyes against the blue and white geometric tiles she knew as intimately as everything else in this house.

Gidd hesitated. "Kaya."

Kaya's head jerked up. She dropped her hand and narrowed her eyes. He never hesitated. Not once, not over anything. Gidd planned her life as methodically as he planned a troop engagement on the field of battle.

"Yes?" She stiffened, neck aching from the sudden tension knotting her muscles.

"I wanted to wait, but Derya's death—" He paused. Kaya frowned. "I know you wish to see Derya one last—" He cut himself off. Kaya's unease grew, a swell of apprehension tightening her chest. "Please don't leave the house, Kaya. Not even for Derya. The Ottomans have returned."

Her stomach dropped, as if the ground had fallen from beneath her. The anger and grief burning in the pit of her stomach froze in terror.

"What?" The question sounded weak and frightened. Rigid with alarm, struggling to breathe past the fear closing in on her, Kaya curled her fingers into the hard tabletop. She refused to be cowed. "When?" She asked, stronger. "It's been—you said they left Cairo. Hadn't asked questions in over a decade. Why now?"

"I do not know." Face lined with weariness, Tahir rested his arms on the table and held her gaze. "Perhaps they suddenly remembered the price on your head. Maybe the famine offered an opportunity. Money, greed, is a powerful motivator, Kaya."

She nodded, or thought she did, but she didn't feel her head move. Her fingers numbed in the afternoon heat. "Why—what—" Kaya struggled to find the logic she prided herself on. "The riot in the souk, was that planned by the Ottomans?"

"I don't believe so." Gidd took her hands again, but she barely felt the pressure. Still, she was grounded by his touch. "It wasn't the first riot, and with the crop failures, it won't be the last, either."

No, the Ottomans needn't encourage rioting, not with the ever-depleting stores of grain. Though, considering they wanted a return to power over Egypt, anything was possible.

"Derya." Kaya licked suddenly dry lips. "Did she know of the Ottomans' return?"

"Not to my knowledge." Gidd's voice softened, and he squeezed her fingers, warming them slightly. "I found out only yesterday morning."

Derya died just after sunrise. She had ventured to the souk in search of food. Tahir stood—she didn't remember him sitting—and rested his large hand on her shoulder. She covered it with her own, comforted by his touch.

"Gidd."

"I have already made plans, Kaya."

"Plans?" Her head jerked up, and she stared at her grandfather in the twilight. "What plans? What—"

He stepped into the shadows of the doorway. "An old friend from India. I've arranged your marriage to Sergeant Paul Hartley, who will escort you from Cairo to England."

Kaya opened her mouth, but no words emerged. She blinked up at Gidd and tried to stand, but she fell back into the chair. Her legs betrayed her, weakening under the absurdity of his declaration. Determined to confront him, Kaya pushed against the chair but stumbled over it.

"Marriage? Friend?" Annoyed with her unusual display of inelegance, she untangled her legs and skirts from the chair. Before she managed to do so, Tahir disappeared into the house. She raced after him. "What do you mean? Gidd—"

"It's done, Kaya. You leave tonight."

He moved much faster than he had when guiding her into the gardens. By the time she reached the entryway, he had already slammed the front door closed. Tempted to yank it open and follow him into the streets, Kaya hesitated. Her hand rested on the wooden locking bar, fingers tightening around it in indecision. Long years of locking herself away from the outside world tempted her to slide the beam home.

In the end, habit had her reaching for the wooden mechanism, then securing it. Once more, she stood on this side of the door, locked away from the world.

"Marriage?" Kaya blinked at the door.

She backed away, as if it might catch fire. Her back hit the far wall, and Kaya stood alone in an empty, echoing house with no company except the sound of her breath. Hands limp at her sides, mind racing for answers, she slid down onto the floor.

Derya would never have allowed such actions. Neither this show of weakness nor the coarseness of sitting on the entryway floor.

The granddaughter of an Egyptian general did *not* sit on stone floors.

"Derya." Kaya closed her eyes against the well of grief.

She pressed the heels of her hands hard against her forehead. Slowly, the tightness in her throat eased and the pricking behind her eyes stopped. Resting her head on her drawn-up knees, Kaya wiped away the dampness and dug in a pocket for her handkerchief.

As quietly as possible, she cleaned up, finding the noise disrespectful in the mournful dusk.

Eyes on the door, which was only a faint outline now that the sun had disappeared behind the surrounding buildings, she stood and stepped noiselessly to the entrance. Her exit. Her escape. Kaya's fingers brushed over the gold gilt she'd long ago memorized, even in darkness.

"I can leave." Her words barely reached her ears. "I can walk out these doors, and no one will ever know who I am."

Her heart beat too loudly, too painfully. How could she run from her grandfather without even saying goodbye? Kaya hated the hollow, cold feeling, but fear tightened its fist around her heart. Her entire life, Gidd had dictated her actions—her studies, her training, her every movement. She'd learned, she'd practiced, but she had never experienced.

"You taught me how to survive," Kaya whispered, though her grandfather had long ago left. "I know more about strategy than the greatest generals; I speak five languages; I am an expert markswoman. I do not want to hide anymore,

Gidd." She opened her eyes and straightened her shoulders. "I refuse."

A hot breeze rushed through the house. It was the first breeze in days, and it struck her like a slap. Tendrils of hair escaped her intricate braids and stuck to the base of her neck.

Kaya blinked and lit an oil lamp, letting the flickering light illuminate the entryway.

For most of her life, she'd dreamed of leaving Cairo and exploring the world. Embracing freedom. Now, the moment she'd waited for danced before her, an enticement she didn't know how to ignore. Or grasp. Kaya always imagined Derya at her side, despite the woman's insistence that she had grown too old for such travel.

Her fingers brushed the khanjar at her waist. She didn't need the reminder that she knew how to defend herself, but the weight of the dagger comforted her.

"Marriage." The word sounded foreign. "To an Englishman?"

Derya had discussed such a concept, of course, but neither of them had truly believed marriage would be in Kaya's future. Anyone her grandfather contracted her with would need to know who she was, and those secrets could never be revealed.

Marriage was a problem Kaya had never anticipated. Never worried about. Now that it lay before her, she didn't know what to do.

Kaya whirled from the door and headed for the stairs. On the first step, she frowned and looked around the dimly lit hallway. Flickering shadows amplified the sound of her skirts—that had to be the odd noise she heard.

She listened but heard nothing further.

She breathed shallowly and shifted her weight, listening, waiting. There. Scratching. Not a rat or a dog scavenging for food. She couldn't place it.

Chills danced over her arms, and Kaya reached for her khanjar. Without a sound, she pulled it from its scabbard and turned tightly in place, careful of her skirts. Crouched low, she angled her back to the wall and listened. Annoyed now that she'd lit a lamp and therefore lost the element of surprise, Kaya looked to the tightly shuttered windows.

It happened so gradually she almost didn't catch it. The lock slid back, and the front door eased open. A thief! Shocked that anyone in Cairo would dare enter this house, Kaya tensed and waited for the intruder.

A sliver of light slipped across the floor, immediately blocked by a body. Kaya tightened her fingers around the hilt of her dagger and eased into the shadows of an alcove. The door closed so silently, if she hadn't witnessed it herself, Kaya would've thought it hadn't happened.

She calculated the distance between her and the door, then the approximate distance the intruder had already moved. Before the person had the chance to fully step into the entryway, Kaya leaped across the space He faced opposite her, staring into the darkness of the inner quarter.

Kaya pressed the knife to the man's back, over his kidney, just beneath his ribs. He stood a head taller than she, and Kaya steadied her stance and pressed the dagger harder into his back.

"Who are you?" she demanded.

"Ah, hello." The stranger spoke in English, hands slowly rising.

Shocked, Kaya faltered. "English?"

Movements even and slow, he turned but made no move to disarm her. Kaya backed up two steps, refusing to take her eyes off this person who had casually broken into her home like a thief.

The man turned slowly to face her. He held his hands out, much as Gidd did when she managed to best him in a sword fight. Dressed in a faded red coat far too warm for an Egypt summer and boots in need of a good polishing, his direct gaze followed her every movement.

At a loss, she scrambled for what happened next. Never, not once in all her years, had she ever spoken to a stranger. Exposed, uncertain, Kaya straightened and met the man's gaze defiantly.

"Who are you?" Kaya picked up her khanjar and balanced it in her palm. She spoke in the precise English Gidd had taught her. "Why did you break in?"

In the faint light, she couldn't tell if his eyes were blue or green. His sharp nose twitched, his thin lips twisting in a semblance of a smile. He gestured to her dagger, but Kaya ignored him.

"Hmm." His lips curved slightly, and Kaya wondered why. "I came to see General Tahir ibn Zanki ibn al-Nafis."

He said Gidd*'s* name carefully, pronouncing each syllable. Kaya's eyes narrowed. "Why?"

"He invited me." The words came quick and smooth, but then the man stopped and cleared his throat. "I'm Sergeant Paul Hartley with the East India Company Army."

Sergeant Hartley. Kaya made a noise she couldn't identify. The anger that flushed her cheeks felt all too familiar. Gidd brought this man here to marry her. Kaya stilled—the East India Company? They had no one in Cairo. Had the sergeant traveled from India? When, exactly, had her grandfather written this man?

Sergeant Hartley didn't drop his hands, in fact he held them as steadily, as if he did so often. Kaya tilted her chin and refused to allow this man to keep her so off balance. "Why break in? Why not knock like polite society?"

His lips curved into a smile she couldn't decipher, but his eyes stayed on hers, watchful. "I'm an Englishman in Cairo after sunset."

"That does not explain you breaking into my home." Kaya balanced on the balls of her feet, ready for an attack. Or *to* attack. "How do I know you are Sergeant Hartley?"

"I have the general's letter, if you'll allow me?" He gestured to his coat with one hand, and Kaya nodded.

He withdrew the thick paper she knew Gidd used. He often wrote correspondence at the table while she studied. Kaya knew much of his work, but apparently her grandfather kept secrets from her. Important ones.

Sergeant Hartley held out the paper but didn't step closer. Eyes on his, Kaya took it without lowering her khanjar. Stepping out of arm's reach, though she suspected this man could easily traverse the distance, she opened the folded missive.

It was written in Tahir's hand, with his seal at the bottom and a line just above that in Egyptian that granted the sergeant permission to enter the city. It seemed legitimate. Kaya skimmed the English words, but the substance of the letter mattered less than the letter itself.

"Sergeant Hartley." Kaya met his gaze again. He hadn't moved, but he held himself at the ready. "I am not marrying you."

Chapter Two

Paul's eyebrows shot up, and he barely swallowed a chuckle. The sound came out in a strangled burst of smothered amusement. Well, he hadn't anticipated *that*. Considering the dagger the woman before him held, perhaps he should have.

"I see." At an unfamiliar loss for words, Paul watched her.

She was taller than he expected—and armed. She met his gaze straight on and refused to back down. Respect. That was the feeling worming its way through him, a surprising respect for Tahir's granddaughter.

She lowered the letter, but not the dagger. Impressed, he kept his hands raised. He still clearly felt the tip of her dagger digging into the small of his back, directly over his kidneys. She would stab him, of that he had no doubt.

No, he had nothing to say to her confident pronouncement. Instead, he flexed his fingers and smiled one of his most charming grins. She didn't so much as blink. "May I lower my hands?"

For a long moment, she stared at him, watching him carefully. Paul all but heard her internal debate. He fully expected her to refuse his request.

"You may." She did not, however, sheath her dagger.

"I promised your grandfather I'd see you out of Cairo." He glanced around the foyer, eyes bouncing from the woman to the gold-encrusted door, then to the bejeweled credenza next to her and back before she blinked. "I understand the city is in the midst of famine."

Her chin tilted up again, lips pursed, dark eyes shadowed with anger she couldn't quite hide. "Be that as it may, I'm not here to debate obvious facts. I've no desire to marry you. I've no desire to marry *anyone*. I've no *need* to marry anyone."

Paul's lips twitched at her confident pronouncement. He'd expected a lot of things upon entering Egypt and finally walking through the imposing gates of Cairo. He had not expected such fire in the woman before him. He'd expected a meek, slight thing, though Paul had no idea where that image came from. The beauty and passion of the reality warmed a part of him he'd thought long dead.

Nonetheless, he was standing in her home, at knifepoint, and he had obviously broken in. At least she hadn't asked where he'd procured the general unlocking mechanism.

"You plan to walk out of the gates on your own?" he snorted, entirely uncertain why he was arguing with her. Part of him acknowledged she was the first to argue with him in so long, he couldn't remember the last person to say no to him. He found it refreshing.

"Yes."

"And your grandfather?"

He knew the moment he said it that doing so had been a tactical error. Her dark eyes narrowed, the light from the oil lamp dancing in them, and her fingers tightened on the hilt of her dagger. She drew herself up, shoulders back, and looked every bit the warrior he knew her grandfather to be.

"Do not speak of what you don't understand." Her words, clear and crisp, snarled across the distance. He felt their power as forcefully as a slap. "Why did you break into my home?"

Not one to forget anything, was she? Paul shrugged, but the movement did nothing to ease the stiffness in his muscles or the cramping in his belly. Hands loose at his sides, he forced them not to shake or brush his own dagger. Then he met her gaze and lied.

"I had been warned that Cairo does not like outsiders

after dark. I have no papers, I don't speak Egyptian, and am clearly"—he waved a hand down his red coat— "an Englishman."

She watched him with a steadiness he envied. So still, so vigilant, Paul wondered why Tahir thought she needed protection—other than the obvious, of course. A woman? She'd be killed before she left the gates. Or worse.

"I'm afraid we haven't had a proper introduction." Paul formally bowed, holding her gaze as he did so. "I am Sergeant Paul Hartley of the East India Company Army. To whom have I the pleasure of speaking?"

The flickering lamplight highlighted her sharp cheeks, her elegant nose, the slight point of her chin. Her eyes, however, captivated him. Dark even in the lamplight, they held a longing she couldn't quite hide.

"Kaya." Her lips parted, as if to say more, and her gaze flickered—just slightly, barely enough to notice.

Paul noticed. "*Madaam* Kaya." Damn if he didn't enjoy the way her name rolled off his tongue. "I brought fresh goat's milk." He pulled a small jug from his satchel with one hand and dug around for the bundle of cinnamon with the other. "And cinnamon."

Kaya blinked. "Where did you find milk and cinnamon?"

Ah. Yes, that. Paul held out the items. He hadn't intended on using them as an offering, but needs must and all that rubbish. "I am very resourceful."

"Thank you." Kaya crossed the foyer, dagger still in hand, and accepted the gifts. Paul admired her alertness.

"I think it's best we leave as soon as possible." He lowered his hands, once more careful not to touch his dagger. Her gaze flicked to his, there and gone in the beat of a butterfly's wings. "Before anyone suspects."

Kaya scowled and opened her mouth to argue. Paul

had the feeling she had questions—and a lot of them. If Tahir answered her questions like he'd answered Paul's, no wonder Kaya resisted this marriage. In the day and a half since Paul had stumbled through the gates, half dead from dehydration and that damned desert, Tahir had offered his hospitality at a grand house on the other side of town, but he had not offered answers.

"Why did you come to Cairo?" Her question was a sharp bullet intent on finding its home.

Paul only half lied. "Tahir requested my presence."

"Why did you agree to this marriage?"

His gaze found and held hers for a long moment. He hadn't expected her protests or reluctance or, for that matter, to find her here. Then again, Paul hadn't expected to go through with this marriage, either. Caught now, he saw little choice but to proceed.

It seemed both their wishes were dust in the desert.

"It was time for a change." The honesty in those words surprised him far more than Kaya.

"Change?" Kaya repeated and shook her head. "I do not understand."

Eyes burning in the darkness, he stepped forward. "I swear to you, *Madaam* Kaya, I'll see you safely out of Cairo and into England."

Stunned at his declaration, at the certainty and conviction behind it, Paul locked his jaw against any further vows. What was he thinking? What the hell had he meant by those words, and where the hell had they come from?

Tahir.

Paul owed the man much, though the general didn't realize it. Or maybe he did. Maybe Tahir knew what had happened in the ten years since their last meeting. Paul hoped not. He wanted no one to know what those years had been like—he didn't want to remember himself.

"Change," he repeated just as a short, coded knock sounded on the door. "We'll work it out, *Madaam* Kaya, I promise you. But I respect Tahir"—not a lie at all, that—"and have vowed to see to his wishes in this matter."

"I'm not to have a say in this at all." The words, whispered almost too softly for him to hear, nonetheless slapped him in the face.

Kaya ignored him and set the small jug and spices on the side table. She waited until the knock came again and opened the already unbolted door. Tahir stood in the darkness and slipped inside before Kaya offered a greeting.

"Ah, Paul." Tahir bowed in greeting, a smile in his voice. "I had hoped to return before you arrived. Kaya, my child. It's time."

* * * *

It all happened before she realized the magnitude of the change. One minute, she and Tahir were arguing over her impending marriage to Sergeant Hartley. The next, he reminded her of the Ottoman price on her head and the very real threat to her life.

That particular weight settled around her shoulders and chilled her to the bone.

"You taught me how to survive." Kaya lifted her chin and very deliberately did not look at Sergeant Hartley. She also refused to speak in either English or Marathi, the two languages Tahir believed the sergeant knew. Petty, perhaps, but with her world spiraling out of control, Kaya felt very irrelevant. "I shall honor that and do so. I shall survive."

Tahir nodded and reached for her hands, holding tight. "I wanted you to be able to defend yourself if the Ottomans found you. Kaya, I want only the best for you." He sighed, sounding as defeated as she. "You can no longer remain in Cairo, and England is the safest place, the farthest from the Ottomans."

One hand ran tiredly down his weatherworn face, more aged now than she remembered. These last months had been hard on all of them, most of all on Tahir. Fear for his health clenched a cold fist around her heart. Leaving meant leaving him alone.

"Why?" Kaya demanded, that fear making her voice harsher. "I know why we must leave Cairo." She waved an impatient hand. The sergeant's eyes burned into her, a flame as cold as the realization she was fighting a losing battle. "But why now? Why England? Why this sergeant?"

"I trust him."

Kaya narrowed her gaze at her grandfather's simple words. Unease fluttered in her stomach. She broke her promise to herself and looked at the sergeant, watching him watch them with detached curiosity.

He stood, back straight, hands clasped behind him, silent. Oh, he'd greeted Gidd well enough; she sensed no tension or deceit in that welcome. Gidd believed his story about being a stranger in Cairo after dark and entering the house.

Kaya did not.

Then again, she'd been raised to mistrust everyone, save Tahir, Derya, and Tahir's manservant, Abdul. Three people. Suddenly being told to trust this man, who would be her husband, grated along her skin.

"What do you mean, you *trust him*?" She held up a hand to forestall his comment. "I'm sure you would trust *any* man you contract me to marry, but why an Englishman? Why *this* Englishman?" Marrying an Englishman with instructions to smuggle her out of Cairo was *not* part of the plan for her future.

"If you trust me, Kaya, then trust I've chosen a strong, trustworthy man as your husband."

"I'm trading one prison for another." Annoyed, Kaya

pressed her lips together. She had not wanted her deepest fear revealed. "When did you contact the sergeant?" She narrowed her eyes. "For him to arrive now, you must have written him months ago. If the Ottomans had returned then, you would have told me immediately."

Gidd looked guilty, an expression that so shocked Kaya she momentarily forgot her question. A cold stone of understanding settled in her stomach. He had planned this for months. Longer. He had planned this and never told her.

He'd planned to marry her off and see her out of Cairo without so much as a day's warning. Alone, as untethered as the boats she longed to see, Kaya swallowed around a dry, tight throat.

"I wrote Sergeant Hartley when the rains did not come and famine swept the city. I heard of the Ottomans' arrival only this morning." Gidd's shoulders slumped, just slightly, but Kaya noticed. Her heart twisted. "Of course, they don't ask after you specifically; they never do. But I am once again under great scrutiny."

Pushing back her pain, her betrayal, the sheer loneliness crushing her, Kaya looked to the sergeant. "How do you feel about this?" she asked in English.

Sergeant Hartley met her gaze, and the conviction in them struck her anew. "I owe Tahir my life. I promised to take care of you and ensure you safely to England. I mean to do that."

The sergeant sounded sincere; Kaya couldn't fault him for that. But his pretty words didn't answer her question—or make her any more comfortable with this mad scheme.

"Oh, Kaya." Tahir squeezed her hands and offered a tired smile. She absently noted he'd reverted to Egyptian. "I did everything in my power…bribery, threats, misdirection—" He broke off, softened, and looked at her wistfully.

Her heart beat too loudly, too painfully. She already

knew what his next words would be.

"I did everything possible, and I would do it all again if it meant keeping you safe. As your grandfather, my child, I only wish to see you happy and alive." For a heartbeat, Kaya swore tears shone in his eyes, but then he breathed a fatigued sigh. "I'll stay in Cairo and see they know nothing of your escape."

How could she fight against that? Kaya capitulated. She hated the hollow, cold feeling, but fear tightened her chest. Fear and that crushing isolation.

Kaya was to be denied even a marriage ceremony.

* * * *

Mere hours later, dressed in her traveling clothes and hijab, she stood in the main room and stared at Sergeant Hartley as he signed the marriage papers. The English marriage license Gidd had somehow procured and already signed. She did not read it to see who her grandfather had bribed to be witnesses.

Now, her farewells said and her tears swallowed back, she stood at the threshold of the open door of her house. On the threshold of change. She tried to gather her thoughts, but they raced as fast as the wind, and she couldn't leash a single one to make sense of it.

Heart pounding, Kaya licked her lips, but her breath came short, her lungs tight. She eagerly peered onto the deserted street and, for only the second time in her life, stepped outside.

Darkness obscured her view of Cairo. She longed to see her city, embrace the sights, the souk, feel the desert sun blazing down as she walked the crowded streets. She wanted to weave through the world with the grace of a kite flying in the wind.

They needed to leave before the city woke.

Kaya tried to dislodge the lump of sorrow and fear and

anticipation. Her entire life, she'd yearned for this moment, and now, with it literally beneath her feet, she hesitated. She looked to the ground and tentatively tapped the toe of her boot onto the dirt street.

"Are you all right?"

Jerking her foot back, she glanced up at the sergeant. He watched her with a patience she didn't understand.

"This is only my second time out of the house," she whispered. Kaya placed her foot on the street and stepped forward.

Away from the door and her life. Into the new and unknown. She looked over her shoulder, remembering the brush of Tahir's kiss on her cheek as he'd guided her out the door. Then closed it firmly behind her. Kaya sniffled back tears as discreetly as possible and stepped from her home.

She purposely ignored the man beside her.

Swiping her cheeks, she lifted her chin higher. Eyes shadowed in the darkness, her new husband gently took her elbow. Inky stillness settled over them.

"I'm sorry." Sergeant Hartley's whisper barely dented the night. His fingers squeezed her arm in what she took as a sympathetic gesture. "I never meant—goodbyes are…" He trailed off. "Tahir is a good man."

Unable to speak around the lump in her throat, she adjusted her hijab, hoping the movement covered her tears. "He is."

The sergeant adjusted his pack and the long wooden beam strapped across his shoulders and stepped onto the street. Kaya breathed in deeply of the cooling night and followed him. They crept among the shadows like purse thieves.

The fear and famine gripping the city hung heavy in the air and smacked Kaya in the face. Every story Derya ever told her about people hiding in the shadows, scavenging for food or waiting to rob an innocent for a piastre or *akçe* or a bit of gold, flooded her mind.

People who didn't care who they hurt.

Kaya braced but heard nothing to indicate an attack. She knew how to protect herself.

Her hand brushed over her waist, where Derya had apparently sewn their gold and jewels for later in their journey. Derya had known of this marriage. Known of it and readied for Kaya's clandestine journey out of Cairo. That knowledge, along with the jewels, weighed on her.

She didn't know what to think of that. Everyone knew about this marriage but her. Swallowing against a strange mix of excitement and terror, of sorrow and betrayal, she focused on the city, the newness of being outside.

Her attention drifted to the sergeant.

He had traded his uniform for civilian clothes: dark-colored trousers and coat, a plain white shirt, and the black hat he wore when he'd broken into the house. Annoyed with her drifting attention, Kaya tried to ignore the enigmatic man just as she ignored the oppressive, underlying scent of decay.

Her first real foray into Cairo was nothing like she expected.

Saddened, at a loss as to what she should feel or how to cope with this disappointment, Kaya hurried beside the sergeant.

Freedom lay before her. Despite the close streets of Cairo, it spread before her in an oasis of hope.

Her lifelong dream was now truly within her grasp. Kaya stumbled, knees giving out, breath rushing from her lungs. On the deserted street, a cold hand of terror settled in her veins. For that single heartbeat, the vastness of her new reality overwhelmed her. Fear froze her blood and squeezed her lungs.

"Are you all right?" The sergeant stopped, held her

elbow solicitously.

"Yes." Kaya cleared her throat. The ground beneath her feet righted itself and she nodded politely. "I am fine, thank you."

Even in the shadows, she saw his eyebrows raise in disbelief. The sergeant slipped his fingers down her arm, sweeping along her inner wrist.

Her heart skipped at the unexpected touch, and she jerked her hand away. Kaya tried not to notice his warm, calloused hand against hers or the gentleness of his touch.

"I always wanted to see Cairo." Mouth dry, throat closed with goodbye, Kaya barely heard her own words. Sergeant Hartley guided her along the streets, keeping her close. He remained deferential despite their circumstances, which confused her even more. "I wished to be a part of the city."

As suddenly as her fear of being on her own had closed around her, this new future exhilarated her. The challenge of it, the task of seeing every day on her own terms. It beat wildly through her.

"I'm sorry." His tone conveyed a sincerity she hadn't expected. His hand, large and warm and oddly comforting, rested on her shoulder then dropped almost immediately. She shivered at the thrill of his touch.

No stranger had ever touched her.

Warm and dry around hers, his calloused fingers brushed the back of her palm and sent an odd tingling up her arm, along each nerve, to finally settle low in her belly. Derya had told her many stories from her time as odalisque in the sultan's harem. She had even managed to smuggle out scandalous books for her education.

But reading about such things had not prepared her for the feel of a man's touch.

The sergeant didn't give her time to dwell on it. They

raced down darkened alleyways and across wide, abandoned terraces, past waterless fountains and cracked streets unattended and covered with sand.

"Hurry," Sergeant Hartley said, a bare brush of sound against the shell of her ear.

Her heart tripped over itself then pounded in her chest. The rush of his breath over her skin jarred her, amplified the tingle his touch had kindled.

"Oh," she breathed, then shook her head at her absurdity.

He was the first stranger she'd spoken with. Of course her skin tingled with his touch. Kaya swallowed useless annoyance and frustration and quickened her pace, easily keeping up with his longer strides.

They neared the western gate and the Mamluk guards tasked with keeping out the frantic, starving people seeking shelter. They stopped at the next crossroads, and the sergeant cocked his head, listening.

What incentive drove Sergeant Hartley to risk his life, to *not* turn her over to the authorities? As a non-Egyptian trying to leave past curfew, he'd be arrested and taken to the Citadel—if not shot on sight.

The jewels, of course. Then again, he could easily kill her, strip her of the jewels, and no one would be the wiser.

No. For all Gidd's secrets, he trusted Hartley to keep her safe. The sergeant wouldn't turn on her or turn her in.

Suddenly, he pinned her against the wall, knocking all the breath out of her. Her heart jumped, fingers curling around her dagger. Shocked at the abruptness, Kaya opened her mouth to demand an explanation. The fear she'd been wrong about him was slithering coldly through her veins.

"Someone's coming."

Her heart stuttered. Over its pounding, Kaya tried to listen for what he'd heard.

Sergeant Hartley moved with predatory stealth until only his head peeked around the corner. He crept along the streets and made no noise at all. Suddenly she understood why her grandfather had trusted this Englishman to keep her safe.

This was not the first time Paul Hartley had used the cover of night to steal out of a city. Sneaking into her house had been no accident.

She pressed her lips together to stop from asking what he heard. Instead, she strained for any sound.

Long minutes passed before he released her and let out a long, silent breath. Whatever he heard or saw, the danger had passed without incident.

Kaya's shoulders sagged, and she curled her fingers into a fist. The memory of his touch continued to prickle along her skin.

They hurried down several more labyrinthine streets. Squeezing Sergeant Hartley's arm, Kaya stopped. The El Kadi Yehia Zen El-Din Mosque loomed ahead, the gleam of its arches and columns, the glittering central dome muted in the night. Even in the darkness, the proud minaret stole her breath.

"Here." Nerves knotted her stomach. Fear, excitement, grief, and sorrow warred within her. Kaya adjusted her scarf, draping it across the lower half of her face.

"*U^caf!*"

Chapter Three

"Damn it." Paul pressed her against the wall and covered her body with his.

No need for silence; the guard had already spotted them. However, he couldn't resist touching her, breathing her in, brushing his lips against her skin. His body tightened at her closeness, and arousal heated his blood.

Torture. Sheer torture.

Sheer stupidity, wanting Kaya.

The mystery around her tempted him, much as her lips did. The curiosity with which she asked questions, the confidence in her stance while she'd held him at knifepoint. The adamant way she spoke, declaring herself quite unwilling to marry him. It all danced over his skin in excitement.

"You speak Egyptian?" Kaya's breath brushed his neck, and Paul had to work harder than he should've not to react to it.

"I know the basics—'stop,' 'Englishman,' 'thief.' Everything a foreigner in Cairo should know." Paul looked down at her, meeting her dark eyes in the shadows. Even without the benefit of moonlight, he knew she was frowning at him.

"You have an odd choice of basics."

Amused, he snorted and eased back from her, hoping physical distance would help his foolishness. Normally he wasn't this sloppy, this reckless. With the threat of the Company finding him, as remote a possibility as that was, Paul hadn't the chance to truly plan their escape with Tahir. Not that he had intended to go through with the wily old man's plan.

Yet here he stood, hiding in the shadows with his new wife.

He was the greatest fool ever.

Married to the beautiful and intelligent Kaya, a woman with callouses on her fingers and a dagger at her waist, he'd used her for reasons far more simplistic than hers. Nonetheless, he'd married her and promised to keep her safe.

Paul scrubbed his hand over his face and carefully released his hold on her. She tightened her grip for a moment, and he turned sharply to look at her. Her expression gave nothing away—she looked toward the gates.

He didn't want to think about being so close to her, but the soft feel of her body against his tempted him to forget any thought of keeping his distance.

Greatest fool ever.

Paul swept the area, eyeing alcoves to hide in. With this ridiculous wooden beam strapped to his shoulders, they'd be far too conspicuous. He eyed her dagger. She'd pressed it well enough into the small of his back, but could she wield it skillfully enough to protect herself?

He gripped his own dagger and blew out a deep breath. He had few options other than this less-than-honorable specialty.

When in doubt, lie.

A young male voice called out just Paul stepped forward. Kaya's cold, stiff hand landed on his arm only to immediately drop. He stopped mid-step.

"It's only a child with supper for his father." Her voice broke.

Paul frowned at her obvious fear and looked at her over his shoulder. "A child?"

He blinked. Either his luck had changed—so unlikely it almost made him laugh—or Kaya had better luck than he did.

He bet on the latter.

"We'll wait for the boy to leave." He kept his voice as dispassionate as possible.

A single oil lamp illuminated the small guardhouse, and he just made out the pair of men on either side of the gates. Paul watched the guards along the wall, tracking their progress to perfectly time their escape. From his limited vantage, he couldn't assess their positions without losing the shadows.

Tahir's voice pounded in his head: *Keep Kaya safe.* The letter would work.

"What are they saying?" Mouth temptingly close to her skin, he breathed deeply of her scent, the clean freshness of blossoms he couldn't name.

"Nothing of import." Kaya spoke so softly he needed to lean closer.

Paul jerked back, jaw clenched. How stupid could he be?

"Kamil's father asks where they found so much food."

Guilt tugged his gut, but Paul ignored it. He'd stolen quite a bit of food in the short time since he'd arrived.

"The child has gone."

Paul shrugged off the heavy pack and, careful of the beam strapped along the top, handed it to her. If the guards attacked or raised the alarm, he'd need to move freely to protect her. Unease prickled along his spine, but his steps remained measured as he closed the distance, Kaya at his back. When the guard called out again, he was ready with Tahir's letter.

"General Tahir ibn Zanki ibn al-Nafis sends his greetings and best wishes." Paul spoke steadily, in carefully memorized Egyptian, his eyes on the guard's.

The other man hesitated, and Paul stilled. He reached back and felt for Kaya's hand, ready to run. Cairo was a big city. They could hide well enough in the darkness. An abandoned building or a closed-up shop.

Kaya's hand tightened around his. Paul didn't know

what Tahir had offered these guards—food, he assumed, given the famine sweeping the country. Still, there were always those who had a stronger moral core than he, those who couldn't be bribed.

Most people had a stronger moral code than he.

The guard simply took the letter. He tilted it into the faint light from the single lamp hanging along the wall and quickly broke the seal. As if he already suspected what it said, he skimmed the parchment.

The men atop the wall walked back into view. Paul felt their window of escape narrowing with every breath.

The guard carefully folded the letter and slipped it into his waistband. He waited another moment—one entirely too long in Paul's opinion—then stepped from the gate. As if on a preplanned signal, the gates ponderously opened. The large hinges groaned faintly in the night, well-oiled despite the desperate times.

Paul angled his body to better protect Kaya, so she did not stand in direct sight of the ground guards and remained partially hidden beneath the parapet.

Too easy.

They demanded no additional bribe. Asked no questions. What had Tahir offered these men?

The guards didn't so much as look at Kaya. They didn't leer or make lewd comments, let alone question him about her. A cold fist tightened around Paul's chest, and he eased her in front of him.

"Move," he whispered. "Quickly."

Kaya, either sensing his urgency or wanting out of the city as much as he, slipped through the narrow gap. The beam clanged dully against the gate. Hand on the small of her back, just brushing her bow and quiver, Paul hurried her beneath the walls and away from Cairo.

He didn't look back.

The moment they stepped through the gate, it slowly closed again. The heavy click probably wasn't as loud and as echoing as Paul imagined. Without looking back, Paul quickly marched them down the hard-packed dirt road.

Not bothering to pause, he simply took his pack from Kaya and swung it around, slipping the straps over his arms. The wooden beam scraped his shoulders with every step. He didn't care.

Kaya easily kept up with him.

"The wall guards had their backs turned." He kept his voice low in the darkness. "Do you know if they carry muskets or bows?"

"Oh. I—both, I think." In the night's illumination, he watched her nod. "Yes. Both. And swords, of course."

"Muskets have about a three-hundred-yard range," he muttered. "What's the distance for your bows?"

What did he know of archery? History lessons from his schooling, when he bothered to attend. Paul glanced at the bow on her back. It was smaller, shorter than sketches of the English longbow. Less distance then, yes? He had no idea how that worked.

"There are stories that the *tirkeş* war bow shoots up to a thousand yards," she said softly. She neither slowed nor looked back. "But Gidd always claimed at most six to seven hundred."

"Damn. Walk faster." Paul expected an arrow in his back. "What do the guards use?"

Those guards might not have demanded additional bribes, but that didn't mean they weren't above looting bodies in the desert.

"The war bow," Kaya said decisively. "We should be out of range in moments."

Paul didn't slow. Couldn't afford to. The middle of his back itched as if someone had painted a target there.

No arrow found his back. No musket ball pierced Kaya's flesh. The cloudless night sky replaced images of blood-stained sand. Kaya, equally unharmed, walked steadily beside him. Behind them, the meager light from Cairo faded.

Only the stars and half-moon lit their way.

Paul ran a hand over his face but ignored the exhaustion tugging his limbs. He needed wine. Wine Cairo did not have. It made surviving the nights difficult.

Damn near impossible.

With each step forward, his tired body threatened to collapse, yet his mind raced, and he counted off their steps. How many steps in a yard? In a thousand? Oh, the things the army didn't teach.

He counted another twenty before the tension knotting his shoulders relaxed. They'd escaped. Paul breathed out slowly, letting the band tightening his lungs ease as well. He stopped to adjust the pack against his shoulders. Kaya paused beside him, silent and watchful across the barren landscape.

Everything about her lured him closer. Her innocence and curiosity. The passion she restrained tempted him to learn more about her. Hell, the way she watched him, as if he were beneath her, drew him in.

The mystery of her past shouldn't interest him.

Why had Tahir taught her to defend herself? The memory of her knife digging into his back returned. That dagger hadn't moved. Without a doubt, she would've slipped it into his kidney as easily as slicing through butter.

Paul cleared his throat and re-shouldered his pack. Walking northeast, he turned toward the mountain range and away from the more heavily traveled Nile.

Beside him, Kaya studied the night sky. The ends of her headscarf fluttered in the wind, and she easily kept pace. Above them stretched the endless black expanse of freedom. His heart stumbled at the sudden realization. Freedom. A fresh start. For him.

He clenched his jaw and glanced at her from the corner of his eye. This was her first night outside the walls of her home, yet she was still trapped. With him.

Paul struggled to say something—words usually came easily. Meaningless creations that held no true value.

"Did you expect trouble?" Kaya asked eventually.

He caught another faint whiff of her soap, or maybe perfume. Whatever it was, it suited her, the fragrance light in the darkly beautiful night. He bit back *those* words.

Those words held value.

"Yes." He shrugged, and the beam rubbed awkwardly against him. "Your grandfather didn't expect any. He believed his plan and the letter would work. But I find it's always best to anticipate trouble. Saves on surprises later."

"You are a curious man, Sergeant Hartley." Her voice remained low and flat. A far cry from the furious passion she'd used to argue with Tahir, to announce her refusal to marry him.

Given the circumstances of their acquaintance—well, marriage—Paul didn't blame her. Though he really hated when she called him "Sergeant Hartley." It reminded him of the army.

"Because I expect trouble?" he heard himself ask.

"No." The word lay quietly between them. Kaya didn't elaborate, and he didn't press.

The desert extended endlessly before him. Over a hundred miles between Cairo and the coast—how many steps was that?

The desert path wasn't made up of the loose, shifting sand he'd expected when he'd finally stumbled into Egypt from Bombay. This was hard-packed, sandy dirt. Paul didn't look back or turn around, just kept moving forward.

The story of his life.

He adjusted the uncomfortable pack and cursed the beam, which was knocking his left shoulder with every step. He and Kaya were stuck with each other, for weeks, months, probably more. He didn't want to spend their time in polite snippets of useless conversation.

"Thank you." Kaya's words caught him off guard.

"For what?" He turned to look at her, but Kaya watched the sky. Paul should've expected that.

"For seeing me out of Cairo." She paused and cleared her throat. "For promising to keep me safe."

Paul wanted to tease her that he'd vowed much more than that when they'd married, but the words caught in his throat and choked him with that restless want. No, it was too soon to joke about that, if there was ever a proper time to do so.

They were married in name only.

There ought to be a training manual. If the army had bothered to print one, there really should be one for marriage. Seemed entirely more difficult than marching to the beat of a drum. Or shooting—

Damn. His nails dig into his palms, his fists pressed against his eyes.

The screams echoed in his head. Despite the darkness, Paul saw the sunbaked Bombay dirt road covered in blood. The eyes of the dead stared up at him, their lifeless hands reached out.

Not now. He needed to focus. Concentrate.

Silent as the night, Kaya handed him his hat. Paul stared blankly at it and then blinked at her. They'd stopped, or he had. Without a word, he took his hat and settled it on his head. Unable to look at her, he resumed their pace.

Looking only on the moonlit ground, Paul quickened his step. His world had shifted with Tahir's proposition, and now all he thought he knew lay in shards at his feet. He'd grasped Tahir's letter and ran from British India faster than he'd run into the army.

Meeting Kaya had changed something in Paul he didn't understand. It pushed forward a side of himself he still doubted truly existed. What did Tahir expect to happen once they arrived in England?

What did *Paul* expect to happen? Hell if he knew.

He'd deserted the East India Company Army, ran to Egypt, married a woman he didn't know, and sneaked her out of the city. The future lay one step in front of him. Always one step ahead.

"Damietta," he said abruptly.

"Pardon?" Her sharp question bit into him.

Once upon a time, he'd known how to woo a lady. At least keep from talking rubbish with her. Rubbing a hand over his face, Paul blew out a breath.

"We'll stay in the mountains." Paul kept his voice low. "It'll take us an extra day or so."

Kaya's gaze pinned him in place, but he didn't meet her eyes. She didn't comment, and they moved steadily east, away from the Nile. In the half-moonlight, creatures he had no name for skittered along the rocky sand.

"It occurs to me." He eyed a four-legged creature with eyes that glowed in the darkness and huge ears that twitched. "I should've asked before. How dangerous are desert animals?"

Beside him, Kaya breathed deeply, not quite a sigh— not quite anything but a show of exasperation. Paul wanted to see her fathomless dark eyes, the slight turn to her lush lips.

He kept his eyes on the ground, scanning for whatever lived here.

"How did you arrive in Cairo? You must've encountered desert creatures then."

"Oh, we—I walked." Paul shuddered at the memory of

tremor-filled days and a relentless sun. "I don't remember much of it."

"We?"

He didn't look at Kaya but swallowed and kept moving. One step then the next.

"However did you expect to survive the desert?" Yes, that was very clearly exasperated annoyance with a nice sarcastic lilt thrown in. "If you know nothing of it, how did you think to walk through it? At night?"

"It wasn't a great plan," he freely admitted.

Kaya merely snorted.

Chapter Four

"What do you know of Damietta?"

The sergeant's voice startled her. She focused on keeping a steady pace, unused to walking so long. Her legs ached and her shoulders stiffened with carrying so much weight. Refusing to show him her pain, Kaya breathed deeply of the cooler night air.

When she spoke, she did so in a crisp, clipped tone. "I know it's at least a six-day walk north."

"They have a beautiful market," he offered.

Surprised at the statement, she pressed her lips to stop from asking. Instead, she looked to the sergeant, who muttered to himself and tried to ease the wooden beam sitting across his shoulders.

"It's a port town. Busy, loud, constantly moving, always awake." His words flowed easily, simple constructs that nonetheless created a brightly colored world for her gray landscape. "With wares from across the world. There's Chinese silk and Indian spices, pottery from Morocco, and hides from interior Africa."

"It sounds wonderful. Vibrant." Kaya couldn't keep the wistful longing from her voice and cleared her throat against the yearning. "Do they play music?" She tilted her head and looked up at the sky, closing her eyes. Kaya envisioned the goods spilling from the stalls, the scent of spices, the gleam of silver and malachite.

"Yes. There are many *Alateeyeh*."

Kaya's lips twitched, and she looked at him. He pronounced the word carefully, elongating each syllable. The sergeant met her gaze, and she saw he knew he'd pronounced it wrong. Kaya's lips curved wider, and a warmth she hadn't expected spread through her. He'd tried.

"I thought you only learned the basic words? That is not so basic."

"Oh." He cleared his throat and grimaced. "No. Learned that one by accident."

He didn't elaborate, and Kaya let the subject drop. "*Ala-tee*-yeh." Kaya emphasized the *yeh*.

Sergeant Hartley dutifully repeated the word. "*Alateeya*."

"*Yeh*," she gently corrected. "*Alatee*-yeh."

Head cocked toward her, he carefully repeated her pronunciation. "*Alateeyeh*."

"Much better." She smiled at him, pleased that he'd bothered. "I used to listen to them play from our courtyard." Kaya tried to stem her wistfulness, but it slipped through. "I'd sit in the gardens for hours and listen to them. Abdul once bought me a lute."

She laughed, a full, free sound that burst from her. Oh, but it felt wonderful to laugh where no one could hear her, where it didn't matter how loud she was. Kaya slowed their pace, enjoying the desert, the open air, the lack of walls.

Freedom.

It sang through her blood, and she breathed deeply for the first time in days. Years.

"I didn't know how to play, and, oh, the noises it made! Harsh and loud." Grinning, she covered her ears at the memory. "I kept trying, but I couldn't make it sound like the smooth melody I heard from the *Alateeyeh*."

Sergeant Hartley smiled at her, an encouraging grin that made her heart skip. "Who taught you?"

"Derya." Kaya stopped, her laughter a lump in her throat. "She tried to teach me. She played so beautifully, but I could never replicate it. I am far more proficient with drawing than an instrument."

Her chest ached and her eyes stung. Kaya slowed nearly to a stop and met the sergeant's gaze. He looked at her with sympathy, an odd understanding. Or maybe that was the half-moonlight, glinting off his features. He merely waited for her to continue walking.

Kaya shook her head and tilted her chin. Derya. Tears pricked her eyes, but Kaya refused to let them fall in front of a stranger, no matter how sympathetically he watched her. Picking up their pace, she kept her eyes straight ahead once more. Damietta wouldn't come to them.

"I'm sure Damietta has lute players, or an *Alateeyeh*—"

"*Alatee* is singular." Kaya cringed and cleared her throat. "Sorry."

He snorted and huffed a small laugh. Perhaps she'd offer to teach him Egyptian. It'd certainly pass the time.

"I'm sure Damietta has an *Alatee* we can listen to. We'll find one on our way to the docks."

Surprised, Kaya jerked her head to stare at him. A nicety she hadn't expected. Warmth she didn't understand eased through her chest.

They walked in silence, one far more comfortable than when they'd first left Cairo. The tension in Kaya's shoulders loosened. Perhaps Gidd had been right to trust the sergeant. Kaya tried not to grin at the way Sergeant Hartley constantly scanned the path or jumped at every skitter of desert animal.

As exhilarating as it was to walk among the desert life, she kept a careful ear out for the many creatures who'd rather attack than scurry away.

"Why are we not walking the riverbanks?" Kaya paused and listened but heard nothing to be concerned about. "Other than the crocodiles and hippopotami. We could pay for a boat. Is there a reason we're taking the mountain road?"

"Too many people." He glanced to the west, toward *en-Nīl*. Kaya followed his gaze, desperate to see the water. "It's the most traveled route. I prefer a bit of privacy."

"Privacy?"

"Not—no, not like that." He stumbled over his words, eyes wide as they met hers. "Don't worry, I didn't mean…" He cleared his throat, and her momentary alarm receded. He did not mean to kill her then. "No. I didn't mean that. It's just a precaution. In case those guards change their minds and follow us."

In case someone betrayed Gidd. The sergeant didn't say it. He didn't have to. Or in case the Ottomans followed. Not that they knew—still. Just in case.

Kaya suppressed a shiver and refused to look behind them. As much as she wanted a final look at the city, she had no desire to see Cairo's gates. More walls to keep her locked away. She picked up the pace.

"We carry enough coin to find a boat, buy us a private room, but I see no reason to waste money so early in our journey."

"All right." That made sense. Or did the sergeant have another reason? Why had he traveled to Cairo on the strength of Tahir's letter? Kaya had trouble reconciling never trusting an outsider with suddenly being forced to trust this man. "How are we to make our way to Europe? Where are we to sleep during the day?"

He huffed out a laugh. "You ask a lot of questions."

"Gidd did not trust me, but he clearly trusted you." The ache that had eased with their light conversation twisted through her.

"Tahir wanted you safe, *Madaam* Kaya." He sighed, and from the corner of her eye Kaya saw him rub his hands down his face. "And, for reasons that escape me, he trusted me to do so." He cleared his throat. When he spoke again, he sounded like a military man. Crisp, on point, offering details but no more than what she asked. "I have a tent in my pack. Tahir assured me it'll keep the heat of the desert at bay."

"A desert tribe tent?"

"Um…yes?" He shrugged, and the beam shifted with him. The sergeant grumbled and tried to adjust it. "It stinks like a dead animal, but he swore it would keep out the sun."

"Is that why you have a plank of wood?"

"Yes, and it gouges my shoulders with *every damn step*."

"They're made of goat's hair." Kaya nodded, relieved to have one point addressed.

"That explains the smell."

She giggled, surprised at both herself and at the sergeant's quip. "Perhaps, but they are very efficient. We shall be quite protected from the desert sunlight."

Once again, they walked in silence. Kaya thought they'd walked for hours, but the moon barely rose in the sky. They had several more hours before sunrise.

"Do we sail directly for England?" Kaya glanced at the sergeant, who mumbled words she didn't understand and shifted the wooden beam again.

Sergeant Hartley paused for so long, Kaya thought he wasn't going to answer her. She watched him but couldn't discern his thoughts. "We sail for Lisbon or Cádiz, maybe Calais. We'll find a ship—Spanish or French or Egyptian, it doesn't matter. Then take her to whatever port she sails for."

"It sounds lovely." Kaya hadn't meant her voice to sound quite so longing. The very thought of seeing so much of a world previously to denied her set her imagination a-flight. Shaking her head, she changed the subject. "Have you no wish to sail for England?"

"No."

Startled, she met his gaze, but his own remained shuddered and hard in the silver moonlight. "We could sail for the south of France. It's warm there, sunny."

Kaya hummed in acknowledgement but not agreement. "We sail anywhere."

At their destination, she'd explore as far and wide as she wished. Standing straighter, she picked up her pace.

Anywhere. Everywhere.

Damietta couldn't arrive soon enough.

* * * *

"How are you holding up?" Paul guided Kaya deeper into the eastern mountains, careful to keep his voice low.

The last thing they needed was their conversation echoing throughout the valley and ravine. He had no idea who else used these mountains, and he did not want to meet them.

"I am well, *shukran*." Her voice dragged, each word precise but rung-out.

In the mountain's darker shadows, he easily found her. Her pace had slowed in the previous hours, and now she forced herself forward, shoulders drooped, head bowed, breathing labored. Paul hated to push her when she clearly had no experience with their brutal pace.

What was worse: running away at fourteen and seeing far more of the world than any man ought? Or being trapped in one place all your life, never allowed to see anyone or anything? There had to be someplace far happier in between their extremes.

The sun blazed along the mountaintops, making the already warm air hotter. He didn't know how Egyptians worked during the day. The sun baked the ground, the houses, the people. The stifling humidity and endless rainy season of Bombay did not compare to the unbroken Egyptian heat.

Paul blinked the sand from his eyes and tilted his head, letting the slight breeze cool his face. Kaya needed to rest, even if she was too stubborn to admit it.

He needed a drink.

Much as he'd searched Cairo, not even the secret side streets or illegal gaming dens had held any wine. How did anyone survive without alcohol?

"We need to climb up to the high ground and out of the sun." Paul spotted several caves and overhangs above them. Hefting his pack higher and cursing the wooden beam that continued to dig into his back, he stepped on a rock and hoisted his aching body up.

Paul grunted at the exertion and looked to Kaya, who mimicked his movements. She grimaced as she pulled herself up, and he felt a pang of sympathy. Probably the first time she'd climbed anything, too.

"Are we spending the day in a cave?" Kaya's voice dragged and slurred with her fatigue. Each gasp for breath showed her exhaustion, the way her arms shook as she steadied against the rock face. They should've stopped before the sun topped the horizon, but he hadn't wanted to lose the cover of night.

"No. Can't hear anything in caves." His shoulders and back protested, but Paul bent and offered his hand. Kaya ignored him and, grunting, clumsily hauled herself over the ledge. "Besides, don't things live in caves?"

"Yes." Kaya frowned at her palms. She wiped them on her gown and looked around the plateau. "That's why I asked."

Paul suppressed a grin. He enjoyed her determination. Finding her stubbornness arous—*interesting* was not a good enough reason to let his heart feel anything. It was the exact opposite of a good enough reason.

One level up from the rocky mountain floor, the long plateau seemed perfect for their daytime rest. It wasn't a difficult or high climb, and they both made it up the mountainside in minutes.

The sun hit the plateau, blinding him.

His damp shirt moved against his skin when he dropped his pack. Tempted as he was to collapse, he knew once he did he wouldn't move. Ever again.

"No, no, no! No sitting!" He grabbed her arm as Kaya made to do just that.

She looked at him with large, dark eyes. Fatigue pinched her mouth, and the dark circles beneath her eyes made her cheeks paler than normal. She blinked slowly. Paul's heart clenched.

"I'm sorry. You're exhausted."

"It is *Fajr*."

"All right." He didn't know what that meant. "We'll stop earlier tomorrow."

Kaya used a little of their water and cleaned up, then awkwardly knelt along the ledge. Paul turned respectfully from her and knelt in silence, unwilling to disturb her. When she stood, he did as well.

Sharply turning from Kaya, Paul yanked the wooden beam from its hold and went about twisting it into the packed dirt. The damn thing didn't twist easily, nor did it go very far into the ground.

"Fig roll?" Kaya asked as Paul pushed a peg into the ground.

Breathless and sweaty, he purposely averted his gaze. "I want to get the tent up first."

Too tired for anything else, Paul leaned the beam between two outcroppings. *Good enough.* Arms shaking, he pushed the wooden pegs into the ground. When that didn't work, he stomped them in.

Tying the ropes to the pegs and stretching up the goat's hair tent, he draped it over the large beam so the opening faced outward. Paul waited a beat, just to make sure it didn't collapse. It slid, settling against one of the outcroppings, but didn't fall.

Good enough.

Gratified, he sank to the ground beneath the wonderfully shaded tent.

"Whatever I said about this tent—" He stretched his aching legs in front of him. "I take it back. It's so much cooler in here."

Kaya eyed the tent as if she expected it to fall and knock him out. Not exactly up to Tahir's brief instructions, but it stood. Kaya sighed and sank to the ground. Turning from him, she eased off her boots.

"Ohh," she sighed.

"Probably shouldn't take your boots off." Paul eyed her back and boots where they lay beside her. "It'll be harder to put them back on later."

"I'll worry about that then." She yawned and hunched over her outstretched legs. "I can't worry about anything now."

"Here." His body protested each movement, and he doubted his shoulders were ever going to be the same. Paul reached for his pack and unclasped his bedroll. Shaking it out, every movement a strain, he spread it on the ground. "Sleep on this; it's better than the dirt."

"What about you?" Her eyes opened wide, only to droop again.

"I'll be fine." He wanted to assure her he was used to the punishing pace he'd set, but he couldn't bring himself to utter that partial lie. The truth was, exhaustion tugged his limbs and made him want to curl around her.

Paul shook himself. Curl into his *bedroll*. Not around Kaya. Where had that thought come from? He ran a hand over his face, scraping fine grains of sand into his skin. Grimacing, he looked to the bedroll. Once rested, those crazy thoughts would disappear.

No doubt—well, very little doubt—about that.

Kaya settled on the bedroll and pillowed her head on her arms. She turned toward him, eyes closed.

"How long were you in the army?" The words were slurred, but she opened her eyes and awaited his answer.

"Sixteen years." Paul huffed and stretched his back. His shoulders ached. He scowled at that stupid wooden beam; at least it had served its purpose.

"A long time." Kaya's voice trailed off. "You never wanted anything else?"

"Never really had the chance." Paul looked to Kaya. Her thick black eyelashes brushed the delicate skin beneath her eyes. Her scarf covered her hair, its ends trailing over her folded arms. Half-asleep, voice groggy, she looked beautiful. His fingers reached out to brush her cheek.

Halfway across the space between them, Paul curled them into a fist and dropped his hand. He shifted on the hard ground.

"Why did you stay?"

Restless, Paul wanted to run, no matter how his body felt otherwise. He didn't answer, uncertain what to say. In the silence, he hoped she'd fall asleep, releasing him from a conversation he definitely didn't want to have.

"Sergeant?"

"Nowhere else to go." The words slipped out. "Easier to stay."

"I'm sorry." The words barely made it across the small distance.

"Yeah." Paul looked at her as she drifted into sleep. "Me too."

He stretched on the ground and closed his eyes. By now, he hoped to be exhausted enough to fall into a dreamless sleep. Instead, he watched Kaya, lying peacefully beside him, breathing even, body completely relaxed on his bedroll.

Trusting him to keep her safe.

Eyes drooping, mind wandering, he wanted to curl around her, feel her body stretched along his. Smell the now-sandy fragrance of her skin. Paul's eyes shot open. Forcing himself to sit, he shifted against the mountainside, as far from Kaya as possible.

Chapter Five

The sun had barely disappeared behind the mountains by the time they packed up camp. Hot, hungry, exhausted, Paul cursed the stiff, dry wind and struggled to fold the unwieldy tent in the unbearable heat.

Kaya tried to catch one end, but either the wind tore it from her grasp or he inadvertently did when he finally managed to grab the other end.

"Haboob."

"What?" Paul fought with the tent, cursing its thickness, the oily texture of the fabric, its hugeness as he tried to refold it in some semblance of order. There had to be a secret method he didn't understand. The wind caught the edges and tore it from his grip. "Bloody f—"

"There's a haboob coming up."

Paul stopped fighting the tent and squinted at her. "A *what*?"

Kaya pointed over her shoulder. The ends of her hijab whipped around her head, and she impatiently tucked them in. Her dark eyes met his, wide and frightened.

A wall. A *wall* moved like the jaws of hell had opened.

"What the hell is *that*?" His voice jumped an octave.

"A haboob." More than a hint of fear colored her voice, and Kaya shouted over the wind that pushed against them. She grabbed the flapping tent and squinted at the swirling dirt and sand. "A sandstorm. We need shelter, a cave."

Heart thundering, Paul blinked against the howling wind and stuffed the tent into his pack, haphazardly slinging it over one shoulder. The long beam dragged against the ground.

A wall of sand moved toward them. To hell with the wooden beam.

"We need higher ground." He grabbed her hand and ran.

Fear urged him faster, and he dragged Kaya along the thin, rocky ledge in search of a cave or outcropping. The storm bore down, kicking up sand and dust and obscuring his vision. He may not know anything about sandstorms, but he knew enough to get the hell out of the way of a *moving wall of sand*.

"Will a cave be enough?" Squinting through the swirling dust and rising wind, Paul scanned the mountain for an opening. He looked over his shoulder again. The storm moved unnaturally fast.

"I don't know. One deep enough should be…nothing shallow, or it won't matter if we're in the mountain or in the open."

He only just heard her. Kaya pulled him further along the unsteady ground, through a narrow pass. The mountains towered over them but offered little in the way of sanctuary. The wind whipped sand around every corner, through every crevice.

"This way!" Kaya tugged his arm and made her way toward a particularly jagged ledge, scrambling over the ridges.

He tossed his pack over the narrow ledge and hoisted himself up and over. His bag tumbled in the wind, the beam scarred the ground. Paul snagged it with his foot, hoping the tent didn't fly loose. Turning, he crouched over the outcrop and grabbed Kaya's forearm as she braced herself on the rocks and climbed.

Her foot slipped.

Heart in his throat, Paul clambered across the serrated edges. She held on only with her hands, feet dangling. Paul cursed and wrapped his other hand around her arm, eyes on hers, willing her to stay with him. He couldn't look at the sharp rocks yawning below.

"I've got you!" he shouted and hoped she heard. "Look at me." She was, but her eyes held such a cold terror he wondered if she thought he'd let her drop. "Trust me."

Paul heard his words and ignored their deeper implications.

Kaya's head moved just slightly, and her fingers grasped round his forearm.

Every breath a struggle through wind and sand, heart pounding too loudly in his ears, eyes open to mere slits, he could barely make out Kaya in the thickening air. Paul held tight and waited until her feet found temporary purchase before pulling her over the edge.

His left knee ached and his palms stung, but he moved with her. They had another wall to climb.

Boots teetering on a rock he wasn't sure would hold, Paul caught her round the waist. Kaya rearranged her grip, planted her boots on the thin ledge, and leveraged herself up.

Avoiding her bow and quiver, he shoved her gorgeously rounded arse upward. *Damn.* Eyes closed against the swirling sand, Paul tried desperately not to think about the feel of her in his hands.

Now was *not* the time.

He grabbed his pack from the ledge below and tossed it beside Kaya. The tent bounced on the ground, the beam beside it. Even in the rapidly fading light, he saw Kaya snatch them as he hauled himself up and over. His knee protested, and his torn hands caught on rough stone. Lungs burning with every shallow breath, eyes tearing, Paul forced his aching body to stand.

In the swirling sand, he could barely see Kaya. Her scarf had molded against her face, its ends concealed by the wind. He blindly reached for her hand. Safety. She gripped his fingers and tugged him along a small, uneven ledge. How she saw in this storm, he didn't know, but she walked steadily and purposefully, and he followed.

Panting, they ducked into a cave, where he leaned against the wall and retched.

She didn't release her hold on him, even as she leaned next to him and wheezed, taking in deep, gasping breaths. Her fingers spasmed around his with every cough, but she never let go. Still puffing, Kaya tugged him deeper into the dwelling, away from the opening, where sand continued to swirl in an obscure mass.

Taking cautious, tentative steps, she looked for the creatures they'd briefly discussed last night. Paul carefully brushed sand from his stinging eyes and listened for any sound over the scream of the wind.

Suddenly, she stopped. Paul looked at her in the darkness but saw only the faint outline of her body. Hand still wrapped around his, Kaya turned a sharp corner a dozen or so steps from the cave entrance.

The curve angled enough that as soon as they rounded the corner, the howl of the wind died. Each hesitant step brought them deeper into the shadows until they turned again, and Kaya dropped his hand.

Willing his heart to slow, his lungs to ease, Paul collapsed against the cave wall. His hands stung, and his arms throbbed. Blinking painfully, he could barely see from the sand and dirt coating his face. Every desperate breath brought fresh dirt with it, burning his lungs.

"I hate the desert," he rasped.

Kaya laughed, a short, breathless sound that echoed harshly around the narrow area. She coughed and cleared her throat, though he still heard each pant of breath. Her laugh, despite the situation—and the fact she was probably laughing at him—eased around his heart.

"I am suddenly not as fond of the desert as I once

was." Her voice wheezed, and she coughed again. "Sheltering at home during a haboob is quite different than running through one."

"I imagine," he offered dryly.

Though none of the late afternoon sunlight trickled into this alcove, he thought he saw her grin widen, and he wondered if her dark eyes danced.

"That is the first time I've climbed a mountain." She laughed again, more a giggle of delight. Music to his ears, sand-clogged though they were. "Last night we marched, but today—" She broke off and coughed again. "Today was real running. It was *exhilarating*!"

Paul couldn't help it. He laughed with her, not a polite chuckle, but a true laugh. It burst from him in a surge of surprise and joined hers. Oh, it felt good. Even if it took them each several minutes to catch their breath and stop coughing.

"I haven't laughed like that in a long, long time," he confessed through a wracking cough.

"Nor I." She spoke so softly he only thought he heard her. Her words, real or imagined, sparked his curiosity. No matter how he wished to hear her laugh like that again, he bit his tongue and halted the flow of words crowding his dry mouth.

A vicious wind howled across the narrow opening of the cave. They sat in relative silence. Trapped a middling distance between Cairo and Damietta, between a dying city and one that offered a promise of life.

Paul scrubbed his hands over his face. Damn. His palms stung, and now that they weren't running or climbing, his knee ached. Pulling his hands back, he tried to look at them in the gloom. He couldn't see but intimately knew the slickness of blood. Now he'd smeared it across his sandy face.

Perfect.

"What's wrong?" Kaya shifted slightly closer.

"Nothing." The lie slipped easily from his lips.

Paul curled his hands into fists, which only made his hands sting more and did the bleeding no good.

Kaya sighed as if she knew he was lying. Shuffling the few steps across the narrow space, she reached for him. Her fingers slid over his chest, to his arms, then down. Paul shut his eyes against the contact, however fleeting. Her rough fingers closed around his calloused and cracked hands.

"You cut yourself." She dropped his hands. The sound of her satchel scraping over her clothing shot through the darkness.

"Don't." Paul grabbed her wrist to stop her from taking one of their water skeins. "Don't waste our water on my hands." He wasn't worth it, and the sooner she realized that the better.

"Your hands will fester," she said in clipped, practical tones. "Then what good will you do us?"

"I'll be fine."

"Perhaps, but I've no desire to find out. I'm not setting up that tent alone."

Paul grinned, another laugh tickling his throat.

Kaya poured a thin stream of water on each palm and carefully wet the sleeve of her dress. Her hands were gentle around his as she wiped them clean of blood and sand. Paul forgot how to breathe.

"I have pomegranate root." She said it as if he'd know what that meant.

"For what?"

His voice barely reached his ears. He was too transfixed by the shadow of her movements, the soft brush of her fingers over his palms and inner wrist. Paul tried not to react, but the darkened alcove heightened his sense of her.

The one woman to whom he'd made promises he

intended to keep was also the one he couldn't have. Paul hoped her forbidding nature was making her more attractive. That once they left the desert and found a ship to sail them away from here, he would no longer want her. But he strongly suspected it was Kaya herself he found so enticing.

From the moment they met, she'd riveted him. The steady way she held her dagger. Her pride and anger when she'd refused to marry him. He wanted to kiss her full lips and caress the soft skin of her neck and chest. Paul tried to back away from the temptation.

Every moment in her presence, he failed further.

Now, trapped in a small cave by a ferocious sandstorm, his conscience ate at him. His promise to keep her safe tasted bitter on his tongue. Where had he left his senses? Probably in the desert.

"Pomegranate will help inflammation." Her voice barely carried over the howling wind.

She splashed water on her hands and briskly rubbed them together. Paul closed his eyes as she smeared a thin, cool layer of paste over his palms. The scent tickled his nose—the same lovely perfume he'd smelled on her skin. Pomegranate. It suited her.

"I have nothing else; I did not think to pack—"

"Kaya." Paul heard the nerves in her voice and stopped her. When had he grown so attuned to her?

"We should check for scorpions."

He jerked back and hit his head on the rock wall. Paul swallowed a pitiful moan. He shook his head, which only made the ache worse and settled sand in his ears. Perfect. He sighed. What was a little more sand in the grand scheme?

"Scorpions?" he repeated.

The sting of his injured hands eased, though the throbbing of his knee hadn't. He prodded the soreness with the backs of his knuckles. He'd ripped his trousers, but his knee hadn't swelled.

"They normally hunt at night."

Kaya moved from him. He felt the slight breeze of her body against his, the touch of her dress. She swept her booted feet over the ground, kicking up dirt and sand.

"What hunts at night?"

"Scorpions," she said, as if he were daft. Maybe he hit his head harder than he thought. "With the haboob and these caves, I am uncertain they remain dormant."

"I thought scorpions only lived in hot, wet climates."

"They live in the desert. As do a variety of snakes," she stated clearly, and he wondered what else lived in desert caves. "Do scorpions also live in Bombay?"

"Yes." He said it softly, but it sounded like a musket shot in their small enclosure.

Kaya stilled, and he knew she wanted to ask about his time there. After a heartbeat, she resumed her movements, faintly shuffling across the dirt. Paul breathed a sigh of relief. He had no desire to speak of Bombay.

"Keep your boots on." Her voice sounded hoarse and rough. "If you feel one on you, don't make any sudden moves."

"Easier said than done."

He kicked the area where he planned to sit before resuming his position on the cool, hard ground. Paul stretched his left leg out, biting back a groan. Silence settled over them again, he on one side of the alcove and Kaya on the other. Paul closed his eyes and let the constant wind lull him.

The wind sounded like screams.

Horrified screams of the dying, begging for their lives. The echo of musket fire into a screaming crowd. The dirt grated along his skin—the rough dryness of the ground as he fell. Hot and bloodied, he stumbled from the bodies. Clawing at his legs, their dead eyes accused him—

"Sergeant!"

* * * *

Sergeant Hartley jerked awake.

He did not flail or gasp or latch onto her. In fact, Kaya barely made out the outline of his body in the dark cave. He was muttering in his sleep, calling out names she did not understand. When she shook his shoulder to wake him, he seemed on high alert.

"Are you all right?"

Kaya brushed her fingertips along the beginning of a rough beard over his cheek, offering what little comfort she had. Derya had often stroked her cheek when she had nightmares, terrified the Ottomans had found her and dragged her away from her home to be killed before a faceless sultan.

The touch always eased her breathing and calmed her. Kaya hoped the sergeant found some consolation from whatever plagued him.

He flinched, and she dropped her hand. Her fingers tingled from touching him.

"Fine." The word sounded as jagged as the rocks they'd climbed.

Kaya snorted and sat back on her heels. "Let me clean your eyes. Don't move your hands."

She rooted around the cave floor for her satchel. The area they sheltered in wasn't large enough for her to lose anything. However, the darkness made it difficult to see her hand, let alone her bag. Kaya closed her fingers over a water skein and tugged the sash from her waist.

As she performed the simple tasks, her mind raced for conversation. She had questions, so many, yet had no idea where to begin. Conversation skills hadn't been one of her many lessons.

"Don't bother." His voice shuddered over her, strained.

Kaya paused but couldn't leave him with sand in his eyes, and she didn't know what to say to soothe him. Derya always knew what to say when Kaya had been hurt training with Gidd. Then again, Gidd ensured she did not complain—a warrior never bemoaned the injuries they received in honorable battle.

"Close your eyes." At a loss, Kaya wet the edge of her sash. "Cleaning the sand will ease your strain and help you sleep."

He snorted, but she felt the flutter of his lashes against her fingertips. With slow, soft dabs, she brushed the sand from his eyes, off his cheeks and lips. She tilted the water skein over the material again and retraced her movements.

She didn't try very hard not to think about how close she sat to him, or the warmth of his breath over her lips. A chill raced over her arms, but she attributed that to the coolness in the cave. What else could it be?

Licking her lips, Kaya sat back. She couldn't see him open his eyes, but she knew the sergeant had. His gaze followed her, a heavy intensity that pressed against her chest. Questions burned the tip of her tongue, but she swallowed them back.

Suddenly, she remembered his hands on her, touching her as no one ever had. His hand closing around her own hand, lifting her onto the ledge. A rush of heat burned her cheeks, but Kaya didn't think he'd touched her so intimately on purpose. Improper though it might've been, she had struggled up the rock face, and he had helped.

"Thank you." Grunting those words, the sergeant pushed off the wall and stood.

Surprised, Kaya fell back, catching herself on a sharp rock. She grimaced, then carefully wiped her bruised palm along her filthy skirts. "You are welcome, Sergeant."

He moved to the mouth of the cave, but the shuffling

surprised her. Had he injured his leg or foot in the climb? "Paul."

Confused, Kaya made a sound in the back of her throat.

"My name. It's Paul. Please call me that." He paused, looking around the corner of their alcove. "Instead of sergeant."

Kaya nodded even though he couldn't see her. Paul. She supposed if they were married, she should call him by his proper name. Paul. Even so, it felt strange to do so. Strange to speak to anyone she did not know.

"Can't see anything in this hubbub." Kaya was about to correct him when he did so himself. "What did you call this sandstorm?"

She stood and closed the short distance to the opening of their alcove. No light penetrated the storm, and the wind howled along the cave entrance. "A haboob. We have many names for sand." Kaya chuckled and closed her eyes. Her muscles ached from the long night's walk and the unaccustomed climb. "And many for a storm of sand."

"I'm sure." He sounded as if he were smiling. "I had no idea sand could do—" She saw the shadow of his hand wave. "That. It's…amazing."

"Sitting in the house, I never thought so." Kaya tilted her head and stared at the storm. Even here, around curves and bends, sand pelted her. She closed her eyes and stepped back. "The desert is a dangerous place."

"Everywhere is dangerous. No place is safe. There's always someone trying to kill you."

Frowning, Kaya looked at him. Of course, she couldn't see anything of his expression. "Someone?"

"Someone, something." He corrected himself, but his words tumbled over each other. "The world is dangerous."

"Yes." The word stuck in her throat. Kaya swallowed,

but her fear of being discovered didn't go away. Instead, she searched for the thread of their previous conversation. "From home, I always thought the sand an annoyance, trapped in every crevice, blocking the light."

"Oh." The sergeant snorted. "It most definitely is."

Kaya laughed again. "When you crossed the Sinai, did you not experience a haboob?"

"No," he whispered. "No haboob."

In the darkness, standing in a nook off the larger cave, Kaya saw him relax. She didn't know what else to say. She wanted to ask about his past, about Bombay and how he knew Gidd—about any piece of him.

"Why did—" He stopped. "You speak English perfectly. Who taught you?"

"Gidd." She noted the change in subject. "He insisted I learn as many languages as possible. He taught me English and Marathi. Derya…" Her voice caught, but she pushed through. "She taught me Turkish and French. Of course, they all taught me Egyptian."

"Derya, she's your maid?"

"She's—" Kaya cut her words short, throat burning. "Was. She was my mother's *odalik*." She whispered the words so faintly, they barely broke through the howling of the storm. "Her personal maid."

Kaya dug her fingers into her skirts, holding as still as possible. She hadn't expected the storm of grief to choke her. What a horrible woman she was, forgetting Derya in so short a time. Sniffing back tears, Kaya swallowed hard, again and again and again, against the lump in her throat. Against recriminations she lobbed at herself for enjoying the night's travel and not mourning the woman she'd considered her mother.

"Kaya." The sergeant stopped and coughed. "*Madaam* Kaya, are you all right?" He stopped again. "I'm sorry. I—"

"She died in a riot at the souk." Did the sergeant know that? Kaya couldn't remember if he knew, if Gidd had told him before she met the man, or even if she had told him herself. So much had happened since yesterday.

Had it only been yesterday? The day before?

"I'm sorry." His voice sounded so sincere, so genuinely sorry, Kaya believed him.

They sat in silence for a stretch of time that did nothing to ease her grief or stop her gnawing guilt.

Finally, the sergeant—Paul— shifted. "Is that why Tahir insisted on England? You sound more English than I."

"He made sure I spoke each language like a native." She closed her eyes and smoothed her fingers down her skirts, letting the touch order her thoughts. "Why did you join the army, Sergeant?"

"Paul."

Kaya nodded. "Paul." She hadn't realized how comfortable saying his name would feel, how it rolled off her tongue.

"I wanted to leave London as quickly as possible." He answered so fast, Kaya knew he'd done so before thinking it through. "The East India Company, and Bombay, was about as far from England as I could get."

"You joined to travel?" Kaya sounded so wistful, so envious, but she couldn't help it. "I wish to travel the world."

"I joined for a lot of reasons." His voice softened. "I'd forgotten I wanted to travel." He stopped again. "India sure isn't England."

"Why did you leave England?" As soon as she said the words, Kaya knew they were too intrusive, too intimate.

"It was time for me to. I needed to…leave. Get away."

She wanted to ask from what. Who he'd run from and why. Kaya crossed the distance between them. Her new husband possessed so many secrets, she didn't know where to begin. Tentatively, she reached out.

"Kaya?"

She took his hand and squeezed. The shock of skin on skin jolted through her. No matter what she thought or how she had railed against it, she and this man, Paul, were now married. She could touch him.

Clearing her throat, she hoped he understood what she had no words to express. Her curiosity and sympathy. Her understanding and interest in him and his life.

"What else have you seen?" Kaya whispered in the breath between them.

"Blood."

She didn't flinch or pull back. She waited. Listened.

He jerked his hand from hers. "I've seen streets covered in it and lands soaked in it," he snapped. Arms folded over his chest, he leaned against the opening and kept his back firmly to her. "I'm not a nice man, Kaya. You'd do well to remember that."

Chapter Six

Kaya leaned against the cool wall, as far from the sergeant as possible. Did the darkness of the cave allow him to see her mortification?

She had no logical reason for why she'd touched him. Offered him—a stranger—comfort. That he was the first man she'd known outside her family sounded as idiotic the fifth time she thought it as it had the first.

Thankfully, she hadn't done more.

Blood rushed through her, roaring in her ears. A different sort of pounding from when she'd climbed the rock face. Kaya rubbed her fingers together, the memory of him beneath her fingers a rush of—something. It warmed a part of her. She wanted to touch that place now, explore it.

Kaya looked to Paul and flushed with more of that forbidden warmth. She wanted *him* to touch her. She sat heavily on Paul's bedroll.

When she imagined new experiences, she envisioned traveling the world, meeting people, talking to them. Walking a souk and purchasing whatever she wished. Not *this*.

"How long do haboobs usually last?" Paul's question startled her, and Kaya blinked open her tired eyes.

"Several hours." She struggled for more to say, but her mind blanked. "Sometimes several days."

"Days?" The sergeant snorted. "Of course."

The wind whistled past the mouth of the cave. The sand clashed against the rocks and dislodged pebbles and larger stones. Kaya focused on her own breathing, on the stinging in her palms from her haphazard climb.

Legs crossed beneath her, Kaya curled her fingers into tight fists. She wanted to run again. Expend this energy thrumming through her. Run from her embarrassment and her foolish need to experience.

Her feet and calves ached from their midnight trek, and her back and shoulders ached from a day's sleep on the hard ground. They still had days before they reached the coast. She needed rest.

She needed to forget how Paul's skin felt beneath her fingers.

Slowly stretching, Kaya listened to the haboob. The silence and loneliness in this cave reminded her of isolation in her house—only her and her studies. In the company of another, who might actually speak with her instead of insisting she train, Kaya found herself at a loss for words.

"Hungry?" Paul asked into the silence.

Kaya started and banged her elbow on the cave wall. Paul crouched before her and held out a small, wrapped bundle.

"Where did you find so much food?" Kaya opened the cloth and inhaled the safflower-spiced dried lamb.

"It wasn't easy."

She snorted disbelievingly.

He sighed. "I stole it."

"Oh." Kaya supposed she'd expected that. Even vast amounts of money bought paltry quantities of food during the famine. "How else were you to have found so much food in a famine-ridden city?"

He awkwardly cleared his throat. "Yes. Well." He cleared his throat again. "I didn't realize how bad Cairo was until…well, until we left."

Confused, she tilted her head. She chewed the meat and tried not to shove the entire thing in her mouth. Kaya may have lived like a recluse, but she had manners, even if she showed them in truly abysmal ways—such as touching strangers.

Not that she'd ever met another recluse. There wasn't a reserved table for them in the coffeehouses. She grinned then sighed. Really, she needed conversation with someone else.

"How long were you in Cairo before we, ah, met?"

"A few days. Tahir directed me to his house; I had not realized he owned more than one."

Kaya frowned, and a familiar longing stabbed her heart. She set the lamb aside, no longer hungry. Paul had seen Gidd's home, the grand establishment he entertained in, lived in. Where people knew him and visited.

Where the rest of his family visited. Had Paul seen them? Met them there?

Hot embarrassment swamped her. Kaya sat in the dark silence, lonely and alone. Isolated.

"It was a nice house. Bit empty," Paul said slowly, as if he knew her sorrow and seclusion.

Maybe he did. Maybe he'd guessed it from the separate house she lived in.

"Only Tahir and Abdul there, no other servants. Nice place. Good food." He coughed awkwardly. "I didn't realize—famine affects people differently. I didn't realize this one affected the entire city."

Kaya had no idea what he meant by that. How could famine affect people differently? Famine affected everyone, did it not?

"You are not who I expected," she admitted.

Paul stretched his legs, his feet resting beside Kaya. Their alcove was just large enough for them to sit against opposite walls, so long as neither minded their legs touching. Paul watched her. She felt his gaze, steady and assessing.

I'm not a nice man, Kaya.

He laughed, a dry, low sound that danced over her skin. "What did you expect?"

"I do not know."

She considered him a burden to her plans. However,

she had spent the previous night's walk reassessing her feelings. "You came at Gidd's summons, promised to keep me safe. Why?"

Her trust in him had grown with every step from Cairo, trust she had not expected. Trust she certainly didn't understand.

"Tahir is a good man. His letter arrived at the right time."

Paul stopped, and Kaya wondered if he meant to go on. He'd said that before, about the letter, and she wondered what he meant. Clearly, the arrival of the missive meant a great deal to him.

"Ten years is a long time, and I had not expected my life to turn out quite the way it did."

She still didn't understand but nodded in the darkness. Her life hadn't turned out as she wanted it to, either.

"I think you are a good man." Kaya paused, then said softly, "Paul."

He snorted but didn't contradict her.

"I admit I have no experience, but you gave me your bedroll this morning and the safflower lamb now. You could have kept both for yourself."

"I don't sleep much," he said. The words lacked bite. He didn't mention the food, and in the darkness her lips curved upward.

"You also could have left me to my own strength while climbing the mountain, a feat that surely would've left me badly injured at the base of that ledge."

If not dead. No sense dwelling on what-ifs. She'd spent her life doing so, and it had only seen her here. In a mountain cave, with a stranger for a husband.

"I—" Paul stilled. Even in the darkness, she saw him shake his head and run a hand down his face. "I suppose, yes. Hadn't thought of that."

"You also haven't thrown me into *en-Nīl*. You could have drowned me over the side, and no one would've been the wiser."

No one would've known except him. Derya was dead, Gidd had cut all ties with her when he married her to this man. Alone. That was what this crushing in her chest was. She was alone with a stranger, and no one would know if anything happened to her. No one.

"Again, yes, I suppose." He chuckled. "Hadn't thought of that, either."

"You may claim to not be a nice person, but you are more honorable than you believe."

He also hadn't taken advantage in close quarters. Kaya frowned and rubbed the back of her hand against her eyes. She needed more sleep. She needed—she didn't even know where to begin.

"Don't believe that, Kaya." She keenly felt the heaviness around him.

She pressed her lips in annoyance. "You said you had nowhere else to go. Gidd considers you a friend. You helped him in Bombay. Why had you not visited Cairo before?"

Paul didn't answer, but then, Kaya hadn't truly expected him to.

"The haboob should dissipate in the night, but it'll be dark." Kaya stood, brushing her greasy hands over her sandy skirts. She grimaced. Now she had greasy *and* sandy hands. Wonderful. "Hard to see climbing down the mountain."

"No. We've lost the night." He followed her from their alcove into the slightly larger cave, but he didn't touch her. "We'll have to stay here. Don't want to risk climbing in the dark."

Kaya leaned against the wall. Hands loose at her sides, she looked around the corner to the entrance. The air was still heavy with bits of dust and rock, and her lungs ached if she breathed too deeply.

"I don't hate the desert." His whispered admission surprised her. "It's unlike any place I've ever seen. It's vast and empty during the day, but at night it's full of life."

"Yes. It is." Not that she knew. Kaya sighed and willed away her bitter anger. She was so very tired of being angry. Closing her eyes, she rubbed her temple, trying in vain to ease the pounding tension.

"The wind is dying down," she finally said. "It should only last another hour or so."

"Left my timepiece in my red coat." Paul sounded amused—and closer than she thought.

Her lips curled into a quick smile, there and gone. In the unrelenting darkness, he couldn't see her, and that small comfort alleviated some of the tension tightening Kaya's shoulders and neck. Not, however, the warmth spreading through her limbs and making her fingers tingle with anticipation.

"Even after the haboob passes, the sand and dust will be everywhere." She strained for any sound over the pounding of her heart and her too-fast breathing. "It's best we stay here until the air clears."

"Right. Yes." Paul moved another step into the main cave. "I trust your judgment in this." He breathed out a huff of laughter, strained in the intimacy of their cave. "It's my first haboob."

The man made no sense. Kaya was used to her life being ordered, practical. Dull and monotonous, perhaps, but regimented. Kaya pulled back. Physically, as far as the alcove allowed. Mentally, even farther.

"It's my first haboob in a cave." She straightened, stretching sore muscles. "We should be more careful. Many animals take shelter in caves."

"I'm surprised we haven't run into any," he said. From

the faintness of his voice, she could tell he once again stood at the curve between their niche and the main cave. As far from her as possible.

"Or snakes. We ought to be more cautious." She stood and wandered to the curve. "There are dozens of poisonous snakes in Egypt."

"Do snakes live in caves?" His question sounded sharper, and she tilted her head.

"They live anywhere," she told him. "And I've no wish to learn anything new about snakes firsthand."

Paul laughed, a choked sound that echoed oddly between them. "I doubt anything moves about in a haboob, even snakes."

"No." Kaya frowned at the ground, though she couldn't see anything. She hoped he was right. "We'll need to hunt soon. Closer to the river will be our best chance."

"We have enough food to see us through a couple nights. We'll make our way west to the river, but I don't want to lose the protection of the mountains." Paul cleared his throat, and she heard a strain in that sound she didn't understand. "Rest. I'll wake you when it's clear."

Kaya stilled. There it was, that inherent trust. She had always relied on others and knew very little about the world, but why trust a man she knew nothing about?

At a loss for answers, she carefully stepped into their alcove. She shuffled along the dirt and kicked the bedroll. No matter how she listened, she heard no skitter of tiny legs, no hiss, no yelp of a larger creature. Still, she carefully crouched down and grasped the edges of the fabric. Giving the roll a firm shake, she settled it back on the ground.

"What are you doing?" Again, his voice was tinged with humor.

"Checking for scorpions and snakes. Or anything else that might live in here or seek shelter." She sat on his roll and made herself as comfortable as possible. "I have no desire to be bitten by anything."

He snorted, and she wondered if she detected a note of caution in that action. "No, no, I can't say I do, either."

Kaya massaged her legs. Her cramped muscles were unused to such long walks or climbs of any sort. Tempted as she was, she didn't dare remove her boots, no matter how her feet ached. Not after this evening, when she'd forced her poor feet into boots she'd rather never see again.

Paul had been right about that much.

Closing her eyes, fingers clenched around the hilt of her khanjar, she did her best to blank her mind and sleep.

* * * *

"Kaya." Paul shook her shoulder but didn't let his touch linger.

Here he was, reduced to fighting his desire for a woman he barely knew. He almost missed the days of charming women, having sex with them, forgetting they existed. At least that had sated his desire for another's touch without the complications of intimacy.

"Is it time?" she asked, voice husky with sleep.

In truth, he had been charming until Egypt. Between Bombay and Cairo, the sun had baked away whatever charm he possessed. Or thought he possessed.

"The sun will fully rise in an hour or so. If we leave now, we can cover a little ground before we need to stop."

If they left now, they could flee this cave of confessions and secrets before he did something momentously stupid. Like kiss her.

"All right." She stood and stretched.

The predawn light refused to dent the darkness of their alcove. Nonetheless, he watched her back arch, her arms raise high over her head, her hips thrust out as she bent backwards. Then she bent forward and let her arms hang down, fingertips touching the ground.

Paul tore his gaze from her and grabbed the bedroll. He was not looking at her arse, at the perfection of her hips. He was not. He strapped the bedroll to the bottom of his pack. Even if he'd already clearly envisioned both her arse and hips. Felt them beneath his fingertips—

"Water?" Without looking at Kaya, he offered her a skein.

She silently took it and drank, adding in a small ritual. Paul paused. She stepped into the larger opening and looked at the sun, which was just peeking over the horizon. Then she turned and knelt.

A large part of him wanted to ask about her prayers. She'd asked him to wake her around noon so she could pray as well. He hadn't said anything, merely done as requested. Now, listening to her morning prayers, Paul wanted to hear her voice as she told him everything. But the more practical part of himself hesitated.

For the first time since meeting Kaya, Paul listened to that practical voice. Instead of asking, he waited for her in the curve between their alcove and the cave's entrance.

"You repacked the tent." She sounded surprised when she joined him.

"Yes." He hadn't been able to sleep and needed something to occupy him. In the darkness, it'd taken forever to repack it, but doing so had passed the time. "It's still fairly dark," he warned as they exited. "Watch your step."

In the heavy, still air, they made it to the base of the mountain with minimal problems. It was far easier climbing down in the predawn than it had been scrambling up during a storm. He opened his mouth to say just that when Kaya skidded, and his heart stopped.

"Kaya!"

Visions of her landing in the crevice below haunted

him. Paul hadn't realized he'd moved until she looked at him as she righted herself.

"I am all right. Unharmed."

"Right. Good."

Stepping back, he clenched his hands around the straps of his pack. His scraped palms rubbed mercilessly against the leather, and his jaw clenched against the pain. Kaya merely dusted her hands on her skirts and continued to descend. Swallowing heavily, willing his heart to slow, Paul kept the respectable distance he'd forced between them and followed.

At the base of the mountain, once more on solid ground, he led them through the winding valley. They walked in silence, sometimes side by side, but more often single file as they wound through the narrow crevices.

"I admit, this might've been easier on the river."

Kaya's soft giggle lightened his mood. "I've never seen the mountains. Either way is a new experience for me."

Paul grunted. "Not all new experiences are good ones."

"No." She drew the word out, huffing slightly. "But they make a person, do they not? Derya always said her experiences at the palace made her the woman she was." Kaya cleared her throat, and Paul stopped, then turned to face her. She shook her head and met his gaze. "Experiences make us who we are, yes?"

"Yes," he agreed, when he saw she was waiting for his answer.

"Then I do not know who I am, as my experiences are quite limited."

"Kaya—"

She stopped him with a hand on his arm. Voice suddenly thin and quiet, she asked, "Did you hear that?"

He looked at her sharply, startled by the uncharacteristic wobble in her voice. All he heard was the pounding of his heart as he replayed her falling down the rock face, but he listened.

"No." He drew out the word, not more than a breath, only to cut himself off.

He backed Kaya against the rocky wall, hand cradling her head. Shrugging off his pack, careful not to let the wooden beam clatter against the rocks, Paul drew his dagger. Someone had found them. Balancing his weapon, Paul braced for a fight. Had the English found him already? And in the middle of the Egyptian mountains?

A betting man to be sure, even Paul acknowledged those were impossible odds.

Two men turned the base of the mountain, chatting quietly in Egyptian, a bound and gagged woman stumbling weakly between them.

Not the English. Slavers.

Chapter Seven

With her breath knocked out of her, Kaya blinked at him. Sharp points of rock face jabbed into her back. Heart racing as quickly as her mind, she didn't move and wisely kept silent.

Paul removed his dagger and braced his feet wide. Fingers numb, Kaya removed her khanjar and prepared to defend herself as she'd been taught.

The whisper of footsteps, the even lower murmurs of conversation grew louder. Her thoughts tripped over themselves—the Ottomans, smugglers, bandits who killed and robbed their victims. Kaya hadn't expected the woman stumbling between the two men. Clearly terrified in the faint morning light, her hands had been bound in front of her, her mouth gagged, her face a mottled mass of bruises.

Blood dripped from the woman's wrists. Her steps dragged unevenly. The men held the rope tied to her neck. When she stumbled, they viciously yanked her upright.

Fury, the likes of which Kaya had never known, ripped through her.

The disgusting way the men treated the injured woman made her want to tear them apart. It welled from deep within her, a place Kaya hadn't known existed. She pushed off the rocks, everything in her frantic to hurt the men for treating the woman so—so—she didn't have a word.

"Appallingly" wasn't nearly strong enough.

It burned in the pit of her stomach. Disdain or scorn. Despise. She *despised* them for their treatment of the woman. It choked her, a vise around her lungs and throat.

Logically, Kaya knew what might happen to an unprotected woman in the desert. Derya warned her of the dangers and had refused to venture anywhere near Cairo's slave markets. But logic had no place in the *anger*, the suffocating *fury* that wiped rational thought from Kaya's mind.

She clutched her khanjar in anger and shock and with a beating desire to help. Paul stood in front of her, back straight, arms loose at his sides, dagger balanced in one hand.

This woman could not protect herself—Kaya vowed to do it for her.

Paul snarled, and it beat deep within her. An answering sound to her own angry ferocity of hatred.

"Leave the woman," Paul growled.

Either the dagger was a widely recognized sign between opponents, or the savage, challenging look on Paul's face translated well enough. The men dropped the rope and lunged.

Kaya, torn between joining the fight and helping the woman, chose to help. The stranger obviously needed it more than Paul, who circled round the pair of men, keeping them in sight. He purposefully drew them away from Kaya to the other side of the small ravine.

Paul's steps reflected his lethal certainty, a predator set to pounce. He moved with a fluidity she envied. She marveled at his grace but tore her gaze away.

Kaya knelt beside the trembling woman and ignored how the hard, rocky crevice dug into her knees. She set her dagger in her lap, glancing at Paul before gently removing the gag. The dirty, gray cloth had dug into the skin around the woman's mouth, rubbing it raw. When Kaya pulled the fabric away, droplets of blood splattered the woman's cheek.

Paul grunted. She flinched at the sound, her head whipping up.

Maneuvering around the woman, Kaya kept Paul in her sights. He prowled around the men, silently focused, not so much as glancing at her. Awed at his smooth movements, the way he deliberately jabbed his dagger at the men, retaining their attention, Kaya nonetheless turned back to the terrified woman cowering on the ground.

"Shh," she whispered. "I won't hurt you." Kaya spoke in Egyptian. The woman showed no recognition.

Another grunt, another hiss of pain. Unable to resist, Kaya looked again. Paul was using the rocky mountain base to his advantage, keeping his back to it so neither man could circle around him. The two men attacked in tandem, but Paul parried each blow.

This clearly wasn't his first fight.

He'd said he'd seen blood. She shivered at his words: *I'm not a nice man.*

Heart leaping at each grunt, each fall of rocks, she fumbled for her bag. Kaya turned the woman's head to face her so she couldn't see the fight and removed a water pouch. It was nearly empty, but she offered it anyway. A small kindness in a life that had clearly endured too much. The woman drank greedily.

"Can you tell me your name?" Kaya asked, again in Egyptian.

The woman whimpered as she drank but gave no answer. Kaya tried Turkish and Marathi, then her halting, limited Greek. Still no answer.

One of the men growled, and Kaya gripped her dagger. Her shoulders knotted, and she braced herself as a lifetime's training emerged. Vigilant, Kaya watched them from the corner of her eye. She tried to help the woman sit, but she cried out in pain.

Kaya gasped at the bloodstain on the woman's gown. "You're injured." She spoke more to herself than the woman, though she hoped it eased her somewhat. "Stabbed. Did they do this?"

Blood seeped through the rough gray fabric, spreading from her side down her left hip. Kaya's mind raced with what she knew about treating wounds. There was too much blood for her to stop it.

Paul shouted, a grunt of pain. Kaya jerked, and her fingers clasped around the khanjar, prepared to defend him. Only one man fought Paul. He panted, hands shaking, as if he'd rather run than continue the battle. He backed up and looked madly around the narrow crevice, but there was no escape—Paul cornered him.

Kaya refused to look at the first man, now a crumpled body on the ground, and returned her attention to the woman. She'd never witnessed death. Never witnessed one man killing another, though Gidd had prepared her to defend herself in such a situation.

It was not as she expected.

"I need to see your wound." Kaya said the words as gently as possible. She repeated them in English, French, and again in Egyptian. The woman stared blankly, tears streaking from the corners of her eyes.

Kaya placed her dagger beside her and raised her hands, palm up, to show their emptiness. Dark, wild eyes looked back at her. Kaya didn't think they truly saw her—or anything other than untamed fear. She ignored the still-too-tight ropes around the woman's wrists and neck and carefully prodded the immediate danger of her bleeding wound.

The woman whimpered in pain, weaker now, and Kaya's heart ached.

"I need to see your side," she said softly in Egyptian. "I want to help."

Listening to the fight behind her, it amazed Kaya how easily she could pick out Paul's smoother movements over those of the slaver's. Even as she slowly reached for the woman's side, she listened to ensure the slaver didn't defeat Paul and attack her.

Paul grunted in pain. Stomach in knots, Kaya glanced

at him. He had the other man cornered. Kaya knew what was going to happen next, and she looked away just as the other man screamed. She did not want to witness his death.

Kaya was still trying to assess the woman's wound, pulling gently at her sodden gown. The fabric stuck to her bloody side, and Kaya stopped. Why had they injured her so fatally only to force her on this march?

"I'm sorry," she whispered, tears blurring her vision. "I'm sorry."

The woman smiled, a slight tilt to her cracked and bloody lips. Kaya didn't know if she understood the words or the tears now falling along her cheeks.

"Kaya."

Her head jerked up, khanjar in hand, ready to defend herself and the dying woman.

Kaya looked up at Paul. He'd backed away, hands raised in surrender. She barely saw that, even as he slowly lowered his hands. All she saw was the bruise blossoming on his cheek, his bloody knuckles, the blood staining his brown coat.

"You're hurt." She pushed herself off the ground and reached for him.

"No." He shook his head, tired and weary, and slumped against a large rock near the abandoned pack. His hands dangled loosely at his sides, and a drop of blood fell from his fingers to the dirt. "It's not my blood."

"Oh." She didn't think any sound had emerged.

Paul's gaze, tired yet suspiciously bright, stayed on hers. His shoulders collapsed; his entire body caved in on itself. She wanted to go to him, offer some sort of comfort or touch or—

"How is she?" he asked before Kaya could decide what to do.

"She's dying," Kaya whispered.

Paul watched her, those blue-green eyes so alert in his dusty, bloodied face. Nodding at his unspoken understanding, she turned and knelt beside the woman, whose breath struggled with every gasp. Paul would watch over them, guard them from anyone else who might wander down this ravine.

She knelt by the stranger. Kaya didn't know what to say, so she sang some of the songs she'd heard the *Alateeyeh* play over her wall. Beautiful songs of far-off lands, of love found in unlikely places. She didn't have a voice like the singers she long admired. It wobbled and broke, but Kaya hoped the melody eased this woman's suffering even a little.

"I'm sorry."

Paul's voice cut through her singing, though Kaya already knew the woman had died. She nodded and slowly released her hand. Sheathing her khanjar, she took another minute to stand. Her legs shook, but she straightened her back and sought Paul's gaze.

His eyes, no longer bright, met hers. She didn't know what killing another felt like, but suddenly she understood the shadows darkening his eyes. It broke her heart.

Kaya didn't think, she simply moved.

In two steps, she met him, wrapped her arms around his neck, and held tight. The comfort of another. She buried her face in his neck and breathed in his scent, stale sweat and blood. Kaya closed her eyes, willing away the images of death.

Paul's arms tightened, as if he never wanted to let her go. With the comfort of him wrapped around her, Kaya didn't want to let him go, either.

He moved just enough to frame her face with his large, warm hands. Enough to move his mouth over hers. His kiss was rough, hard, and it sent a thrill through her that Kaya wanted to feel always. She opened her mouth to him, felt the sweep of his tongue against hers as he deepened the kiss.

Kaya wanted it to last, wanted more of everything, all of it. Of him and the charged feeling of being *alive*.

Gradually, her breathing heavy, she pulled back, stepped from his arms.

The sun rose high in the desert sky, high enough to pierce their small area of shade. They had lost another day in this ravine between mountains and desert. They needed to leave, continue toward Damietta, but she hadn't the strength.

She barely had the strength to stay out of Paul's arms. She cleared her dry throat and licked her cracked lips. She still tasted him there and wanted to again.

Paul watched her for another moment. "Come on."

He turned for his pack and shrugged it on, each movement slow and painful. Kaya adjusted her hijab and shouldered her bow and quiver. When had she dropped them? She didn't remember, she only remembered her burning need to help the woman.

Paul had moved the two dead men off to one side, slightly deeper into the mountain. She stared blindly at their bodies, they who thought this woman's life less than their own.

"We can't bury her." Paul took her hand. "I'm sorry." He snarled the words, anger and something else tingeing them. Helplessness, maybe. "I don't know if there are more slavers nearby, waiting for their friends."

Kaya looked at him, truly studied him, but he turned from her. She understood, she did. It didn't make leaving the poor woman any easier. They had no shovels, no tools to dig through the hard-packed sand. And while there were plenty of rocks, they were either far too large for them to lift or too small to cover the nameless woman.

Her head shot up. "I need another minute."

Paul frowned but nodded. Angry with herself for

forgetting, for putting her own comfort above this woman's soul, Kaya knelt beside the body. She recited the *Ṣalāt al-Janāzah*, the prayer for the dead.

Her family was not religious—Abdul claimed, at one time, Gidd had been, but lost his faith after the death of his youngest son, her father. However, Derya taught her all the proper prayers. After Derya's death, Kaya never thought she'd have to recite it again so soon.

Standing, she returned to Paul's side. He watched but didn't ask. Kaya sniffed back tears for a woman whose name she didn't know and met his gaze. He took her hand, and they walked out of the ravine.

Tired, hungry, in desperate need of further comfort, she hiked beside him.

"We won't be able to walk long in the desert sun," she said, for lack of anything else, as they navigated the narrow path. Kaya kept her voice low in case the dead slavers' comrades searched for them. "We won't make it far, not in the heat."

"We need to get away from here," Paul insisted and continued walking.

He hurried her along, pulling her through narrow passes and slightly wider ones. Not that she needed hurrying. Kaya was eager to leave the bodies, the death, behind. Keeping an eye on the sun's position so as not to lose their way, they climbed over low ridges, careful not to dislodge too many rocks or make too much noise.

They moved north, deeper into the mountains as they ran from Cairo and from the dead.

The sun rose higher, topping the mountain peaks. Their pace slowed, but Paul moved them inexorably forward. Kaya didn't protest and silently trudged beside him.

Paul looked up as they exited the small path and came back into the desert. The sun seared her skin. It was so blindingly bright; even with her eyes closed, it burned. Kaya forced her feet to continue through the scorching sand.

"There are too many places to hide in the mountains, too many little caves like the one in which we waited out the haboob."

"Are there many?" Kaya panted. Her voice sounded unnaturally loud. She was so very hot and wanted nothing more than to stop and rest. Drink—oh, she desperately wanted to drink the rest of their water. "Slavers, I mean."

"Probably." He cleared his throat. "I won't let them take you, Kaya."

Kaya whipped her head round to stare at him. The movement made her dizzy, and she stilled while the world righted itself. In the glaring sunlight, he looked straight ahead, his impassive face sweaty, resolute. Incredulous, she waited for him to elaborate. But Paul offered no addition.

"I know you won't," she whispered. "Thank you."

Not a nice man.

Yet he'd protected her and the nameless woman from the slavers. Not just protected. The snarl in his voice, the way he attacked them, told her how much he hated what those men stood for. He hadn't paused, he had only reacted.

They walked slower as they moved along the hot, rocky road, the mountains looming to the east. Kaya focused on placing one foot in front of the other, trying not to think about the nameless woman or how close they'd come to sharing her fate. Worse for her—she might've ended up a slave, sold who knew where.

She watched Paul from the corner of her eye. She owed him her life.

The energy pumping through her after the fight now exhausted her.   Kaya desperately wanted sleep.

They walked along the edge between mountain and desert. She used her sleeves to wipe her face, but it did little good. Eventually Paul stopped, breathing hard, red-faced, and limping.

"Your knee bothers you?" Frowning, Kaya looked down at the tear in his trousers and the exposed skin of his left knee.

"It's fine." He didn't look at her.

"You are limping."

"We'll camp here for the day." He looked at the sky, then to the mountains. "How much further before we lose the protection of the mountains?"

"The mountains give way to the delta in…" She tilted her head as Paul dumped their tent onto the ground. "I'd say two days' walk? That's barring haboobs, men trying to kill us, and the desert heat."

"Which is also trying to kill us."

"Yes," Kaya agreed softly.

Paul snorted and held one end of the tent out for her to take. Kaya moved clumsily; every movement took all her energy. They quickly assembled it, as best they could in the hard-packed sand, and ducked under its shade. Kaya sighed in relief. Paul shook out his bedroll and sat next to her, stretching his legs.

Blood stained the trousers of his left leg, the fabric torn and dirty. His face remained caked with blood, as did his hands. She couldn't bring herself to look at his coat, which he'd carelessly tossed to the side.

"I'm sorry I can't clean your hands and face," she said in the sudden silence between them. She tried to ease her breathing, but she was unbearably hot and so very thirsty. Kaya threw propriety and caution away and rolled her skirts up to her knees. There was no wind to cool her. "We only have enough water for two days."

Paul made a small sound in the back of his throat. His eyes were already closed. "Thank you."

"For?"

"Trying. Caring." He turned to face her, his eyes still closed. "Being you."

"Oh." She had no idea what that meant.

He looked exhausted, far more tired than she. Had he not slept in the cave? Or had he stayed awake—and what? Watched for trespassers? Watched the swirling sand of the haboob? Watched her?

Kaya would've laughed at her own preposterousness if she weren't so drained. She eyed his bedroll but couldn't bring herself to use it when he so clearly needed sleep.

"We should sleep." The words fell from her lips, a slurred mumble. "Once we reach the delta, we'll lose the protection of the mountains."

"You sleep." His eyes focused on her now, startling in their force. "Take the roll; I'll be fine."

"I doubt that," she shot back, annoyed with him and herself. She had not thought to pack for sleeping. But then everything had been so rushed that night. "You are injured and exhausted and walking in the desert heat. The roll is large enough for us to share."

Paul shook his head, grimacing at the movement. He didn't argue, and Kaya thought him even more exhausted and pained than she'd originally believed.

"We need to sleep if we're to walk more than an hour tonight. We'll hunt on the road."

Paul only huffed. "I was right." Movements slow and measured, he maneuvered his pack deeper into the tent and leaned it against one of the rock formations to the rear. "You are stubborn."

Kaya raised an eyebrow. "When did you think this?"

"The moment you refused to marry me. Again when Tahir entered the house and you two argued. I'd never seen a chin rise up so fast in anger. And your eyes…" His own met hers, and he let out another small huff of amusement. "Thought you were going to shoot fire from them."

She sniffed and moved to one side of the bedding. "I had very few choices in my life." She meant the words to sound flippant, but they came out low, wistful. "I hoped one decision to be mine."

He looked up then, all exhaustion gone. Paul reached out and brushed rough, dry fingertips over her cheek. "I'm sorry."

Speechless, she watched him. After all that had happened in the last day—two? —Kaya had no idea what to say. When had things shifted between them?

They stretched out on the hard sand, each using the bedroll for a pillow. Kaya tried to stay awake, tried to think things through and sort out her suddenly conflicting feelings for Paul. But then her eyes closed, and she drifted into a dreamless sleep.

Chapter Eight

Another morning, another sunrise.

The sun peeked over the horizon in a blaze of orange-gold. Its light spread over the craggy desert and hard brush like questing fingers gingerly seeking their way through unfamiliar territory.

Not unlike her.

In an hour, the sun would break from the horizon and cast its heat over the desert behind them and the fertile ground ahead. Only then would they stop for the day.

Paul had insisted they circumvent the small towns that dotted the desert and avoid the animals that ventured from their daytime dens. Kaya agreed, though she never told him of her own fears—his paranoia served her own.

She hunted in the hours before sunrise, finally putting into practice all Gidd's teachings. They ate well enough once the sun rose and the light from their small fire was no longer visible. Luckily, an oasis lay in their path, and they refilled their water and quickly washed, vanishing before anyone saw them.

This was her fourth sunrise? Third? Fifth? The days muddled together in a whirlwind of heat and walking. Kaya closed her eyes and concentrated—one foot in front of the other. Her legs ached, her feet throbbed, and every breath burned through her.

She righted her hijab over her head, adjusting the material with shaking arms and fumbling hands. Kaya closed her eyes and silently berated herself. She should have been careful about her wishes. These were not the new experiences she'd hoped for.

Kaya wanted to talk to Paul, to recapture the closeness of their night in the cave. Hear stories of his travels and learn about the outside world. Anything to relieve the monotony of this walk. Licking her lips, the memory of their kiss still afire along her skin, Kaya wanted to rekindle the spark of lightning that had flooded her veins when their lips met.

The fertile delta beckoned her, the only reason she kept walking, kept moving forward. The promise of fresh water enticed her, and Kaya swore she already felt the cool river breeze.

Finally, the just-rising sun stretching over the landscape, they crossed into the delta, closer to one of *en-Nīl*'s tributaries.

Eager, hot, exhausted, Kaya hurried from Paul's side to the shoreline. Before she could kneel by the water, Paul stopped her.

"Not here."

She stilled, absurdly afraid he'd spotted an Ottoman scout. An assassin. A slaver. Crocodiles, even. She saw nothing but allowed him to lead her along the river. The water was lower than she'd expected, but Kaya nonetheless knelt by the river and splashed tepid water on her face, sighing at the feel of it on her dry, hot skin.

Paul joined her, removing his pack with a groan and washing. "I have never been so happy to see clean water."

"I need to bathe." Kaya sighed, hesitating. She eyed Paul, then dipped her hijab in the river and wrung it out several times before wrapping it back around her head. Sighing at the cool water dripping down her back, she cupped her hands in the thin stream and rinsed her mouth.

Paul grinned and washed his sunburnt face and hands. "We'll drink up and refill our skeins."

"You plan to make camp nearby?" Kaya paused as she held one of the skeins beneath the river. "There are animals close to the banks."

"And I'm sure they eat people." His voice held humor, but she knew him well enough by now to know he didn't doubt her.

"Yes."

"Of course they do."

They refilled their water and drank as much as they could. Kaya let the river wash over her hands and longed to do the same for her feet and legs. Now wasn't the time. Not with the sun rising and the water beckoning others to its banks.

"Better?" Paul asked.

"Delightful."

Paul took handfuls of water and wet his own head, scrubbing his hands through his hair. His normally slicked-back hair curled loosely against his neck and cheeks. Kaya wanted to run her fingers through it, feel the strands, see if they were as soft as they looked.

"Come on." Paul grinned through dry, cracked lips. The bruise on his cheek had deepened to a mottled purple. "We can walk another hour before the heat stops us."

He dunked his coat in *en-Nīl*, soaking the wool. Kaya didn't watch to see if the water washed away the bloodstains.

"We haven't much food left." Kaya stood and gathered her items. "We can fish here, or hunt the banks."

"Two fig rolls and a lamb kabob." Paul stood and strapped his pack over his shoulders. He wrung out his coat and settled it over the pack, then dipped his hat in the water and placed it on his head. Water dripped onto the wooden beam, *plick plick plick.*

"But we have fresh water."

"Yes." She blinked in astonishment.

"Always pays to keep track of one's provisions."

"Yes, I suppose that makes sense, always knowing what one has to eat so one can ration a day's meal—"

"In case you need to barter for something better."

Kaya blinked again. "Oh. Yes, that makes sense, too."

Paul Hartley was full of surprises.

A breeze cooled the morning air, and she closed her eyes against the sun's glare, tilting her chin toward it and simply enjoying the feel. She'd been too weary during their nighttime walks to appreciate her surroundings and too exhausted during the daytime to notice much.

"Let's make camp here." Kaya pulled her hands from the water though she desperately wanted to bathe then sleep in a clean bed. Or maybe sleep first. No, definitely bathe first. "Not here, on the banks, but close. I can't walk anymore."

Despite the water and the breeze, fatigue tugged her shoulders. It was clouding her brain, and she'd no wish to speak more than necessary.

"Kaya," Paul drew out. He stopped and nodded. "All right. We'll head away from the banks of the river and set up there."

"Thank you."

He helped her shoulder her things and led her away from the water.

"How many more steps until Damietta?" She prayed once they arrived she could finally stop walking.

"We'll be in Damietta tonight," he promised.

Her legs protested the very thought.

Paul no longer struggled with the wooden beam or scoffed at her offer of help. Together, they set up the tent as far from both the river and the road as possible.

She wanted to cry every time she raised her arms. Or breathed. Or blinked. But she was too exhausted even for tears. In silence, they secured their goat's hair shelter and sat beneath it to watch the day.

Kaya slowly chewed her fig roll and offered the last one to Paul. Without touching her, he accepted. Kaya stretched her legs in front of her and moaned.

She eyed her boots longingly but resisted.

"Don't," Paul warned, a hint of humor in his voice.

"I have learned my lesson," Kaya assured him. A hard lesson, to be sure, but one she clearly remembered. Never again would she cram aching, tired, slightly swollen feet back into shoes they did not wish to be crammed into.

"Until today, I'd never seen *en-Nīl*." She spoke softly, massaging her poor calves.

"No," Paul muttered. "I supposed you hadn't."

"I tried once, sneaked out one night when I was maybe ten." Why hadn't she kept her mouth closed? Now that she'd started, the words refused to stop.

"What did you do?" Paul chuckled. Kaya felt his eyes on her but didn't meet his gaze. "Jump out the window?"

Feet firmly encased in her detestable shoes, Kaya flexed her toes. She tore her gaze from her boots, offering a slight smile. "Yes."

He laughed, a rich, deep vibration. The sound wound around her so intimately, she wanted to hear it again.

Kaya licked her lips, her brain scrambling. "I wanted to see *en-Nīl*. Abdul told stories of the crocodiles and hippopotami, and I was young and tired of being hidden away. I didn't—I wanted to see more than the walls of that house or the books I read. I wanted to—"

Kaya cut herself off. She'd already told Paul how she wished to see more than her house, more than three people. Implied it, at least. There was no point in rehashing the same, pathetic story.

"It's good we set up camp here," she said instead. "River animals devour people who venture too close to their territory."

"Of course they do." Paul sighed and shook his head. He immediately pressed his fingers to his eyes. He hadn't said anything, but she knew his head pained him. "Nothing in this country is easy."

"Do they not have dangerous animals in England?" Kaya frowned. "I don't know much about England."

"It's colder. Not as much sun. Lots of rain." Paul paused. "Badgers. We have badgers and boars." He frowned but didn't elaborate of the dangers of badgers and boars. She knew what a boar was, of course, but she couldn't place a badger.

Kaya tore her gaze from the landscape to Paul. He didn't look at her, just stared at the scenery, eyes unfocused and distant. His hands rested on his thighs, fingers curling upward. She didn't ask about badgers, keeping quiet in the hopes he'd talk.

"Bombay has tigers." His softer voice captivated her, a mesmerizing quality she'd not heard from him before. "They're so graceful when they attack. It's like nothing I've ever seen. Sleek and deadly. Silent as the night. But so beautiful." He inhaled sharply and shook himself. "And snakes—they have snakes so large they'll wrap around a man, choking him to death. The *ajgar*."

"I have no wish to meet this *ajgar*." Kaya shook her head decisively. "Are there snakes in France and England?"

"Yes, but nothing like in India or here. I don't think there's anything poisonous, but I didn't live on a farm or in the woods."

"Where did you live?"

Paul didn't answer. Kaya hadn't expected him to.

"We have no snakes that wrap around a man," she said into the silence. "Though I would not wish to meet an asp, either."

Paul shuddered. "No."

He turned to face her, surprising her. His eyes, the beautiful blue-green that so captivated her, locked on hers. All his barriers dropped for a heartbeat, and his gaze softened, opened, steadily watched her. The constant focus, the trust, the understanding.

It trapped her, captured her so completely it hurt to breathe.

Her heart twisted, and Kaya abruptly stood, turning her back to him. She closed her eyes and willed away the emotion clogging her throat. Stepping from the tent, despite the hot sun, she stretched her arms high over her head. Her back ached, her legs hurt, her muscles pulled and throbbed and stung, and her feet refused to move another step.

She let out a small whimper and gingerly lowered her arms. Maybe moving had not been a good idea.

"You're going to need new shoes once we reach Damietta."

Looking over her shoulder—and even that pulled and ached—Kaya nodded. "Yes." She didn't return to the tent, despite the foolishness of being out from its cover.

Paul shifted closer, and Kaya looked down at him despite her desire not to. He pushed her skirts out of the way to expose her right leg.

Stunned, Kaya stared, open-mouthed. "What are you doing?" She'd wanted to demand, but the words came out quietly, shocked rather than forceful.

"Here, sit," he whispered. "Trust me."

Before she realized what was happening, before she knew what he intended or even found words that weren't incoherent mumbles, Paul tugged her beneath the tent and onto the bedroll. In a single smooth move, he rolled up her skirts and took her calf in his hands. His steady fingers massaged her sore muscles.

"*Oh.*" She melted into his touch.

His fingers were long and sure. They dug in with just the right amount of pressure. Captivated, she watched his darker, tanned fingers move confidently against her lighter skin.

She licked her lips and tore her gaze from the sight. Kaya wanted to ignore the way his touch lit up her nerves from her shin to her belly, but she found it impossible to do so. Newly familiar warmth spread through her with each stroke.

This was nothing like their kiss.

"I should've done this before," he said. His fingers dug into her calf, and she moaned. "You aren't used to walking so long."

Kaya ignored the awareness dancing over her skin. Or tried to. She wanted his touch. His kiss. Wanted to explore the temptation heating her blood and pooling low in her belly.

Crouched in front of her, she felt the caress of Paul's gaze as surely as that of his fingers.

Without a word, he took her other leg and offered the same long strokes, the same care and touch that had sparked a wildfire in her. His fingers brushed the sensitive skin behind her knee, and she gasped. The heat melting through her intensified, and she ached for more.

Kaya abruptly pulled her legs back.

Paul's fingers dropped to the ground, now nothing more than a phantom touch. She hastened to cover her legs and slipped them beneath her.

"We'll—" Paul cleared his throat and avoided her gaze. His hands curled into fists and pressed to the tops of his thighs. "We'll find you another gown in Damietta, too."

Unable to tear her gaze from him or find any reply that didn't sound as if she'd pulled random words from the sky, Kaya pressed her lips tightly together. He met her gaze, and, for the briefest of moments, she thought she saw hunger burning there.

The same hunger clawed within her, an agitated animal Kaya didn't understand. It burned just beneath her skin, a fire threatening to consume her.

* * * *

"Kaya."

His hand was large and warm on her shoulder, his fingers faintly brushing the side of her neck. She sighed and leaned into his caress.

Then she shot awake.

"Is it time?"

Kaya cleared the clouds from her brain, the sleepiness that tried to rule her movements. She hoped Paul took it as a sign she was waking up, not wanting more of his sinful touch.

"The sun will set in an hour." He stood and looked to the road. "There's a caravan a few miles off. I want to be in Damietta before they catch up with us."

Stilling, she looked to the south, toward the barely visible caravan. She licked her lips and casually stood. "Do you think they're more slavers?"

Her calves felt gloriously loose. Her feet still throbbed, and her thighs wanted the same wonderful massage her calves had received—as did her back and arms and shoulders. But Kaya resolutely kept those wishes to herself.

Voicing them would lead to madness.

"No idea, but it's best we move ahead of them." Paul knelt and rolled the bedding, his eyes shadowed beneath the tent.

The memory of his touch sent that same yearning anticipation tingling sharply through her. She wanted his fingers on her bare flesh, exploring this tingling need.

The sun blanketed the ground and made the air heavy. Kaya sipped from a water skein and made sure they didn't leave any of their paltry belongings behind. The coolness of the river breeze barely tempered the heat.

If they—and by *they*, Kaya meant *she*—maintained their pace, maybe they'd arrive in Damietta in several hours. Her feet protested.

In the distance, the caravan made its meandering progress toward the fertile plain. More and more of them crowded the road the closer they crept to the coast, and Paul seemed nervous every time he saw so much as a dust cloud.

How many transported slaves? How many women had been bound and gagged and beaten? Were any of the riders from the sultan's court, sent to hunt her? Her grandfather had promised to keep them otherwise occupied, but even Tahir's influence didn't reach into the desert.

Kaya shuddered in the heat and curled her suddenly numb fingers into fists.

No matter how often she reminded herself that no one knew who she was, that it was impossible for the Ottomans to discover her identity, the fear remained. Her too-many years spent listening to warnings, spent preparing for an attack, curled cold through her.

Beyond the caravan, she fancied she saw the outline of Cairo. She closed her eyes and breathed out a prayer for Gidd's safety.

Pressing a hand to her heart, she attempted to ease its ever-present ache. As much as she mourned Derya and missed Gidd, Kaya was determined to embrace her new life. Taking a deep breath, she turned north.

Paul rolled up the goat's hair tent and deftly stowed it in his pack. He eyed the thick board, but dutifully tied it to the leather pack as well.

"I'll be happy when we don't have to sleep beneath this again."

Kaya felt her lips quirk, there and gone in a heartbeat. "Yes, I as well."

Sleeping in the tent, the wide, square covering that felt so much smaller on the inside than it looked on the outside, had not helped her forget the closeness she and Paul had created in their cave. Not *their* cave—that was a very strange way of looking at a space that was neither theirs nor comforting.

"Water?" She motioned toward a pouch of water and the last of the desert animals they'd caught and cooked the previous dawn, when their small fire couldn't be seen. "We should eat now."

He accepted, his blue-green gaze meeting hers for a long minute. Her movements froze at the hunger in his gaze, the hunger Kaya thought she saw—but Paul abruptly handed her the water pouch and turned away.

"Do you know people in Damietta?" Kaya ignored the abruptness of her question.

He confused her, kept her off guard, and she did not know how to respond.

"No. Even if I did, I wouldn't contact them. It's bad enough I don't speak Egyptian." He paused to secure the pack's straps closed, then straightened. "I don't want anyone remembering they saw an Englishman and an Egyptian woman."

"You think someone will ask?" Kaya frowned dubiously. "Damietta is a small port, not Alexandria or Rashid. If anyone bothers to search for us, they'll do so long after we depart."

"I don't think anyone will," Paul admitted. "But I don't want to take the chance."

Kaya secured her bow on her back, her khanjar at her waist. "You are a very mistrustful man."

"Damn."

Her eyes snapped to his at such a strange use of the word. Paul scowled at his pack, then looked at her, holding her gaze longer than normal. The lightness of his eyes belied the darkness that occasionally overtook his soul. Paul often looked haunted. Disturbed.

After the slavers, Kaya had an inkling as to why.

Now he blinked and scowled, eyes dark with a heaviness she didn't understand. "Give me your bow and dagger." He held out his pack. "It won't do for a lady to carry such things."

Kaya stilled. He was probably correct—she had absolutely no experience with what other women did or carried. However, these were the only things she had from her previous life. The only items that were *hers*.

She stepped back, away from his reach.

"Kaya." His voice broke, a whisper of emotion carrying across the distance. "It's only while we're in Damietta, I promise. But I don't want to draw attention."

Stomach swooping in fear, she looked behind them to the distant caravan. Without her weapons, how could she defend herself?

"All right." Not bothering to hide her reluctance, Kaya lifted her bow and quiver and handed them over. "Not my khanjar." She flatly refused.

Paul opened his mouth, then nodded silently. Passing him her satchel, she lifted his pack, settling it over her shoulders. She tried not to wince at its weight or the wood digging painfully into her shoulders and neck. She didn't want him to know of her pain.

He knew too much of it already.

"Here," he whispered, directly behind her. "Let me."

Paul's fingers brushed the nape of her neck, sending heat flushing through her. He lifted the ends of her hijab, his touch so light it sent shivers along her skin.

Her eyes drifted closed, and Kaya leaned into his touch. Her heart pounded, loud and uneven in her ears, and that same coil of anticipatory warmth tightened her belly. Fingers soft and gentle, Paul tucked in the loose ends.

Each nerve sparked to life, quick and hot and reaching for more of his touch. Another shiver raced through her. Kaya tilted her head. She wanted to let her own walls drop and kiss him again, feel his body against hers.

With one final brush, Paul's fingers left her skin. He tightened the pack's leather straps to shift it higher on her back. The wood still pressed hard into her, but it wasn't as painful.

"Can you manage for a couple of hours?"

His hands rested on her shoulders, and Kaya swallowed hard, her mouth dry. Movements slow and jerky, she turned her head just enough to look at him.

Paul hadn't shaved since Cairo, and the beginnings of a dark beard covered his cheeks. Kaya's fingers longed to run through it, feel the texture. For one glorious moment, he watched her with that same intensity. Open and alive, with that elusive emotion darkening his gaze.

His lips hovered a breath away, and he looked like a wild man who served no lord or sultan. A man who took what and who he wished.

Paul's eyes flicked to her mouth, there and back in a heartbeat. He leaned forward, a small movement she might have missed had they not been standing so close.

She waited, tempted. His fingers stroked her sensitive skin, his breath fanned over her cheek, a warm touch on a hot desert evening.

"Yes." The admission caught in her throat. She hadn't meant that she was able to carry the pack. She meant she longed for his kiss. She hastily looked away, gaze to the north, toward the faint outline of Damietta. "I'll be all right."

She stepped from the power of his gaze, his exciting touch, the heavy feeling still low in her belly. Her stomach jumped with nerves, her legs willing her to run as far from Paul as possible.

Before it was too late.

Kaya turned to the road, the truth sinking in heavily.

It already was too late.

Chapter Nine

Damietta smelled like death and rot and waste. Frowning at this unpleasant realization, Kaya wrinkled her nose and tried to hide her disappointment. She had hoped for life and sound and the remembered scents of a city not in the horrible grips of famine.

Famine clutched this place as well, and it broke her heart.

"Oh." People pushed by her, not bothering to look twice. Despite the unaccustomed contact of so many strangers, Kaya stood rooted to the street.

"Kaya?" Paul tugged her arm, but she only stared blankly up at him.

He glanced around, and she wondered what he saw, if he'd expected this.

"I had not expected this." She met his gaze. "It's dying."

"It's—" He stopped, sighed in realization. "Yes. No."

Frowning harder, she lifted her chin. "What does that mean?"

Rubbish littered the streets and was piled high in corners. Buildings lay abandoned, their doors and windows broken. Cracked stoops were layered with desert sand; shadows moved in darkened alleyways.

"All cities—maybe not all, but those I've seen—have areas like this." Paul paused and tugged her arm again, slipping his hand down to hers. "Come on. The closer to the wharves, the more people we'll see."

None of that made sense, but Kaya allowed him to guide her along the streets. She closed her eyes and breathed deeply, doing her best to ignore the stench. Instead, she focused on her first scent of the sea. There it was— the first salty breeze, the wonderful openness. It transformed the city, so unlike Cairo.

Stumbling into Paul, she hastily opened her eyes. *"Aasif."*

Occasionally, when the rains came, Kaya could smell *en-Nīl*, the freshness that cleansed the city and made her imagine she lived by the river. She was enchanted, and, despite Damietta's stench, curiosity burned within her.

"I want to explore every corner of this town."

Paul merely grinned. He did not release her hand, keeping her close. She appreciated that, not only the solidness of his touch, but the comfort from his protection. As much as she was confident in her abilities, she was still so new to the outside world.

The sun set an hour ago; she'd heard the call to sunset prayers, and still the city bustled with life and sound and a power that pulsed just beneath her skin.

"All right, but I'd like to find a tavern or an inn before the streets clear." Paul guided her, his hand on her elbow.

As much as she desired to soak in the city and its people, the sights and scents, they didn't stop. They strode through the streets, weaving through the masses.

Blending in as if they belonged. Another couple out of the desert, one among thousands. No one looked at them. She almost laughed. Despite the large wooden beam she was carrying, no one looked twice at her.

"Better?" Humor coated Paul's voice, but Kaya only nodded.

"This is amazing," she whispered, her gaze roaming everywhere.

Despite the closeness of the crowds and the noises ebbing and flowing as they hurried up one narrow street and down another, his voice was a whisper over her cheek. A shiver raced down her spine and along her arms. The fan of breath over her hot, taut skin awakened her nerves.

"It's wonderful." Kaya turned a wide smile up at him, unable not to. "I want to spend weeks here, shopping the souk and eating cooked meats on a corner and drinking carob juice and observing everyone who passes by."

Paul smiled even as he watched the crowds. Eyes darting from side to side, he watched everything.

Kaya added softly, "There are so many people." A shiver raced up her spine. Hundreds of people. How many were Turkish? How many knew of the price on her head? How many were searching for her? "Are all cities like this?"

He looked around, eyes bouncing from one corner to the next, over groups and individuals. However, Kaya sensed his attention completely on her.

"I suppose." Paul caught her gaze, as brief as the upward tilt to his lips. "Yes. I never looked at it like that."

"I love it." She looked from him to the crowd. The stalls were just closing, the scents of *kahwa* permeating the air. "Everyone has something to do. They're shopping or walking home or selling their wares."

She paused and tried to swallow her next words, but they burst forth without her consent. "I never knew it could be like this."

Paul's hand squeezed her arm, tender and comforting even as he hurried them through the city. They kept to the main streets, past *kahwa* houses and homes with bright geometric designs on their doors.

"You're right; Damietta is not dying," she whispered. "Cairo was dying. Even within the walls of my home, the stench and silence of death clung to everything."

"Damietta is a port city." Paul gentled his hand on her elbow. She heard his smile, the indulgence in his tone. "There will always be a need. Ships still sail into port, goods are loaded and unloaded."

"I want to see it all." She bit her tongue at the

confession.

Mercifully, Paul didn't comment. The scent of water grew bolder, and Kaya breathed deeply. She didn't care about the decay and mold and unwashed bodies.

Then they turned a final corner and she saw the sea.

"*Oh.*" Kaya stumbled to a stop.

The sea didn't spread out before her like the desert, vast and empty. In fact, she barely saw the water in the starlight, crowded with lanterns and buildings that cast long shadows. Ships lined the docks and dotted the shoreline. Large, hulking things, they creaked and swayed in the water.

She didn't recognize all the languages hovering around her, sharp yet transient. French and English, yes, the clipped tones of Prussian, though she didn't understand more than a handful of that conversation. Egyptian, of course, and Turkish and Marathi.

"It's beautiful," she breathed.

She struggled for words to describe the beauty and wonder before her. This oasis of things long imagined but never witnessed. The breeze off the water brought scents she could not identify yet yearned to know.

"Is it?"

She jerked her head around and stared incredulously up at Paul. He cocked his head and frowned. In the uneven light, shadowed by oil lanterns, Kaya clearly saw the lines between his eyes and around his mouth. Slowly, he nodded, bare increments of movement, and looked from the docks to her.

"I never thought so," he admitted with a hesitancy she hadn't heard from him. "Before."

She wanted to say something funny and intelligent. Make him laugh and break the tension drawing them closer. She wanted to sound profound and wise, to say something about how seeing it for the first time made it beautiful.

"Will you show me everything?" She heard her voice say.

Paul watched her for a long, malleable moment. It stretched between them—stretched and stretched. Then it snapped, and Kaya caught her breath. Even though nothing had changed, she felt as if the entire world were different.

"Yes." In that single word, she heard his inherent promise.

She lost count of the twists and turns they took through Damietta. Physically exhausted, she struggled to follow Paul's circuitous path through the city. Her legs ached, and her back protested carrying the beam across it. However, each step thrilled her with the newness of everything.

Kaya wanted to spin in a circle. She wanted to grab Paul's hand and run far and fast until they lost themselves in the city, then wander back and discover all that made Damietta so wonderful.

She swallowed those desires down deep within her, where her hopes and dreams still bubbled inside her, effervescent and wild.

Adventures just waiting.

On a quieter street, Paul slowed their pace.

"What are we looking for?" she asked quietly.

For the dozenth time since accepting the pack, she readjusted it. No matter how she did so, the wood continued to dig painfully into her shoulders. How had Paul carried this for their entire walk? She vowed never to complain again over his arduous pace. His warm hand settled on her shoulder, reassuring in its firmness. Kaya took strength from that touch.

"An inn," he whispered.

Incredulous, Kaya looked up at him, her feet slower with every step. Exhaustion tugged her limbs until her entire body drooped. "We passed a dozen. More."

Paul's lips tilted up. "I don't want one near the docks,

not too fancy, not too obvious. I'll know it when I see it."

"All right." She forced her feet to continue walking, and, while she didn't trip, every step dragged. His hand on her elbow steadied her, and she leaned against him. The wooden beam overpowered her and knocked her into him.

"*Aasif*," she muttered, regaining her balance.

His fingers gently closed over her upper arms, holding her securely while she found her footing. Kaya nodded, too exhausted for more, and they continued. Finally, he stopped and turned to face her.

"Good?" His fingers brushed along her cheek, rough and dirty but every bit as comforting as his touch on her shoulder, her elbow.

Before she realized it, Kaya leaned into him. Paul's fingers grazed her cheek once more, and he stepped back. He adjusted the pack on her shoulders, a frown etched deep into his face.

"Not much longer, promise." He took her elbow again and steered her further from the sea.

The ancient inn sat on a corner, two roads back from the docks, in a quieter neighborhood. No steady stream of sailors passed as Kaya had seen them do by the water.

The inn beckoned her. Warm lantern light glowed through windowpanes in desperate need of washing, but the faded, blue wooden door stood open to the faint breeze, and the walkway in front looked swept clean. Kaya nearly grinned at what she now considered *warm* and *welcoming*.

Tonight, any structure with an actual bed, one that offered food she hadn't carried for a week or had to trap herself, one that had water to wash with, looked welcoming. Her standards weren't very high.

A glance told her Paul watched the area as observantly as he had the desert. The street remained oddly silent compared to those they'd walked down on their way here.

The silence made her skin tingle.

Kaya wasn't alone in Damietta. Now that they were standing still in the open street, not locked behind closed doors, unease fluttered through her.

Still, she trusted Paul. He had saved her life, protected her. Held her after the woman died and comforted her when she had no words to express her sorrow and rage.

She was not alone here.

Only a pair of cats moved in the shadows, stealing along the street in search of scraps. The shadows flickered, but she heard no noise from the hidden corners and alleyways.

Heart roaring in her ears like a haboob, Kaya couldn't shake the feeling of being watched—by something other than the cats.

Being watched might have been a new experience, but it wasn't one Kaya enjoyed. She tried to ignore it, quite unused to the feeling of being seen. It pricked along her shoulders, walked along her skin. A cold sweat broke out on the back of her neck, and she shivered.

Paul squeezed her shoulder as if he knew.

Long used to hiding her feelings and wishes, Kaya refused to meet his gaze. She forced her legs to carry her those few remaining steps to the inn. It smelled of lamb and falafel, fava beans and hot *kahwa*, and her stomach growled.

Inside, she allowed the relative coolness to settle over her sandy skin. Two men sat by the windows at small, round tables, reading newspapers and smoking *shishas*. In the kitchens, she heard movement despite the late hour.

A large pot hung along the opposite wall over a banked fire. Dozens of tables were pushed so closely together, Kaya wondered why they'd bothered with separate eating areas if people were to sit on top of each other.

Several niches in the walls held unlit candles and

lamps. A large wooden chandelier hung from the ceiling with dozens of candles. It gave off enough light to see by, but kept the corners shadowed.

"*Aywa?*"

An old woman was perched on a high stool along a wooden counter that stretched the length of the wall. Beside her sat a small oil lamp and a long-handled copper *kanaka* and empty cup. Behind her hung shelves lined with sturdy looking tankards. Huge barrels lay on their sides with spouts of some sort protruding from them.

Fascinated, Kaya tried not to stare. Did those barrels hold *alcohol*?

Kaya took a breath and wondered at the tangy scent she didn't recognize. Not the *shishas*. Gidd never smoked one, but her neighbors had, and the smells would drift over her wall. Ignoring the odd, unidentifiable scent, she looked at the woman to offer an Egyptian greeting. Paul gripped her arm, squeezed just hard enough to stay her words.

"*Ahlan.* My wife and I need a room." He spoke very deliberately, enunciating each English word.

Wife. Luckily, Kaya was far too tired to flinch at the mention of that word. *Wife.* She had not thought so on their trek through the desert. Hearing Paul describe her as such sent her mind buzzing with questions.

Questions her too-tired brain could not grasp.

The woman watched him, her eyes nearly black in the flickering lamplight, then looked at Kaya with that same dissecting quietness. Kaya didn't know if the other woman spoke English. As a tavern owner in a port city, she thought it best to learn other languages, but Kaya was new to this thing called life.

"'*Engelīzi?*" the old woman spat in Egyptian.

Kaya waited and clenched her jaw to stop her reflexive reply in Egyptian. Paul's reminder, the heavy warmth of his hand on her arm, was entirely unnecessary.

They didn't know anyone here. If the previous days had taught her anything, it was that one never knew what corner danger might lurk around.

Kaya remained silent. Once more, her complete lack of outside education had robbed her of an experience she wished to enjoy. Resentment bubbled in her throat. However, she swallowed her annoyance, her anger, and schooled her features into some semblance of hopefulness.

"I'm sorry," she whispered in English just loud enough to carry. "I'm sorry, neither my husband nor I speak Egyptian." Kaya refused to dwell on calling Paul her husband. Or the lie that chafed her tongue. *"Parlez-vous français?"*

The old woman's eyes narrowed, and Kaya wondered if she heard something in her voice that sounded Egyptian rather than English. She didn't know how she could have. To Kaya's ear, the words sounded as crisp and clipped as Paul's.

"English gold only." The sharp English words shot between them, cold and decisive.

Paul nodded and, eyes on the woman, dug into the small pouch by his belt. At his move, the men in the corner stood, chairs scraping the floor.

The hairs on the back of her neck prickled. She reached for her khanjar. Fingers closing on the hilt, Kaya looked to the men now standing ominously in the corner.

She couldn't see them in the gloom. They kept to the darker corners, and the thin haze of smoke added to their concealment. It looked as if they melted into the walls.

Paul shifted. It surprised her how well she already knew his movements, almost as well as she did her own. He moved until he stood between her and the men, blocking her line of sight—which meant he blocked theirs, too.

"We're not here for trouble." His voice remained

steady. Though she couldn't see his face, she knew he was watching the other three occupants, gauging their next move. "Only for a bed and a meal."

And a bath. Kaya desperately needed enough water to scrub her skin clean of sand and sweat and blood.

No one moved. The stillness scraped along her bones, tense and loud despite the hush. Kaya straightened and readied herself. She didn't draw her dagger but waited. Watching the woman, whose eyes flicked to the dagger at her waist, she strained for any sound behind her. The quiet stretched out, beating louder with every second.

"Yes." The woman nodded and, like that, the tension dissolved.

The men sat back at their tables, picked up their newspapers and their *shishas*, and filled their cups from their own copper *kanaka*. Kaya wasn't fooled—the men watched them as clearly now as they had a moment ago.

Beside her, Paul relaxed, body easing slightly. She breathed deeply, smelled the decay—yes, that was it. Even in this small tavern she sensed death. She suspected it clung to Damietta as it had to Cairo.

Ignoring the putrefaction, she focused on the smell of fava beans and pita. Suddenly, she was starving.

Chapter Ten

"English coin only," the woman reiterated.

Paul held her gaze. By memory, he searched his coin pouch for the English sterling the innkeeper demanded. Het set an exorbitant amount on the counter between them. More than enough for a room and food for a week.

He suspected they'd get no more than a few days.

Hard gaze on him, the woman reached for the coins. They disappeared beneath her gnarled hand. Paul noted the ease with which she moved. His eyebrow twitched, the only sign he let the woman see.

Her own lips pursed, as if in acknowledgement, and the coins fell into her pocket. She slid off the stool and jerked her head toward the stairs, walking as smoothly and silently as he. Impressed, Paul settled his hand on Kaya's arm and gently steered her after the woman.

Frankly, he didn't care how much money the woman tried to take them for. The price was worth it to see Kaya safe. He'd dwell on that need to keep her safe later.

They followed her up to the first door on the right. She looked them over. In the uncertain light of the single wall lamp, he couldn't tell what she thought. Kaya swayed on her feet, and Paul forgot about the woman.

"Easy," he whispered. "I've got you."

The woman snorted and unlocked the door, leaving the wooden mechanism in the door. She shoved a single candle at him and turned for the stairs. Paul ignored her and helped Kaya into the room.

As fascinated by the Egyptian lock as he was, his first concern was Kaya. He'd pushed hard the last days, driven by Tahir's unspoken worry to see Kaya out of Cairo as quickly as possible, and then by the very real fear of slavers in the desert.

"Here." He gently turned her around. "What does *El Reyah* mean?" The name of the inn. He asked more for conversation, to keep her focused for a few moments more. He gently lifted the pack and slid it off her shoulders. Paul dropped it to the floor and instantly turned back to her, watching her for any signs of pain or discomfort.

"*Strength* or *power*." She stretched and winced but didn't voice any pain.

"How are your shoulders?" He gently rubbed them, and she sighed. "Your back?"

"I'm all right."

She didn't sound all right. She sounded as if she slept where she stood. Paul set the pack against the table to deal with later and turned Kaya toward the bed. "Sleep. We'll talk in the morning."

Apparently, she didn't need to be told twice. She lay in the dubious bed. He eyed it as Kaya curled onto her side, slid her dagger from its sheath, and rested her head on one arm. Paul didn't think she even realized she was holding her dagger—she was already asleep.

Despite her wishes, she hadn't bathed.

Grabbing the single wood chair, Paul shoved it beneath the door handle. Not much, but he took what he could in this small, sparse room. He wandered to the square window and looked out to the alleyway.

He rubbed gritty eyes and leaned against the rough wooden wall planks. His body begged for sleep, but his brain stubbornly refused. Closing his eyes meant seeing the massacre, the blood-stained streets, hearing the cries of the dead. The echoes of his own conscience screaming at him.

Basu.

Kaya dead. Her accusing eyes condemning him for failing her.

He watched her in the faint light from the single candle

spluttering in its own wax. Kaya sighed in her sleep but didn't move. Shadows danced over her pale skin, deepening the bruised exhaustion beneath her eyes.

The knock at the door startled him. Paul slipped his dagger free and crossed the short distance. He set the chair aside, then moved the locking piece in and unlatched the sliding bolt. The innkeeper stood there with a tray of food and a scowl worthy of the finest British drill instructors.

"Food," she spat and shoved the tray into his hands.

Eying her, Paul took the tray and used his foot to close the door. She huffed and stormed away before it completely shut. Paul shook his head—of all the odd and interesting things he'd seen in his life, Egypt proved to be the most interesting yet.

He set the tray on the floor and quickly relocked the door.

The table lay littered with their things, and Paul hadn't the energy to shift them. Instead, he settled on the floor, back against the door. Not the most comfortable of positions, but not the most uncomfortable, either. The *ful medames* with flatbread, a meal quickly becoming his favorite, disappeared. Though he couldn't identify all the spices, the fava beans, garlic, onion, and peppers tasted delicious. Then again, he suspected hardtack might taste just as wonderful after a week in the desert.

Kaya hadn't so much as twitched at the intrusion. His heart ached for her. He'd pushed her too hard these past days. Ran from Cairo as he had from Bombay: terrified the English were tracking him.

He punished her for his sins.

His gaze drifted from Kaya behind him to the door— his instincts assured him the owner wasn't going to kill him and steal Kaya.

The landlady was observant, shrewd, and abrupt, and

would no doubt take them for as much sterling as possible. But his skin didn't crawl, and the hairs on the back of his neck didn't scream at him to turn and leave.

He snorted. Maybe Kaya was right. Maybe he was more than a bit mistrustful.

"Hell."

Boots soundless on the uneven floor, Paul left the rest of the meal for Kaya. He'd already walked two steps across the narrow room before he realized he was heading for her. Curling his hands into fists, Paul stopped mid-step and watched her sleep.

Tahir had assured him Kaya knew how to protect herself.

As true as that may have been, Paul didn't want her in danger, and leaving her alone did not sit well. Especially while she slept. In the short time they'd spent walking through the desert, he'd grown to—to care for her.

Yes. Care.

Paul ignored the way his heart sped and the mocking laughter inside his head. He'd grown to care for her far more than he ought to, more than was wise.

"Damn." He pressed his fingertips against his eyes and returned to the window. It did nothing to alleviate his pounding head. "Damn."

The sea breeze cool on his face, Paul looked at Damietta through Kaya's eyes. The wonder and newness, the excitement in each step and around every corner. Every new experience an adventure she never thought to have.

He wasn't going to be the one to burst Kaya's enthusiasm.

Keep Kaya safe—and him out of a British noose.

On the small bed, she breathed evenly, unmoving in her exhaustion. His lips curled upward.

Oh, he was in trouble. Paul scrubbed his hand through

dirty, matted hair. Grabbing the wooden beam, he unstrapped it from his pack and maneuvered the thing onto the floor. Careful not to look at Kaya—a feat he lost time and again—he placed the beam along the gap between the floor and the door.

He was much better at carelessly tossing money at women and drinking their wine. At pretty words and forgotten promises and leaving before the sun cast its bright light on his ugly life.

Kaya made a slight humming sound, but she hadn't moved on the filthy bedding, nearly as filthy as they. In the morning, he'd pay the proprietress extra for clean sheets.

"Damn stupid schoolboy," he muttered.

He'd also taken to talking to himself. While Kaya slept during the long, blazing days in the desert, he'd tried to keep his demons at bay with the sound of his own voice.

With one last glance at the locked and barred door, he sucked in deep breaths of sea air and forced his mind to focus. Paul closed the distance to the bed and knelt at its foot. Gently, so as not to wake her, he unlaced her half boots. Kaya didn't move, and his heart twisted.

That was his fault. He'd pushed them through the desert, set a brutal pace running from his past and the mysterious threat to Kaya.

"I'm sorry," he whispered into the silence.

He didn't want to stay in Damietta longer than a couple days, three at most, but she needed rest.

Hands resting on her ankles, he debated untying her garters and rolling down her stockings. Far too intimate, that. His fingers clenched around her calves, and Paul forced them to release her.

Sandy, sweaty, still clothed in a dress that had seen far better days, she stole his breath. Her enthusiasm for life, her starving curiosity tempted him.

Paul found himself at the head of the bed, fingers shaking as he brushed her cheeks. She slept half on her back, half on her side, shoulder against the wall. One arm curled beneath her head, the other lay on the bedding next to her, palm flat. His hand brushed the back of hers, faint as a butterfly's kiss.

The proprietress had to know a shop or stall where he could, ah…*purchase* a new gown for Kaya. She deserved that, at the very least. New boots, too, and stockings.

Clearing his throat, Paul stood, hands clenched at his sides. He shook his head, eyes closed, jaw locked. He needed a decent night's sleep to banish these damn fanciful thoughts.

Paul shook out his bedroll and made himself moderately comfortable alongside the bed. He checked his precautions once more, unease slithering up his spine despite their relative safety.

Kaya's dagger, curved and lethal, lay on the bed between them. Her fingers had loosened around the bone handle, which was inlaid with silver and carved with markings he didn't understand.

"What a mess." He shoved the blanket she'd left him into a makeshift pillow. "What a damned mess. And not one drop of wine to stop it."

He closed his eyes and willed himself to at least a few hours' nightmare-free sleep. He'd hoped for that every night since leaving Bombay.

"Paul!"

His eyes snapped open. His heart raced, his head pounded, his chest ached. The screams of death. The cries of abandonment. Hands slick with blood. Blood slipping beneath his boots. Basu.

The screams of children and horses. Musket shots. Shouting. Chaos. Basu's mangled body, nearly unrecognizable in the muck. He saw Kaya. Running.

Panicked. Too late. Kaya's beautiful dark eyes staring up at him. Her body bloodied. Dying at his feet, her hand reaching for him, her unseeing eyes condemning him.

You promised. You broke your vow.

I'm sorry. I'm sorry.

"Paul! There's no one else here. It's safe. Just us."

Kaya. He looked at her, pale and frightened. Alive.

Gasping, heart racing, ears ringing, Paul focused on Kaya, not the images burned into his mind. He blinked again, willed away the horror.

Damietta. They were in an inn where no one knew them. In a town no one knew them. Not Bombay. Not with the Company.

"It's all right." Kaya's soft voice washed over him. One hand squeezed his, the other gently brushed his cheek. Her eyes were steady on his. "We're safe here. You made sure of that."

Slowly, her voice pierced the roaring in his ears. The room came into focus in the indistinct light of predawn.

The muted colors of memory sharpened. In the light of day, the bodies and the dying and the bawling hysteria faded.

As much as they ever did.

Paul purposefully relaxed, eased his back and shoulders, and tried to slow his frantic breath.

"What happened?" Kaya's whisper-soft voice swept over him, and he shuddered. He opened his mouth to dismiss her question, to pretend all was well.

Only then did he realize she was holding his clenched fist, her fingertips brushing his dirty, bruised knuckles.

He jerked away, burned by her touch. A fire threatening to tear him apart. Scrambling onto his knees, his stomach revolted.

Paul swallowed bile and self-hatred and the lingering scents of decay and blood and excrement.

At the still-open shutters, he forced his broad shoulders out the narrow window and gulped in air. The sea breeze, the rubbish, the decay and rot—anything to wash away his sins. The death that clung to him.

"Paul?" Kaya's voice hesitated, closer. "What happened?" Her hand, dry and calloused, lay on the back of his neck.

"Nothing." He swallowed hard. Every bit of him craved a drink and promised oblivion. It itched along his skin, clawing for a drop of wine. "It's nothing."

Kaya dropped her hand. Paul didn't need to see her to know her lips were pursed and her eyes flattened, their normally expressive brown now dull and distant. He didn't want to see that empty, shuttered look.

"Just a dream."

From the corner of his eye, he saw her nod, a slow half movement that conveyed more understanding than made him comfortable.

"Once the sun rises, I'll head to the docks. Find a ship. We'll leave as soon as it sails."

"All right."

Kaya backed away. She didn't turn around, as if she didn't want to turn her back on him. Paul didn't blame her.

* * * *

"No." Kaya raised her chin and glared at Paul. "I'm not staying in this room while you search for a ship."

"Kaya—"

"No, Paul."

She didn't care how tired he sounded or how worn-out he looked. Well, yes, she did. During their trek from Cairo, she suspected he'd stayed awake while she lay exhausted beneath their tent.

When she'd woke him before the sun rose, her heart had lodged in her throat. Even now, the sounds of his screams rang in her ears—pain and anger, harsh, guttural sounds of fury and fear. Kaya had wanted to hold him close and ease him back to sleep.

This, however, this was her limit.

"I am *not* staying indoors. I am not *hiding*." She pointedly looked around the sparse room and knew his gaze followed hers. "I'm done hiding. Hiding away as if I were nothing, a secret to be kept, a—a *problem* to shove beneath the bed and forget about. If you won't show me Damietta as you promised, I shall explore myself."

His jaw tightened, and his hands curled into fists. Paul's anger fascinated her, though it did not scare her. She knew it wasn't directed at her.

"Kaya—" Paul cut himself off. The tension didn't release his shoulders or unclench his jaw, and his beautiful eyes hardened. He gave a short nod.

"I promised to show you the city." It was more statement than capitulation. "First, I want to find new clothing. *I*," he reiterated, "want to find fresh clothes. I don't want you wandering around in that dress."

She raised an eyebrow in confusion. "And you are presentable?"

"Not in this lifetime," he muttered. "But men aren't—please just—" He ran a hand down his face. "I've arranged for *Madaam* Nephthys to bring breakfast and hot water." He looked at her again, that long, penetrating stare she couldn't read. "I'll be gone an hour, no more. We'll walk the souk after. Spend the morning exploring."

Kaya studied him, waiting for additional restrictions, more on what he planned. Another reason to argue with him. But Paul remained silent.

"One hour."

His lips twitched. Pressing his fingers to his eyes, he tilted his head to the ceiling and huffed what might be called a laugh. Finally, he shook himself and dropped his hands.

"I won't be long." He turned and left. Before the door closed, Kaya swore she again heard his laughter.

"What's so funny?" She frowned at the closed door and tried to decipher that man. He confused her.

Kaya turned from the door to the room. Her dagger still lay in its sheath, strapped to her waist. The bow and quiver lay on the table, which Paul pushed to the far end of the room. His pack, bedroll, and her satchel also lay there, ready to pick up at a moment's notice. The chair, previously under the doorknob, now sat innocently at the table, as if it always had.

She knew why he'd wedged the chair beneath the knob and the wooden beam along the door. Despite her current annoyance, her heart did a slow flip. Last night, she'd once more fallen into a dreamless sleep, and once more he'd protected her.

"That does not give you the right to leave me here," she muttered to the empty room.

A sharp, token knock rapped on the door.

Kaya stilled. Her khanjar was steady in her hand before she realized she'd pulled it. Alone. She stood alone in this room. A stranger knocked at the door.

If she wanted to experience the world, she had to experience all of it.

Heart skipping, she crossed the room and slid the bolt free, easing it open. The woman from last night, presumably *Madaam* Nephthys, stood with a small tray of food and a bucket of water.

"Your husband demanded food be brought to you," she said in that snappish voice she'd used when she "greeted" them.

"Demanded?" Kaya frowned. Her fingers tightened around the hilt. "I doubt that."

Madaam Nephthys snorted. "Weak English women."

It took Kaya a heartbeat to realize the woman had said that last sentence in Egyptian, and she was not meant to know their meaning.

Just in time, she stilled her tongue. Fingers still clenching the dagger, Kaya took the tray. *Madaam* Nephthys's eyes flicked down to the khanjar, then back to Kaya, who set the tray on the bed and picked up the bucket of water.

"*Shukran*." Kaya watched the woman's eyes narrow at the Egyptian word of thanks.

Madaam Nephthys left, not bothering to close the door. Kaya slammed it. The echo only momentarily appeased her.

"The first person I speak with outside the household, and she thinks me English scum." Slamming the bolt into place did not offer any satisfaction, either. "I don't believe it."

The silence echoed around her. Amplifying her heart, it settled in the room like a heavy layer of sand during a haboob. Kaya's gaze darted from door to window to chair. She debated wedging the chair beneath the door again.

Smoothing her fingers down her filthy skirts, Kaya instead settled in the chair and ate the food *Madaam* Nephthys had delivered. The window remained open, and she strained for a sound, an out-of-place whisper.

And she wished for Derya.

She missed her friend, the woman who'd raised her, her constant companion. Blinking rapidly, Kaya willed herself not to cry. Grief crushed her chest, and a tear leaked from her less-than-steady grip on her emotions.

"*Sabah al-khair*!" a voice shouted from below.

Startled, Kaya half rose. "Oh." The realization of her mistake knifed through her. "No." Her voice broke, and she shook her head. "Of course not."

Derya was not calling to her from the street. Kaya could not even say why she'd thought the strange voice was Derya's, only that her heart wished it so.

Pushing the half-eaten meal aside, she grabbed her satchel and the pomegranate paste. Quickly swirling the paste into the bucket *Madaam* Nephthys had brought, Kaya stripped out of her dress.

Khanjar on the table beside her, she dipped the small linen cloth into the tepid water and washed.

Kaya didn't even care that Paul might arrive any moment. She took her time unbraiding her hair and rinsing it. Her scalp had never felt so clean. Derya would scold her if she saw her now, quite improper, as she washed in a strange room in a strange city. The imagined argument brought a sad smile to Kaya's lips.

Finishing the last of the fava beans and flatbread, Kaya eyed her gown, stained with blood and sweat and coated with sand. Her skin rebelled at the very thought of wearing that thing again.

Slipping her thin chemise over her head, she shuddered. Hair wet against her back, Kaya settled in the chair, gown over her lap. She refused to wear it again but had no sewing materials to transfer the jewels from this dress to whatever new one Paul was buying.

Before she decided what to do with the gown, someone knocked.

Startled, Kaya snatched her dagger. A day might come when she didn't open the door with her dagger. Today was not that day.

Paul stood in the open doorway. He blinked in surprise, his free hand palm up and away from his body. In his other hand, he clenched a beautiful blue gown.

"You bathed." Kaya tried not to stare, but he had transformed.

He'd bathed but hadn't shaved. Behind him, the door clicked shut. Her hand raised to touch his cheeks, his beard now neatly trimmed. She curled her fingers into a fist and dropped it to her side. Swallowing hard, she lowered the dagger.

Paul eyed her and carefully laid the gown on the bed. He watched her as if he'd never seen her before. His look raced through her, rushing along her skin and flushing her cheeks.

Her fear of being alone and vulnerable vanished.

"I did. I found a dress for you, too."

Kaya glanced at the blue material, but her gaze drew back to him.

Instead of his torn, bloodied outfit from earlier, he now wore a pair of dark green trousers and a plain white shirt that tied at his base of his throat. Even in the autumn morning heat, he'd added a matching green vest and a long brown coat. His black boots came to his knees.

"I see you bathed, too." Paul's eyes darkened, and Kaya suddenly realized she wore naught more than her chemise. A now damp chemise.

Eyes blazing, he stepped closer. Want flushed through her, but Kaya didn't turn. Didn't run. She waited, dagger still clenched in her fist. Paul's eyes locked on hers with a power that stilled her.

Drew her in.

Each step he took went straight through her. Heat flushed along her skin and pooled low in her belly. In a moment of wildness, she threw caution to the desert winds and embraced what came next.

Suddenly, he stood before her, smelling freshly washed and so very Paul.

Kaya licked her lips, hungry for the taste of him. For his body pressed against hers, his hands cupping her face.

Her heart raced.

She moved, closed the step between them, and kissed him. Part of her knew she shouldn't. Giving into this fire would only lead to disaster.

She kissed him anyway.

She craved his touch, the way he made her feel. Clawing need and abandonment. She wanted him, not out of curiosity or a need for new experiences. She wanted to drown in this pleasure overtaking her. Wanted his touch, wanted to know the feel of his hands on her skin.

His hands tangled in her loose hair, cupped the back of her head. His mouth, firm on hers, sparked that fire to life. Kaya wound one arm around his shoulder and tangled her fingers in his soft, curly hair. She pulled him closer, or she stepped closer, until she was pressed flush against him.

Still she ached for more.

Kaya shivered and rose onto her toes. Paul growled against her mouth, kissed along her jaw and down her neck. She gasped for breath but knew it was pointless. His teeth lightly scraped her sensitive skin, and she shuddered.

Oh, she wanted more of that.

His mouth returned to hers, softer now, tender as he tasted her.

"Kaya."

Slowly, his mouth gentled and pulled away. She blinked open her eyes and met his blue-green gaze, darker with a wildness she couldn't name. Her breath caught, heart racing, body longing for him.

His hands cradled her head, holding her to him with a fierce hunger and an infinite tenderness. It closed her throat.

"Get dressed." He sounded gruff but not cross, his voice gravelly but not harsh. "I'll take you to the souk."

Confused, yearning for Paul's touch, his kiss, Kaya frowned. Her hand gripped her dagger hanging at her side, and her lips tingled. Her heart raced, mind struggling for one coherent thought—any coherent thought. Paul pressed his lips to hers once more, then his hands fell, and he stepped away.

"We'll sew the jewels into the waist of this gown." All business now, he produced several needles and a spool of thread, grinning proudly at his purchases, as if the last minutes hadn't happened. "Shouldn't take long."

Kaya swallowed.

She wished for more carob juice to ease the dryness of her throat, but she'd long since emptied the small cup *Madaam* Nephthys had brought with the tray. She wished for steadier ground; her world continued to tilt from that kiss. She wished—

"All right."

"I also bought you fresh, ah…unmentionables," Paul continued, as if he normally held this sort of conversation. As if he hadn't just kissed her to within a beat of surrender.

"Thank you." She didn't know what else to say. Her world tilted and whirled around her. Blinking to try and clear her vision, her Paul-clouded mind, she sat on the bed. She picked up her old gown and glared at him.

Infuriating man.

Chapter Eleven

Kaya laced up the square-neckline gown that revealed a large expanse of her neck and shoulders. A *very* large expanse. The off-the-shoulder sleeves, paired with the daring neckline, teased so much of her breasts, she wondered if she wouldn't pop out of the bodice.

"Do all Englishwomen show so much *skin*?"

From his position against the window, Paul didn't answer. He watched her, gaze moving from her face to her breasts, down to her hips and back up again. She felt his look as if he caressed her, fingers tracing the outline of the dress. The heat in his gaze set her afire.

Clearing her throat, she looked back at the bodice. Uncomfortable, she pulled the laces up the front of her gown, tightening the material to ensure it didn't sag. Huffing, Kaya tugged the bodice to cover more of her breasts. It was no use.

The stiff material didn't budge. Kaya frowned and took a breath. Or tried to—the bodice cinched her stomach so forcefully her breakfast churned.

Taking shallow breaths, she looked down at herself. The fine blue material clasped her body and revealed her curves. Kaya didn't know how to feel about that. She no longer looked Egyptian but, she supposed, like an Englishwoman.

Which was the entire purpose of this *endeavor*.

That revelation settled awkwardly over her. Despite the beautiful material, she disliked so much exposed skin. Smoothing her hands down her hips, over the voluminous skirts that puffed out at her sides, she vowed to remember who she was.

It didn't matter what she looked like for their charade.

"I almost forgot." Paul held up a piece of fabric. His eyes burned with emotion she didn't understand. "A new headscarf."

"Oh. Thank you." She took the plain black fabric and wrapped it around her head and shoulders, tucking it into her bodice. Much better. The dress might be English but she was not.

She flicked the skirts around her ankles. The material was slightly too short and showed far more of her new black ankle boots than she liked. But this wasn't about what she liked, and she had to remember that.

This was about fooling an entire city. About proving to them she was English.

"I want to walk barefoot for the next week." She didn't think she said it loud enough for Paul to hear, but she looked up at him anyway. "With no jewels."

"Under a shade." He chuckled. "And with a nice breeze."

"I've never bought anything for myself." Kaya gingerly raised her hands, feeling foolish.

She turned expectantly to Paul. The heat in his gaze had not lessened. His fingers, light as a butterfly, brushed her cheek. "You look lovely."

Kaya shivered. The touch shot straight through her.

She met his gaze, that burning blue-green fire that seared her. Licking her lips, she held herself from stepping into that fire. For as much as she wanted to leap into the unknown and experience everything, her desire terrified her. Even as it drew her in.

Averting his gaze, Paul reached to the table for the wide-brimmed, lacy hat and placed it on her head. He turned her around, fingers gentle on her hijab-covered shoulders. Her eyes slipped closed. She wanted to turn, step into his embrace, measure his expression, but he moved.

"That hat won't stay without pins, but I don't want to poke holes in your scarf."

"Do all Englishwomen dress like this?" Kaya kept her head perfectly straight, but the hat tilted precariously. She grabbed it, grimacing when the bodice and jewels dug into her.

Keep her head still. Don't breathe too deeply. Don't move too suddenly. Hope her breasts stay in the confines of her bodice.

"Rich ones." He cupped her chin and brushed his thumb over her jaw. Her breath hitched. "Beautiful ones."

That warmth rushed through her again, and Kaya leaned into his touch. She wanted that rush of need, the clawing ache of Paul's kiss. Wanted to know what truly happened between a woman and her man.

Her stomach twisted, and the throb low in her belly spread. Her heart slowly thudded, only to trip over itself and race. Suddenly, she didn't need to worry about breathing so shallowly. She barely gasped a full breath.

She hadn't meant *her man*. She meant a woman and a man. Just any man.

How easily she lied to herself.

Paul dropped his hand and stepped back. "What would you like to buy?" That familiar smirk, a faint twist to his lips, settled in place. The one he used when he tried to keep distance between them. "Ribbons and jewelry?" He instantly shook his head. "No, no jewels."

"No." She laughed in agreement and tried not to think about the space between them. Or the lack of space. "We've enough. Perhaps a gown with longer sleeves however."

"If you wish." Paul abruptly stepped forward and wrapped his hands around her shoulders. Kaya's breath caught. His gaze bore into hers, and he didn't seem to notice the rhythmic stroke of his fingers against the line of her jaw.

She might never understand him.

"Please stay close to me. I don't want to lose you in

the crowd."

Kaya sighed. "I will," she promised. "However, I wish to see this city. All of it."

"I promised," Paul said, as if that explained everything. Then he stepped back and dropped his hands. Turning sharply, he picked up her satchel and draped it over his shoulder.

She had strapped her dagger to her outer thigh using a sturdy length of leather—another of his morning's purchases. How she could possibly unsheathe it Kaya had no idea, but probably wouldn't need it on a simple walk through the souk. She didn't know where Paul kept his, but, until the incident with the slavers, she hadn't realized he carried one.

"How do women walk in these gowns?" Kaya mumbled as they exited the room, all important possessions now either in her dress or someplace on Paul. "The waist is very tight."

Every movement cut into her. The leather chafed her thigh, and each step rubbed the dagger's sheath along sensitive skin.

"I wanted you to look English," Paul muttered as they walked down the steps of the inn. "We can look for another gown today."

The same two men from last night sat at the same table this morning. *Madaam* Nephthys watched from behind the long counter and only snorted when Kaya met her gaze. Neither *Madaam* Nephthys's antagonism nor the heavily suspicious atmosphere mattered.

They stepped outside, into the bright, hot day.

The sun bounced off the dull-colored buildings, momentarily blinding her. Kaya blinked, closing her eyes and letting the rays warm her. It was different from the sun in her walled gardens, even from the sun in the blazing desert. Now that she stood on a crowded street with the sea breeze winding around corners, she felt the vibrant life surrounding her. The pulse she had lacked in her own gardens.

The freedom to stand outside sparked against her skin and lit her heart. Oh, she wished her family stood next to her, embraced her joy in this simple act. Hiding her grief behind enthusiasm, Kaya opened her eyes. She'd enjoy every second of freedom.

Gidd wanted this for her, and Kaya knew Derya had always wanted her to know the outside world.

"It's beautiful!" Kaya breathed deeply of the late morning.

Paul laughed, that elusive sound she longed to hear. "It's still a port city."

"I don't care." Kaya stepped along the stone street, one cautious foot in front of the other.

They'd walked these same streets last night in the dark, slipping around corners and hiding from onlookers. This morning, everything had changed. The street beneath her feet, covered with sand, felt like nothing she'd ever experienced. Purposely slowing their pace, Kaya breathed in every moment.

"The sky looks different." Kaya dropped her head back, uncaring how her hat tilted or her bodice pulled. Her hijab covered her. "The air smells different. I feel the breeze from the water and see the people I hear."

A gust of wind whipped down the street, and she clapped her hand to her ridiculously large hat. Kaya laughed, and a lightness she'd never felt floated through her.

"Come on." Paul's voice still held the humor of his laugh.

Kaya wound her arm through the crook of his elbow, and they walked down several dirt-packed roads crowded with people and animals and noise. Fascinated, Kaya didn't know where to look first. At the small herd of goats and sheep? Or the groups of children running between animals, people, and buildings? The musician on the corner playing an oud?

She tugged his arm and slowed Paul's step even more. "I want to listen."

The string music soothed her. Despite her yearning for experiences, she missed her family. Missed sitting with Derya during the heat of the day and talking about what Derya had seen on her errands. Missed Gidd.

Her throat closed, and tears pricked her eyes.

"Kaya."

She looked up. Paul watched her, his gaze soft and sympathetic and accepting.

"Do you want to stay?" His thoughtful question, the comfort of his hand on hers, wrapped around her heart.

He understood. Despite her vow to keep her pain hidden, he saw. And he understood. Acceptance. That's what this was, warming her from the inside out. Acceptance, support. Acknowledgement of her pain, not simply dismissal.

"No." She cleared her throat and wiped beneath her eyes. "No, let's continue."

Paul tossed a few *akçe* coins at the musician and guided her along the main road, deeper into the heart of Damietta.

"It's wonderful."

Busy and crowded, the noise spilled from the souk— the baying of animals and the call of vendors. Kaya didn't know where to look first. They slowed near another musician and listened to the mournful notes of the lute.

Paul squeezed her elbow, and they turned away. Unaccustomed to so much physical contact, she breathed deeply. She enjoyed Paul's touch. Eyes closed, she soaked up the words and culture as the strangers around her shopped, sold goods, argued, and laughed.

"All my life I wondered what it looked like, how it felt, what it tasted like." Kaya breathed deeply of the rich scents and smiled up at him. "I never imagined this."

"Imagined what?" Paul's gaze caught hers. He didn't hurry her, didn't force an answer or demand she walk faster. He simply waited.

"Freedom. The freedom to walk the souk or watch people, listen to oud players." Her smile widened, and she laughed. "I always thought my imagination an unfettered thing. I've imagined myself walking the city streets, losing myself in the crowd. Stories aren't experience."

Men shouted their wares and haggled over spices and fabrics, silver and wooden boxes, brightly patterned fabrics and beaded baskets. Groups of women roamed the souk, a few dressed as she, others wearing the more traditional clothing she'd worn in Cairo.

Damietta thrived with life.

"Are you hungry?" Paul asked, mouth close to her ear.

Breathless at his nearness, she tore her gaze from the bright colors lining the souk to meet his. "No. Let's walk a little."

He once more offered his arm. "What would you like to see first? Shop for spices? Another dress?"

"I—I don't know." She breathed deeply of the scents and enjoyed the way they ebbed and flowed and combined. They brushed over her skin and wrapped around her, enticing her to explore. Cumin and dill, chili peppers and saffron, parsley and cardamom lined the stalls and perfumed the air.

How was she to pick one activity? One stall, one place to shop?

"There's so—I mean there's—there's—everything. There's *everything* here." Kaya shook her head in wonder. "I don't know where to begin."

A group of men pushed by them, shoving people out of

their way. Heart skipping a beat, Kaya stepped closer to Paul. The men hadn't said anything untoward, just rudely rushed by them.

Had the Ottomans finally found her?

They didn't know her, especially in a new city. Kaya needed to remember that.

Paul, muttering words she didn't understand, pulled her close.

"What did you say?" Kaya tilted her head and tried to translate, but the phrases had no meaning in her vocabulary.

"Nothing." When she looked up at him, he looked embarrassed. Paul cleared his throat. "What were you saying? What did you want to see first?"

Kaya let it pass. His words weren't important in the grand scheme of the riches now laid out before her. "All of it. I want to see it all."

"Let's start with Anatoly."

"Anatoly?"

"The man I need to see about passage on a ship."

Paul took her arm again, careful to keep the satchel hidden between them, and turned down a dirt road. Faded canopies draped between buildings, and fewer people shopped this street. They came to a stall with dresses already sewn. Kaya frowned.

"Is this where you purchased my dress?" She fingered a light green fabric hanging from the stall, the same material and style as the dress she wore.

"Yes." Something in his voice made her look at him.

"I had assumed you found a seamstress," she admitted. "One who specialized in English fashion."

"Ah. No." Paul leaned closer. "Don't ask where the dresses came from."

She opened her mouth to ask just that, then snapped it closed.

"Ah, my *'engelīzi* friend." A tall, pale man appeared inside the stall, Kaya didn't know from where. It wasn't that deep or that wide. "Return for another dress?"

She studied the stranger, only the second man she'd had the chance to study. His blue eyes danced with humor and something else she couldn't place.

Not wariness, not suspicion, but a watchfulness that reminded her strongly of Paul—of Derya, too, who constantly ensured Kaya's safety by being as paranoid and vigilant as Paul.

"With my wife," Paul said in a friendly, easy tone. The tone made her skin crawl, the overly polite, grating graciousness of it. His hand remained easy on her arm, however, and she felt no need to defend herself. "As you can see, the first one fits her almost perfectly."

The dress was too short and far too tight. She adjusted her hijab over her shoulders, grateful Paul had bought it as well.

The man bowed to her, blue eyes sparkling with— what *was* that emotion? His laughter danced only on the surface. Though she longed to embrace this new world, she hadn't expected to do so quite like this.

Exposed, and severely out of her depth. She was overwhelmed by the multitude of new experiences she had not expected.

"*As-salamu alaykum.* A pleasure to meet you." The man took her hand in his hard, leathery one and bowed nearly in half over it. She couldn't place his accent—it sounded nothing like Derya's Istanbul words or Paul's English ones, and certainly not the flowing Egyptian of Gidd. "*Madaam* Conrad."

Kaya blinked and tried not to yank her hand from his. She didn't understand—who was *Conrad*? Was not Paul's surname Hartley? However, she forced her lips into a smile and tipped her head. The hat tilted precariously. *"As-salamu alaykum, sade* Anatoly."

Anatoly released her hand and straightened. Kaya moved half a step back. He watched her with renewed wariness, and she wondered if he'd heard something in her Egyptian greeting. Kaya hoped not; she'd promised she wouldn't give away their ruse.

"Don't wander," Paul whispered, head bent low, breath light and warm on her cheek. "I need to speak with Anatoly."

She met his gaze and saw the silent worry there. The tension in his shoulders. The way his eyes flicked from stall to stall.

"I'll stay close," she promised.

His fingers brushed the inside of her elbow, the lightest of touches that sent a thrill dancing over her skin. Paul hesitated, gaze burning into hers, hand tightening around her arm. He opened his mouth, then snapped it closed, jaw tight, and dropped his hand. With a final look, he walked a few paces away from her.

Kaya turned to the items on display in Anatoly's stall. In addition to the dresses, lengths of ribbon were also laid out in a rich variety of colors. Kaya grinned and separated several strands of delicate material. She didn't wish to buy any; she had little use for ribbons. Still, the texture against her fingers, far different from the rough fabric of her gowns, made her giddy.

She'd never owned such a fancy ribbon. There had been no need. So many new things were laid out before her, and Kaya wanted to see them all.

Looking over her shoulder, she watched Paul and Anatoly speak in low, hushed tones. They hadn't moved far, only a couple steps, and Kaya stepped closer to hear what they were saying. But Paul caught her eye and gave the smallest shake of his head. She stayed back.

Once more, others excluded her from plans that involved her.

Annoyed, she huffed and turned abruptly from both men. Clamping her jaw in simmering defiance, she did her best to ignore how he made her crave things she had no reference for, yet he treated her no better than Gidd. Kaya refused to spare him a glance and examined the wares instead.

The souk wasn't as crowded here, and she didn't have to fight the press of people. Determined to enjoy this experience, she shifted through inlaid silver boxes at the next stall. Stroking her fingers over the items, Kaya breathed in the smells of spices drifting on the hot wind.

A commotion at the head of the street caught her attention. Kaya's head jerked up. Unease skittered down her spine. She scanned the area, looking for the source of the noise. Her hand moved to her bare waist, but she'd listened to Paul's concern about looking English and had strapped her dagger to her thigh.

She stood there, perhaps not weaponless but as useless as if she were.

Chapter Twelve

No means to access her khanjar. She couldn't very well lift her skirts to grab her dagger.

Foolish. *Foolish.*

She spotted a group of five or six men arguing and stilled. A dog barked near them. Paul stood several stalls further than she remembered, nearer the commotion. His head jerked round. Even from this distance, she saw the terror in his gaze.

Kaya stood in the street, alone and vulnerable—unaccompanied, away from Paul, and all too aware of how far he stood from her.

Her heart stuttered at the memory of the nameless woman in the mountains. Bound and gagged, beaten until she bled, then forced to walk through the desert. Paul had been concerned that every caravan might be more slavers, but her immediate fear was that they were hunters sent by the sultan.

How would they know her? How could they possibly find her? An old argument, and yet everything Gidd taught her bounded to the surface.

Swallowing against a dry throat, Kaya examined her surroundings.

Fear curled through her stomach, pricked along her nerves. Warning her. Escape. Run. *Fight.*

A large hand covered her nose and mouth. Cut off her air. An arm banded around her breasts, jerking her backward. Calm settled across her.

Kaya didn't panic—well, she panicked, yes. She could barely breathe; someone had tried to take her off the streets, and the icy terror of being bound stiffened her limbs. Made her clumsy.

Still, she did not yield to her attacker.

Kaya struggled against the hold, but the man lifted her

off her feet. Acrid sourness filled her nose and throat. She couldn't move her head or look for Paul. Shock and anger pounded in her chest, choked her.

How *dare* someone touch her!

Gidd had trained her. He believed in her. Knew her capable of defending herself from just such an occurrence. Kaya clenched her fists and stilled for the space of two heartbeats. She gauged the man to be slightly taller than she. It did not matter.

Shouting in rage and pain and *fury* against the hand that stifled her, Kaya angled her arm and swung her elbow backwards.

Fabric rent. Her hat fell. Despite the constricting bodice of her English gown, her elbow connected with his belly, causing him to grunt and loosen his hold. Good. Moving quickly, she swung her fist backwards into the softness of his throat.

Blood pounding in satisfaction, Kaya heard her attacker cry out, a hoarse sneer of anger. He released her, and she dropped to the ground. Kaya gasped, landing in a crouch. Tangled in her skirts, the tight bodice cutting into her, her breath too short and too fast, she pushed herself upright, then whirled to face the man who tried to—*to kidnap her!* Fury burned through her, and she reached for her khanjar. Once again, she did not find it on her hip.

Aggravated at English fashion, Kaya briefly debated hiking up her skirts and grabbing her dagger. She hadn't the time.

Hands loose at her sides, Kaya circled the man. She wanted to look over her shoulder, find Paul, but she didn't dare take her eyes off the man in front of her.

Thin and pale, and dressed in loose trousers and a filthy shirt, he clutched his throat. He spat, gulped in deep breaths, and grimaced. Hateful, dark eyes, nearly black with anger, bored into her even as he stumbled backward.

"You tried to kidnap me," Kaya spat, backing up to give herself room. "Why are *you* so angry?"

Behind her, Paul shouted her name. Warmth eased through her. He'd fought to make it to her side. She didn't need to look to know that. The sureness of it almost made her smile.

However, Kaya didn't dare look from this man as he lumbered forward. He snarled, but his words caught. Kaya viciously hoped she'd hurt him. She hoped his throat *ached*.

Her mind sped through her options, through each move, each advantage Gidd ever taught her. Stay aware. Assess her opponent. Calculate her advantages.

No one expected her to fight. No one expected her to know how to use a dagger—which she couldn't access. Kaya risked darting a look from the man to a nearby vendor. The vendor, that coward, did not step out of his stall. Kaya sneered at him.

None of them moved to help her.

She spotted a row of candlesticks along the ground and grabbed one.

"*Malesh.*" She offered a quick Egyptian apology to the stunned man staring at her from behind the stall, making no move to help. Infused with confidence, Kaya grasped the poorly weighted pewter candlestick and held it before her, prepared for battle.

Kaya tensed, eyes narrowed on her attacker.

He spat at her again, English words she didn't understand. What was an *English bitch whore*? And why was he *going to fucking rip you to shreds*?

She'd ask Paul later.

Right now, Kaya gripped the candlestick.

Annoyance heated her cheeks. This dress didn't move as freely as her own. Today was supposed to be a lovely outing in a new city, her first souk walk. How dare he interrupt her?

Kaya tensed, prepared to defend herself. Her off-the-shoulder sleeves restricted her movements, and the jewels and boning of her bodice dug into her skin. With every arc of the candlestick, she feared the seams might split.

She gasped for breath, chest tight. Her heart beat faster than a drum.

The man lunged, and Kaya forgot her discomfort. Balanced evenly, Kaya waited until he moved again and swung. The heavy candlestick connected with his left shoulder. He grunted, twisting out of the way far too late.

Kaya shivered in satisfaction. Good. She hoped he suffered tremendous pain. He stumbled and muttered more words she did not understand. Then he lunged again, tried to grab her, but his movements were sloppy. Uncoordinated.

Not at all the fluid grace she'd watched Paul fight with. Or the ease with which Gidd moved when he trained her.

"Sloppy," she taunted the man.

She swung again, but he stumbled out of the way. He wiped the back of his hand across his mouth and spat more strange words. Heart slamming in her chest, Kaya waited…waited…waited. She swung a third time. The candlestick hit his lower back.

He stumbled forward, sprawling onto the dusty road. Without looking at her, he scrambled to his feet, turned for a small alleyway, and fled. Whether it was her skill with the candlestick—doubtful—or the fact he attracted too much attention—more probable—he ran.

Hands trembling, heart thundering in her ears, chest tight as she gasped for breath, Kaya blinked. Suddenly, the roaring in her ears cleared, and the sounds of the souk returned. Legs stiff, Kaya turned back to the merchant and handed him the candlestick.

"*Shukran*." She thanked the man, though he hadn't bothered to so much as shout.

He accepted his merchandise without a word and stared at her as if she were about to attack him. Or maybe as if she were mad. Kaya sniffed. He had no right to judge her. *He* hadn't left the relative safety of his stall.

"Paul!" She jerked around to the last place she'd seen him. Her senses were sharp, narrowed in on the people lining the souk, those who had not helped her. She lifted her skirts and raced down the street. The jewels dug into her sides, and she pressed a hand over them, panting for air.

She truly hated this dress.

Slightly worse for wear, Paul and Anatoly stood at the mouth of the street, looking at seven men now lying on the ground. The men who'd caused the earlier commotion. Chest aching, Kaya stumbled to a stop.

They weren't dead, the men. But one look at their battered and bloodied bodies told her they wouldn't be moving on their own. Even the dog quieted. Breath coming in short pants, heart still hammering in her chest, she looked to Paul.

"I guess you don't need my help." She wasn't entirely sure she would have been able to help, not with the way her limbs shook. Quite unsteady, she ensured her hijab covered her hair and neck, grateful it hadn't slipped. She seemed to have lost her hat.

Paul spun on his heel and yanked her against him. He hugged her tight, face buried in her neck. His lips pressed hard to her shoulder, her jaw, her cheek. He murmured soft words too low for her to hear over the roaring in her ears.

Kaya closed her eyes and sagged in his embrace.

Arms around his waist, she held him tight and simply basked in the strength of him. He pulled away, hands cupping the back of her head.

"Are you all right?" Paul's lips pressed to hers.

His own breath came hard and fast, and a fine tremor shook through him. Kaya held him closer, though she met his gaze. His eyes were a stormy blue, wild and panicked.

"I'm fine." Kaya released a breath as shaky as her legs. She wasn't fine. She needed him, needed him to hold her, wanted to feel his heart thrum against her to assure her they lived. "Yes. I am fine."

Paul cut her off and kissed her again, harder now, deeper. A small part of her thought this quite improper; they were standing in the souk for so many to see. But she kissed him back. What did it matter, proper?

"*Madaam* Conrad." Anatoly stood to the side, his tall shadow blocking the sunlight. "I believe you dropped your hat."

"Oh." Kaya blinked up at him. She supposed she ought to have been embarrassed, but she merely smiled. "*Shukran*." She took the hat, trampled and dirty, and shook it out before settling it on her head.

"Paul, my friend," Anatoly said with a wide, genuine grin. "Your wife is terrifying."

"Aye." Paul looked at her, gaze dark and hungry. It sent a thrill dancing along her skin, curling low in her belly. "I'll find you later, Anatoly." To her, quieter, he whispered, "Let's go."

* * * *

Kaya didn't pay attention to their walk back to the inn. Damietta no longer enchanted her.

Only Paul's hand on her elbow mattered, the warmth of his touch on her wrist arm as he hurried her across streets and around corners. It pulsed through her, wild and frantic, the rapid beat of butterfly wings against her skin. Her stomach clenched in anticipation.

Maybe from the tightness of her bodice.

Either way, she welcomed what came next.

Finally, *finally*, Paul shoved open the door to the inn. The sudden quiet enveloped her. They'd walked from the souk, and she hadn't cared about anything they'd passed. Hand on her lower back, Paul guided her through the stale, dim atmosphere to the long counter. *Madaam* Nephthys sat on her preferred seat, and the two men were at their usual tables. Several other men sat around the inn, hiding in the shadows.

The proprietress looked horrified.

"Our room key, *Madaam* Nephthys, if you please." Voice short, Paul offered a perfunctory bow, fingers slipping to Kaya's elbow and tightening around it.

Madaam Nephthys, mouth slightly agape, reached into her apron and handed over the unlocking mechanism. Kaya didn't know if the woman's scandalized look was because of her crushed and filthy hat, or the fact that the moment Paul took the key the two of them rushed through the main room and up the stairs.

Kaya didn't care.

Paul unlocked their room and walked through first. She'd expected that. Despite the eager anticipation thrumming through her veins, Kaya had expected him to ensure the room was clear and safe. Even with the impatience twisting through her, the craving that pounded in time to her heart, Kaya did not expect Paul to push her against the closed door. Not without searching the room first.

Her back slammed against the door, his body pinning her there.

His hands were hot on her shoulders, his fingers the lightest of touch—bird feathers along her skin. Paul's hands cupped her face and carefully undid her hijab, folding it onto the chair. He never took his gaze from hers, and before she found words, his fingers were threading through her loosened hair. He kissed her, mouth rough. It was a lightning strike along her skin.

"Oh." She tried to say more, but Paul kissed down her neck. Her rather extensive vocabulary vanished. "Paul."

"Do you want this, Kaya?" His lips caressed her neck where her heart pounded wildly. "Do you want me?"

"Yes." She tangled her hands in his hair—where had his hat gone? —and tugged him up to face her. "Show me?"

Mouth hard on hers, Kaya could do nothing but open herself and follow his lead. His fingers traced the tops of her breasts, along the edge of her bodice, up her shoulders. Kaya shuddered and arched into his touch.

"I'll show you everything," he promised.

"Yes." Kaya tried to catch her breath. She never seemed to be able to around him. "Show me everything. I want to know it all. I want to feel you. I want to feel more of this—"

His mouth returned to hers and gentled, but that gentleness did nothing to ease the ache inside her, the tearing need for his touch clawing through her. Paul stepped back, a single step, and waited. Kaya opened her eyes and met his. He watched her, waiting to see if she would follow.

She didn't pause, didn't hesitate to join him.

Paul held out his hand and walked backward to the bed, one slow step. A chance to change her mind. His gaze, bluer now than green, never looked away from her.

The hunger, the focus, the intensity shivered through her. All for her. It stole her breath.

"Paul…" She trailed off, unsure what to say. No. She knew. "Touch me."

He growled low in his throat, and the sound twisted her insides. Kaya whimpered, gasped, tried to say what she was feeling, but her throat closed with such *pleasure*. A sharp need tensed through her, wringing tighter and tighter.

"I want to know what happens when it snaps." Had she said that aloud? Did he know what she meant?

"I'll go slow." His mouth brushed hers again, sealing that promise. "You'll enjoy it, Kaya. I won't hurt you."

Derya had been very specific in her explanations of what happened between a man and woman. Kaya never figured out how, and Derya never said, but she'd even smuggled illustrated manuscripts from the sultan's harem.

Paul unlaced the front of her gown, his mouth trailing along the opening. His lips closed over her nipple, and even through the cloth of her chemise, the warmth of his mouth awakened sensations she'd never known existed. Kaya cried out, one hand cupping the back of his neck.

She arched into his touch, seeking more. She was greedy for this experience, for his touch. His fingers brushed down her body, along the curve of her hips and thighs.

He turned her gently, kissing along the back of her neck, and unlaced her skirts, letting them fall to the floor. She bunched her fingers into her chemise and tugged it upward, wanting him to touch her skin.

Suddenly, she stood bare before him, clad only in her new stockings and boots. Paul groaned again, that same sound from deep in the back of his throat that sent shivers down her spine and intensified the ache between her legs.

He knelt before her, a graceful fall at her feet. Holding her gaze, he untied the leather around her thigh and let her dagger and sheath clatter to the floor. Kaya barely noticed. Paul's fingers brushed the inside of her thighs, his touch a fire through her. He left her garters tied, her stockings untouched, and kissed her belly, hands spanning her hips.

Beneath her touch, his hair curled softly, and she threaded her fingers through it. Paul leaned into her. His lips trailed over her hip, an intimate press of his lips to her skin.

Kaya trembled, breath short, knees weak, stomach clenched in anticipation of—of *next*. He stood, hands gliding up her sides, sending shivers dancing along her nerves.

He held out a hand, incredibly formal given her nakedness. Uncertain, Kaya rested her hand in his. His gaze held hers, burning steady through her as he walked her to the bed.

Breathing heavily, Kaya sat on the clean, fresh sheets. She wanted to unlace her boots, roll down her stockings, feel him against every part of her. She couldn't tear her gaze from Paul as he undressed. Each tantalizing bit of skin he revealed had her digging her fingers into her thighs.

She stood and ran her fingers down his chest. "I want to undress you."

His shirt was fine and soft, but she didn't want to feel his shirt. She wanted to feel his skin, see him as bare before her as she was before him. That knowledge sent another piercing beat through her, a rhythm of need and aching want.

"Later." His voice caught, and his fingers clenched around hers. "You can touch me all you want, I promise."

"Good." Kaya met his gaze, and the heat in his eyes flashed.

Paul released her hand and let his clothing fall beside hers. Bit by bit, he revealed his body to her greedy gaze. Licking her lips, she ran her fingers over his belly.

The muscles contracted beneath her touch. She flattened her fingers, sliding them up to his chest, over his bare arms covered with faint scars. The puckered scar of a musket ball on his left shoulder and a jagged dagger wound on his right thigh. Kaya ran her fingertips over each one.

Paul hissed out a breath and caught her hands, raising them to his lips. He kissed her fingers, gaze steady on her.

"Do you want this, Kaya?"

Chapter Thirteen

Paul knelt before her, hands cradling her hips, cheek brushing her inner thigh. He watched her steadily.

"Yes." Kaya shuddered. "Show me everything."

He barely touched her. Her fingers dropped to his shoulders, dug into the muscles of his arms. She tried to steady herself but didn't know how—if doing so was even possible.

"Paul."

The strong muscles of his thighs flexed as he crouched before her, and Kaya wanted to feel him against her. The hardness between his legs drew her gaze, and even as she watched he grew thicker. She licked her lips, wanting to taste him, to feel those muscles beneath her tongue.

She'd never seen another person naked. She'd devoured the salacious books Derya had smuggled in, but Paul looked far different than she'd imagined. He was beautifully muscled, broad shouldered, with a bit of dark hair covering his chest. Kaya wanted to feel it under her fingertips.

Beautiful.

He opened her thighs and leaned up, pressing against her. Her breath rushed out at the feel of his chest, the smattering of hair against her breasts. Her hips arched against his, seeking contact, touch, anything to ease this piercing ache. His hands danced down her leg, featherlight, which only intensified the ache.

Fingers sure on the ties of her stockings, he rolled them down, dragging his hands along her skin. The slide of her stockings and the slight scrape of his nails on her thighs left her gasping. Shivering. The intimate touch sparked through her and made her want more.

Paul tugged off her boots and tossed them aside,

stockings and garters quickly following.

Once more, her mouth opened to his, her breath a soft moan against his lips. Kaya melted into his kiss. Paul felt warm and hard against her, and Kaya's tongue hesitatingly brushed his. She couldn't stop the little sighs and whimpers that escaped her throat. Didn't want to.

Paul's hand cradled her head, and in one smooth movement he gently pushed her onto the bed. Kaya struggled onto her elbows to watch him. She didn't want to miss anything. He cupped her breasts, gentle and slow, thumbs brushing over her nipples.

She gasped, curved upward into his touch.

"Oh! That feels—I had no idea—"

"I'll show you everything." Paul tugged her nipples between his fingers, and heat shot through her. Her hips jerked against his. He groaned and shuddered above her.

"Yes. Again."

He obeyed, lips trailing along her jaw, her cheek. His nose brushed hers, his warm breath fanning over her cheeks. "We'll learn your body together."

He kissed her, slow and deep and *yes*. Kaya explored, tasted his mouth and all the glorious flavors that combined there. Her teeth sank into his lower lip and tugged. Paul shuddered, and Kaya sucked in a breath.

Satisfaction—no, power. *Power* and arousal shot through her, and Kaya wrapped her legs around Paul's hips, her blunt nails scraping through his hair. She attacked his mouth, wanting all the passion and need and—and *everything* he offered.

"I could spend hours, weeks, tasting you." Paul kissed down her shoulder and shifted so his fingers brushed the wetness between her legs. Her breath caught, and he immediately did it again. "Every sound you make, every sigh. I want to taste you."

"Yes. Paul." Kaya gasped for breath, hips moving of their own accord, desperate for his touch.

Paul skimmed his fingers over her thighs, her belly. She moaned, her body craving his. Her fingers curled into the bedding, but that was not what she wanted to feel beneath her hands. One hand wrapped around the back of his neck, the other skimmed down his spine, over the toned muscles of his bum.

"Kaya," he breathed.

She whimpered his name—or thought she did. She couldn't be sure if she'd formed words. Thinking while he did incredible things with his hands and tongue required more effort than she possessed.

Her breasts felt warm and heavy as he lifted them. Her nipples were hard peaks, eager for his touch. He brushed a finger over each peak, and Kaya cried out. His lips closed over a nipple, teeth tugging it gently.

"More," she cried.

His groan vibrated against her skin, and Kaya dug her nails into the hard muscles of his back. He showed the same attention to her other nipple. That coiling, spiraling pleasure tightened, gripped her hard and fast and she was close to— to—

"I want to worship you, spend eternity making love to you. Touching you." His hands trailed along her belly, mouth brushing over her wetness, and she cried out again. "I want to listen as you cry your pleasure, beg and shatter at my touch. And then I want to start over again."

Kaya's hips rocked against his mouth, against his talented tongue, her fingers falling from his back to the bedding and holding tight. He pressed his fingers to her, and she jerked, crying out as pleasure seared through her. *Yes, yes, more, right there.*

Leaving her bereft, he kissed his way back up her

body. Kaya arched into him, feeling his hardness against her throbbing wetness. She scraped her teeth over his neck and reveled in his shudder of pleasure. Her tongue licked down his neck, teeth nipping at the base of his throat.

"Kaya." His voice broke.

One finger slipped into her heat, and she bucked hard against him. Her hips rolled, and he slipped deeper. He added a second finger, stretching her.

"Oh!" Pleasure tightened in her, and she cried out again. Her mouth moved frantically against his, sloppy as she tried to feel it all. The thrust of his fingers, the brilliant, coiling pleasure. The way his body moved with hers, the bunch of his muscles beneath her touch.

He shifted onto one arm, legs tangled with hers, fingers moving lazily inside her. Kaya cried out, begged, but he didn't increase his pace. Once more, he kissed down her body, tasting her, his tongue pressing against her even as his fingers stretched her.

Kaya sobbed, her body out of her control. Exquisite. Intensely beautiful and yet acutely sharp. She burned and shivered, her skin unbearably sensitive to his touch.

It rushed through her, this exquisite pleasure. She cried out, a wordless shout. Her hips ground against his hand, his mouth, her fingers digging into the bedding in a vain attempt to anchor herself against this storm. It didn't matter. She was lost in the pleasure. Her body bent toward him, into his touch, skin slick with sweat, her limbs boneless.

"Beautiful." Paul kissed up her belly, and Kaya shivered and gasped, the pleasure already winding through her again. "I want more. Are you ready?"

"More?" Kaya heard him chuckle, felt the breath of it along her belly. She blinked open her eyes and tried to clear her brain. "Yes. More than ready. I want it all."

Paul withdrew his fingers and deliberately licked them

clean. Kaya was utterly unable to stop her guttural sound of pure pleasure or the renewed hunger clawing through her.

Kaya tasted her own completion on his lips when he kissed her. Curious, she deepened the kiss, even as his hand languidly trailed up her inner thigh, over her hips, along her belly. He pulled back and watched her. Eyes dark and intent, he paid special attention to her breasts.

He pressed his lips to her chest, lifted her breast. Kaya cried out again when he nipped a particularly pleasurable spot. She sighed when he kissed her shoulder and settled over her.

Kaya hummed and tightened her legs around his waist, her hips slowly rocking against his. She nipped his chin and found his mouth again, kissing him once more.

"You like that?" Paul kissed her jaw. "The taste of yourself?"

Her nails clawed at his back, and her thighs pressed hard to his hips. She took more. All. Everything.

"Yes. It was—I feel—" She shook her head. "I want it all. Now," she panted, kissing him anywhere she could reach. "Now, Paul. Please."

His hard length brushed against her sensitive wetness. Kaya's breath caught. Slowly, stretching her even more than his fingers had, he eased into her.

She shuddered at the feel, at the overwhelming sensations of him above her and in her and around her.

Finally, he stopped. Stilled. Waited.

Kaya shifted her hips a bit, adjusted to the feel of him. There was no pain. A little discomfort, but when she tilted her hips and he slid deeper, all she felt was the sensual slide of him within her.

He slowly pulled out, until only the tip of him remained inside her. Then he eased in once more. Again. Paul braced her legs on his arms and caught her lips with his.

Sloppy and hard and perfect, Kaya felt that decadence tighten in her. Wanted his hands on her again, until she cried out in pleasure and bliss and satisfaction.

Her nails dug into his back, her body urgently moving to meet his every thrust.

"Paul," Kaya panted. Chanted. "Yes, Paul."

"Come for me, Kaya," he ordered. Or maybe begged. She didn't know, didn't understand his words, but wanted…yes, she wanted. "Come for me."

Paul eased her legs around his hips and leaned onto one arm. His other hand slid between them. His fingers danced over her again and she cried out. The pleasure building within her shattered, the world blinding white as her hips sought his touch, more of it. All of it.

"Beautiful," Paul panted, his face buried in her shoulder. "You're so beautiful when you come."

Paul moved harder, faster. Kaya opened heavy-lidded eyes to watch him. He caught her hands and twined their fingers together.

Licking her lips, Kaya tried to find her voice. "Come for me, Paul."

A shudder raced through him, and he slammed into her one last time before pulling out. Kaya whimpered at the loss. Paul stilled over her, his head thrown back. So beautiful as his own pleasure overtook him.

His arms gave out, and he collapsed on top of her. Mind blank, senses filled with Paul and what they'd just done, she wrapped her arms around him and held tight, not yet ready to be away from him. Eventually, her breathing evened out, her heart slowed, and her skin stopped tingling.

Paul opened his eyes and met her gaze. Rolling onto his side, he brushed a hand down her cheek, along her neck and shoulder.

Kaya sighed into his touch and closed her eyes, her

body wonderfully heavy from pleasure. She turned onto her side and whimpered. He climbed from bed and wet a linen in the washbasin, then he gently ran it over her belly and thighs. Paul tossed the linen into the basin and climbed back into bed, tugging her against his side. He held her tight, hands gliding down her back, over her hip.

Warm and comforting and steadying. Perfection.

* * * *

Eyes closed, Paul dozed, holding Kaya close. He had no desire to move, not from her arms or the bed. The bed where *Madaam* Nephthys had, indeed, provided clean sheets for an exorbitant price.

Worth every bob he paid.

Perfectly content in a way he'd never experienced before and didn't quite understand, Paul foresaw no reason to ever leave this position.

Except maybe for food. Possibly. Maybe.

"What is *bitch whore*?" Kaya's voice was soft, sleepy, but still alert.

His eyes flew open and he choked, jerking back to look at her. "*What?*"

"And what does *fucking rip you to shreds* mean?"

Paul blinked down at her. He'd been lost in memories of the sounds she'd made. Those hungry sounds from the back of her throat that urged him on and only made him want her again. Kaya raised her head from his chest and looked at him with those beautiful dark eyes.

The innocence belied their naked bodies currently entwined on the small bed. The curiosity, however, did not surprise him. Innocent curiosity—yes, that described Kaya perfectly.

"Where did you hear *that*?" He thought he'd managed to sound calm, inquisitive. Not stunned.

"The man who tried to—to take me." Kaya shuddered,

and he held her closer.

Paul pressed her head back to his chest despite the midday heat. He felt the warmth of her body against his, the puff of her breath as it fanned over his chest. A small part of the tension curling through him eased with her, alive and close and whole, in his arms.

He didn't want to relive the longest moments of his life. He didn't want his mind's eye showing him that heart-stopping instant when the man had grabbed her. When he lifted her from behind, intent on taking her. Paul had been too far away to stop him. Then the man's accomplices attacked him and Anatoly, and the world went to hell.

Paul shifted so Kaya lay fully against him, one leg over his thighs, her soft breasts pressed to his chest. His fingers flexed on her shoulder, the back of her head, and he tried to find the words to answer her.

His throat closed with that earlier terror.

"They were curses." He swallowed hard and tried to infuse humor into his voice. He doubted Tahir had ever cursed in front of her—if the man did so at all.

Paul had never felt such paralyzing fear. It clawed at his throat and pierced his heart. Different than watching his fellow officers slaughter innocents. Even when he saw his friend in the pile of bodies. That moment when he realized he was too far from Kaya when she needed him—

"Curses?" Kaya lifted her head, frowning. "Like some sort of pagan magic?"

"No." He laughed then but didn't release her, too afraid if he did so, she'd disappear.

Paul kissed her, slow and deep, tasting all the glorious flavors that made her Kaya. He didn't think he'd ever grow tired of that. Of her. When he pulled back, breathing heavily, he was not the least bit surprised to realize he'd hardened for her again.

Seemed to be his perpetual state.

"Curses, curse words…bad words." Paul shook his head and tried to explain, but he knew it was hopeless—especially when her scent surrounded him and her body pressed so intimately against his. "Words one does not normally say in front of a lady."

Her eyebrows shot to her hairline. Paul brushed loose strands of her thick, dark hair behind her ear, off her shoulder.

"Then why did he say those things to me? What do they mean?"

Paul huffed. "The first—" He didn't want to repeat the words, not when they reminded him of how he wanted to rip that man's tongue from his mouth. "It's derogatory. Means you've done something to upset a man and he doesn't like you much for it."

"Truly?" Kaya asked, surprised. "Men call women derogatory names because they're upset?" She snorted angrily. "Do men always call women *bitch*, then? If we do things to upset them?"

He opened his mouth but had no reply. Paul sighed. "Some men do, but they're not men worth knowing."

"Have you ever called women a bitch?" Kaya stared at him, that curiosity burning though him.

"I'm sure I have," Paul admitted. He wanted to close his eyes against the disappointed surprise in Kaya's eyes, but he forced himself to hold her gaze. It took all his willpower to do so. "But I won't ever again, I promise you."

She nodded, satisfied, and returned her head to his chest.

He let out a breath, quite unsure how this conversation had turned. Or where these promises had come from. Or the deep, innate knowledge he'd keep them. "The second word is another derogatory one that means men pay you for sex."

Kaya lifted her head and frowned again. He could

almost see her running those words around her mind, sorting them out. He had a feeling they'd be having a lot more discussions about curse words in the future.

Never had he expected to explain curse words to anyone, let alone his wife, whom he'd just made love to and wanted very much to do so again.

The world was a strange, mad place.

"And *fucking*?" She met his gaze, still frowning. "I know what *rip to shreds* means."

He snorted. He wanted to kiss her. Unable to resist, he did so, enjoying the way her tongue swept along his, no longer tentative but still so new. Pulling slightly away, he ran his index finger between her brows, smoothing the line between them.

"Lots of meanings, that." Paul dropped his hand to his stomach and frowned. "Very versatile word there. Usually used as an adjective to describe something like *I'm fucking tired* or…hmm. Or *I fucking hate the desert*."

Kaya giggled and grinned. He knew she remembered the cave during the haboob. It seemed so long ago now. Her fingers brushed over his stomach and up his chest, as if she couldn't stop touching him, either. He didn't want her to.

"In this case, he used it to show his anger." Paul cleared his throat and wondered if her body was ready for his again. Probably not. Probably best to go slow. After all, he'd promised not to hurt her.

It was damn hard—no pun intended—with her lying over him. Her fingers explored his body, brushing lower and lower with every passing minute. His cock twitched, craved her touch, but he didn't push.

He certainly didn't tell her the other meaning of *fucking*.

"Very strange." Kaya shook her head. "I don't understand the need for them, for these curse words." She shrugged, a half movement while lying in his arms. Paul wanted more of the slide of her skin against his. Craved the feel of her with every breath. "Did you finish your business with Anatoly?"

Just like that, she dismissed both the curses and the man who tried to kidnap her. Whether for ransom from the rich Englishman they believed Paul to be or to sell to a slave boat, it didn't matter. That man had tried to take Kaya from him. His hands tightened on her body.

"No."

When he saw Anatoly again, he planned to find out who the men were. By any means necessary.

"How do you know him? Anatoly, I mean. Did you know him before? Why did he call me Mrs. Conrad?"

Paul laughed and rolled her beneath him. He kissed her, partly to quiet her, mostly because he could now. Her nails scraped down his back and he groaned, shuddering. Her legs opened to cradle him, her hips tilted just enough that his cock brushed her wetness.

Kaya shivered, whimpered against his mouth.

"Kaya." He pulled back to look at her and gently brushed away the strands of hair that were clinging to her cheek.

His heart thudded, slow and painful. Too late. It crashed over him like a monsoon—it was too late for him. He'd fallen for her innocent curiosity, the fierce fighter, the pure beauty. He'd fallen in love with her harder than he'd believed possible. Maybe it wasn't too late for her.

Kaya deserved so much more than a broken drunk like him.

Chapter Fourteen

"Anatoly?" Paul shrugged.

He tried to roll away, but his body refused to move. He needed to stop this unreasonable intimacy, this closeness between him and Kaya. Her fingers flexed on his back, the simplest of touches.

Paul wanted to arch closer, drown in her touch, her essence.

"*Madaam* Nephthys recommended him." Paul told her in lieu of these new emotions crowding his tongue. He bit those back, a vicious yank against his heart. "Introduced us this morning. I thought it best to use an alias."

Kaya narrowed her eyes. "You trust *Madaam* Nephthys?"

He opened his mouth to answer, flippant and dismissive, but her tone caught him. Paul eyed her. "I trust no one save you," he answered honestly, the words pulled from his heart. "Why?" Narrowing his eyes, he shifted, but he didn't pull away. Couldn't. "What happened?"

"Nothing." Kaya stiffened and refused to meet his gaze.

That was a first. Strong, defiant Kaya refusing to meet his gaze? Since when? Fingers gentle on her chin, he urged her to look at him. When he spoke, however, he couldn't stop the hardness in his voice, the nearly physical need to stand up and protect her.

Annoying, unnecessary emotions.

"What did she say to you?"

"Nothing." Kaya sighed, tilted her head away, then met his gaze again. "She thinks me a weak Englishwoman."

He brushed his fingers over her cheek, watched her eyes flutter at the contact. "I want her to think that." The admission ripped from him, gently spoken words that belied the brutal force of his feelings. "If she thinks you're anyone else, we might have trouble."

Her eyebrows rose again in clear disbelief.

He grimaced. "More trouble."

"I've never had a chance to be me." Her words were soft, hoarse, as if each one had forced itself from her heart without consent. "Now I'm forced to be someone else."

Paul opened his mouth to object, to insist she was Kaya—his wife, his lover. Luckily, his brain caught up with his heart before he uttered a word. What business did his heart have in making decisions? It never mattered before.

It mattered with Kaya.

Always with Kaya.

"Why did Tahir keep you in the house?" The words barely left his lips, almost silent in the space between them. "Why did you never leave? See anything or talk to anyone? Why couldn't you be you?"

Kaya watched him. Time stretched between them, and Paul counted the seconds with every breath she took. She never looked away, never moved. Her eyes darkened, as if she had the power to divine all his secrets.

Maybe she could. He put nothing past Kaya. Her probing gaze remained on him so long, he wanted to run.

But he stayed there, in her arms—odd for him. He held steady, warmth winding through his heart. He was a coward around anything resembling feelings, and his ego was maybe a touch wounded by her silence. Paul rolled off her. His skin protested the loss, and he forcibly told his heart to shut the hell up.

Sitting on the bed, head in hands, fingers tangled in his hair, he tried to set aside his jumbled feelings and refocus his thoughts. By that, he really meant stop thinking about Kaya. How she'd felt against him as they made love. Her mystery. The way she moved. How she spoke. All she knew and everything she didn't.

He needed to stop thinking about Kaya. Period.

"I never knew my parents." Her voice sounded soft in the hot room, a gentle breeze on a scorching day. Paul raised his head and met her gaze. "My father died before I was born, and my mother in childbirth."

"I'm sorry," he whispered.

Her depthless eyes studied him, as if discerning how sorry he really was. Kaya nodded, and her lips curved just enough it might be called a smile. She sat on the bed, back against the wall, utterly blasé about her nudity.

"Is that why Tahir kept you in the house?" He frowned. "Because your parents died? He wanted to, what? Keep you safe? Did he think he was protecting you by not allowing you to—well, to do *anything*?"

Kaya nodded, a single long movement of her head that didn't covey agreement so much as—he didn't know. His instincts told him Tahir was many things, but arbitrarily keeping Kaya locked inside? No, there was more to both Tahir and Kaya.

"My father," she continued in that slow, even voice. "He was a trusted soldier attached to the Egyptian delegation visiting the sultan's court. My mother was the daughter of the Ottoman Turkish Sultan."

Paul jerked, ice suddenly running through his veins. "That—that was *not* what I expected."

"She was promised to a vizier, one highly regarded and trusted in court. But she and my father fell in love and married in secret." Kaya didn't look away, even when she licked her lips. She folded her legs beneath her, hands loose on her knees, back straight.

Paul forced his attention from her lovely naked body. From her soft breasts, pink from his mouth and hands and the scratch of his beard. From the gentle curve of her belly, her thighs and the patch of curls that hid her wetness from his hungry gaze. He dragged his gaze up her body and met hers.

"How did they meet?" He knew very little about the Ottomans, but he knew women's quarters. How had a mere soldier met the daughter of the sultan?

"I don't know. No one ever said." She tilted her head and looked up from her hands, which were now folded on her lap. "I imagine they met in the gardens, but I'll never know for certain."

Kaya watched for his reaction to this fantastical story. At a loss, he simply nodded for her to continue. "Go on."

"The sultan found out. I don't know how. Derya, she was my mother's *odalik*."

"What is that?"

"It's what you call a lady's maid." Kaya paused. "Derya never said, and Gidd never, *ever*, talked about it." Kaya shook her head, as if to clear the memories—or wishes. Wishes that her childhood had been different. Paul was quite familiar with that wish.

"You're the granddaughter of the sultan?" He let out a choked sound.

"Yes," Kaya replied calmly.

"Everything about you, about Tahir and his elaborate schemes and convoluted paranoia, it makes sense now." He shook his head and scrubbed a hand down his face. "So much sense."

He laughed, harsh and rough, and it burned his throat. Standing, he paced the length of the bed but didn't look away from Kaya. "No wonder Tahir didn't want anyone knowing about you."

"He feared for my life." Her voice broke, and she sniffed. Paul suspected it had more to do with missing Tahir than the parents she never knew. "The sultan put a price on my mother's head, and on mine. He sent hunters throughout the empire and its allies. My mother, Esme, fled Istanbul with Derya. Gidd was constantly watched; they knew who my father's family was, of course, and threatened his other children."

Paul started. He had no idea Tahir had other children, or that Kaya had an entire family she'd never met or spoken to. The way she said it—*other children*—made it sound as if she didn't care. But the way her hands twitched told him otherwise.

"He never doubted Derya or my mother."

"How—" Paul cut himself off. "How did they survive the desert crossing? How did they know to find Tahir? How—" He stopped again. "I suppose it wouldn't be difficult to find General Tahir."

He had, after all. Every soldier seemed to know of the great general.

"Gidd hid me in the house so no one could ever find me. I snuck out, once, and when I returned he told me the truth and began my training. I was no longer a child, and if something happened…if he could no longer protect me…he wanted—" She broke off and looked away.

He crossed to the bed and knelt before her. All his pretty words dried up in the face of her tears, and he brushed them away. "He trained you to fight for your life? Why not marry you to a merchant, someone outside the military, if he wanted to keep you safe?" Paul stopped at her knowing look. "Oh. People would know. Your husband would know because Tahir arranged it. Or someone—whoever Tahir trusted to arrange the marriage—would know."

"Yes." Her voice barely carried to him.

The only person you trust with a secret is yourself.

"He didn't know what to do with me." Kaya's laugh echoed bitterly around the room. "I realized that on our desert walk. He had decades to plan how to keep me alive, and the only thing he came up with was to marry me to an Englishman. He couldn't marry me to anyone in Cairo, couldn't admit to anyone in the city he knew of me."

"And he couldn't leave you to fend for yourself." Paul sighed and squeezed her hands. "In case the worst happened, and he could no longer protect you. A woman alone in the city like that, you'd be prey the moment they realized it. I'm sure he never expected you to tell me."

To trust him. Kaya's secret wasn't a trifle. It loomed over her life, dictating her every move. Her own paranoia made sense now. The reason Tahir had trained her to fight. It was still highly unusual, but at least it promised to keep her alive.

Her level of trust humbled him, and Paul floundered.

"He trained me in case the Ottomans found me. I had a lot of time to think on our walk." Her voice thickened, and she paused. "He couldn't marry me, as is proper, so he trained me to take care of myself. To defend myself. He did it out of love, I know he did. Love for my father and for me."

"Christ," Paul cursed.

His hand moved; he watched it curl around hers but didn't remember ordering it to do so. Probably his heart issuing orders again. Kaya trembled, the slightest quiver against his fingers. He hadn't noticed until he touched her. After he did, he only wanted to soothe her until the trembling stopped.

"I'm sorry, Kaya." He meant it from his heart—which really ought to stop interfering in things.

"Gidd had a larger house closer to the Citadel." She looked away but didn't release his hand. In fact, her fingers tightened around his. "He entertained there, met his fellow military leaders there, housed his other son and family. I was never allowed to see those rooms, not even when I promised to hide under the bed during a party."

"How old were you?" Paul swallowed against the lump in his throat for the innocent child caught in a deadly political game. "When you tried to leave the house, how old were you?"

"Ten." She looked back at him, her lips twisted in a parody of her previous smile.

Her voice didn't break, but something inside him did. Without overthinking it, Paul shifted them. It was a bit uncomfortable, a bit awkward, but they once more lay side by side. One of her legs rested over his, and Paul tried not to think too deeply about the casual intimacy, the tenderness. She watched him, eyes wide but dry, one hand still holding his, the other bent beneath her head.

"Gidd told me about every meeting." Kaya's voice whispered through the hot space between them, close and familiar. "About the parties and the food, which he always brought with him. Derya tried to make the recipes as best she could so I could taste the desserts from other countries." Her tone turned wistful there, sad. "He taught me about military strategy and shared the latest Citadel gossip. Information from Istanbul. And if there was any rumor, anyone searching for my mother. Or me."

"He had to keep up appearances," Paul realized. "And he wanted to make sure he knew if anyone from Court was looking for you."

"He—" Her voice cracked, thready and broken. "For ten years, the sultan actively searched for Esme, my mother. My father was already dead, murdered by palace guards as he helped my mother and Derya escape."

"How did she escape the palace?" Paul asked, though he doubted Kaya knew the specifics. He'd spent more than a decade in Bombay and knew the security around palaces. Around women.

"She had nowhere else to turn. I don't know how she

made it that far, just her and Derya, and her pregnant. I don't know how two unaccompanied women traveling from the Empire entered the city, or how they found Gidd."

The social mores of the Ottoman Empire sounded much like those of the Maratha Empire when it came to women, and the thought of Esme and Derya alone in that desert sickened him.

"She carried a letter from my father, explaining what happened." Kaya shuddered. "Derya never said, and Gidd burned the letter after she arrived," she whispered. "My father probably had it on him when he was killed. I always imagined it was bloodstained."

"Kaya." Paul pressed his lips to her forehead and tried to think of some way to soothe her. To make her understand he held her and wasn't letting go. That he understood, sympathized.

There he was, thinking with his heart again.

Paul told his brain to shut it.

He raised her hands to his lips and kissed the backs, hoping to convey what he had no words for.

Kaya cleared her throat, made her voice forcibly lighter. "The sultan threatened to invade Egypt, burn Cairo to the ground for the insult."

Paul choked out a laugh. "Good to see he took it in stride."

She looked up with a puzzled expression that instantly cleared when she met his sardonic gaze. "He demanded Gidd hand both Esme and Derya over for proper punishment."

She didn't have to say what *proper punishment* entailed. There was only one *proper punishment*.

The thought made him ill.

"Cairo and Istanbul do not get along, however, and Gidd is very powerful in the government. He has many influential friends as well." Kaya paused then blew out a short breath. "He told the authorities Esme died from the punishing walk through the desert, as did the child—a boy. Derya, he said, overcome with grief, disappeared into the city."

Paul brushed loose strands of hair from her cheeks, her skin smooth beneath his touch. "They believed him?" He had so many questions. Why hadn't Tahir simply said he never saw them? What about Kaya's father? How had Tahir kept the powerful Ottoman Empire at bay all this time?

"Of course. They had no proof otherwise, and when they searched his home, they found no sign of a child or a pregnant sultana. His servants knew nothing, either."

"Where were Esme and Derya?"

"Hiding with Abdul, Gidd's manservant and most trusted friend." She frowned. "You said you met him in Bombay." Paul nodded but didn't interrupt. "Abdul hid both Derya and Esme. It was then that I was born. Abdul and Derya brought me into this world."

"And Tahir?"

"With no proof, and the backing of the Egyptian government, the Ottomans had no choice but to leave Cairo." Kaya stopped again and cleared her throat. "They could've marched to war. Assassinated Gidd. But that was more than I was worth."

Her worth crowded his tongue, but Paul kept quiet.

"That was when he bought the house," she said in a lighter, if far falser, tone. "The one you broke into." She eyed him, but he only grinned. That was a story for another day. "It wasn't under his name, of course. I don't know how he managed it; it was never important. He visited every day he was in Cairo. As I said, he is a powerful man with the backing of powerful friends."

"That's why he could bribe the guards at the gate." Paul snorted and rolled his eyes in self-deprecation. "Of course. He never said."

"I didn't know the extent of his plan." Kaya shook her head, her long hair brushing his arm. "He only wanted to keep me safe."

"I know." Paul drew her close and rolled onto his back to better hold her. To better feel her against him, warm and alive. "Did a damn good job, too," he admitted. "Had me fooled."

"Did you think he would put me in danger?" A thread of outrage contrasted with curiosity. So typical of Kaya. "Did you think my own grandfather would purposely seek out a weak—"

"No," he interrupted. "No, it's not what I meant. He shared none of that with me."

Kaya sighed and relaxed against him "He shared very little of his plans with *me*. But he trusts you, and…" Her breath caressed his chest when she sighed. Kaya lifted her head and met his gaze. "I do as well."

All his air left Paul in a rush of—of pride and fear, of this intimacy that now bound them. It terrified him.

"You shouldn't," Paul warned.

Kaya looked back at him calmly and steadily. He didn't know how to respond, what to say. Instead, he kissed her, let that feeling engulf him. Kissing her was easy. Sex was simple.

So was lying to himself.

Paul willingly submerged in the taste and feel of her. He ran his hands down Kaya's back. He cupped the gorgeously rounded arse he'd been admiring since they met and squeezed.

She made a strangled sound in the back of her throat and broke their kiss. Sitting up and straddling his legs, Kaya looked down at him.

"Why did you do that?" Voice breathless, eyes dark, breasts heaving with each breath, she studied him.

"What?" He was momentarily distracted—well, more than momentarily—when she gently rocked against his cock. Paul wondered if she even knew she was moving. Knew what she did to him. "Squeeze your arse?"

Kaya opened her mouth, but he did it again. Her breath hitched, and she moaned. "I had no idea." Her breath rushed out, her fingers curling into his chest, eyes wide on his. "I had no idea I enjoyed that."

Paul stilled. Her admission had him completely hard for her. Had another woman ever told him what she liked? If she had, Paul hadn't remembered beyond that encounter. Kaya eclipsed every other woman as if they never existed.

"Like this?" He dragged his hands up her back, thumbs brushing her ribs.

Kaya arched her back, thrust out her breasts, and gasped. He trailed his fingertips down her spine. She whimpered and shivered. When he danced his fingers over the curve of her arse, she moaned his name.

Kaya shifted over him, opened her legs wider, and he felt her wetness along his cock. "Do you?" Her voice was strangled, heavy with arousal.

"What?" Paul jerked against her.

"Do you enjoy it?" Kaya clarified. He wondered how she could still speak. "If I squeeze your—your *arse*." She stumbled over the word, flushing. "Will you enjoy it? Will it feel like it does for me?"

Confused, he stared at her. "I've no idea," he admitted. "No one's ever squeezed my arse." He did it again, watched her entire body shudder with pleasure. "How does it feel?"

"I—I don't know. Not like earlier, when I flew through the sky like a kite, wings spread wide." She threw back her head and spread her arms, hips stilled. Her hair brushed his legs, but Paul didn't move. He simply watched her, mesmerized.

Adjusting herself lower so she rested on his upper thighs, she carefully grasped his cock. Paul groaned and forced himself not to jerk in her hand. Kaya looked at him, breath coming fast, breasts flushed, and stroked him. He clenched his jaw, fingers digging into her hips, and sucked in air through his teeth.

"It's like a drum beating low in me. A—a pulsing beat that builds higher and tighter." Once again, she threw her head back and sighed. Her hand left his chest to rest just above her wet curls. "It clenches through me," she whispered. "And I want all of it."

Paul growled. He had nothing to say to her admission, her confession. Her openness, her enjoyment of sex—not only was she so responsive to his every touch, but Kaya turned her curiosity of the world onto something far more intimate. She didn't let anything distract her. Every action focused on him, on *them*.

He'd never been attracted to a woman's mind before. Everything about Kaya attracted him.

She still stroked him, her calloused fingers brushing up and down his cock. Unclenching one hand from her hip, Paul wrapped his fingers around hers.

"Open yourself," he managed. "Guide me in."

Eyes on his, Kaya obeyed. She rolled her hips, fingers slipping between her legs to do as he commanded. Gasping in several breaths, she guided him into her. Perfect.

"Is it always like this?" She rocked against him. Gasping, she did so again, taking him deep into her.

Paul cupped her breasts, pinching her nipples. She whimpered, leaned closer, and he tugged her nipples harder. Kaya clenched around him, slick and hot, her fingers pressed hard into his chest.

"Move faster," he begged.

"Touch me again," she demanded. "Make me fly

again."

"Your wish is my command."

Hands braced on his chest, Kaya lifted her hips, moving slowly as Paul slid his fingers through her curls to her clit. He pressed against the hard nub, and she choked out a moan.

He loved the sounds she made, the breathless sighs and the moans. The way her eyes closed, the way her head tilted back to expose the graceful column of her neck.

"That's it. Take me deeper."

He circled her in hard, tight movements. Kaya clenched around him, erratic. Paul steadied her hips, wanted to cup her arse again, but not yet. Wanted to watch her come as he touched her, showed her yet more new sensations, experiences.

"Paul," she moaned, head bowed. Glazed with passion, her eyes met his. Focused, eager, ready. "Paul."

"Let go, Kaya." He caught her hand and guided her to her own pleasure.

"*Oh.*" Her eyes drifted closed as her fingers slid over her clit, slowly at first, then faster as she found a rhythm she enjoyed. Kaya moaned again, high-pitched sounds that caught in the back of her throat and wound his pleasure tight. Paul clenched his jaw and grasped at the threads of his control.

"Ah!" Kaya cried out as she climaxed.

Her fingers continued to move over her clit, the nails of her other hand digging into his chest. That pain shredded the last remaining hold he had on his control.

He grasped her hips tight and thrust up, holding her to him as he let go. He moved in her, harder with each movement. Eyes closed, lost in the feel of Kaya's orgasm, Paul barely remembered to roll them over and pull out of her as his climax raced up his spine.

Utterly spent, boneless, breath heaving out of him, he

collapsed beside her. He pressed his lips to her shoulder, one arm heavy around her as she, too, struggled to catch her breath. He wanted to stay here, wrapped around her. Nothing else mattered.

Eventually, he felt her move and blinked open his eyes. She hissed and stretched out beside him. Limbs shaky, breathing heavy, he reached for his handkerchief and cleaned her up. She watched him silently, leaning on her elbows, skin flushed.

Paul tossed the linen to the floor and lay next to her, pulling her into his arms. Her head once more on his chest, she trailed her fingers over the marks her nails had made. She didn't apologize.

Good.

He didn't want her to. He wanted those marks for reasons he didn't understand. Or didn't want to admit.

"Is it always like this?" Her voice brushed over him, and he shuddered, still trying to catch his breath.

Paul stilled. "No. No, it wasn't always like this."

He kissed her again—to stop her questions, to stop the words crowding his throat. To stop his traitorous heart from whispering words he never had before. He didn't know how to salvage the situation or his heart or any of it. She sighed into the kiss, her body pressed close to his. Tempting. So damn tempting.

Abruptly, Paul stood.

What was he thinking? More importantly, what was he *doing*?

Kissing her, making love to her. Holding her close and not letting go. Somehow earning her trust, trust he most assuredly did *not* deserve.

He'd needed absolution, and he thought helping Kaya escape Cairo was the way to that. Stupid, stupid fool. Making love to her, promises of—of what? Promises of more than right now.

Of a future.

Her dark gaze captured him, compelled him, and he couldn't look away. Face flushed, lips swollen and red, nipples hard points, she enticed him.

Pulled him back to her.

Paul stepped away. Doing so took more willpower than he thought it should.

"I need to see Anatoly again." Was that his voice? That coarse, uneven sound he didn't recognize? "He knows of a ship with a mostly trustworthy captain that can take us as far as Cádiz."

Kaya sat up, her long hair falling over one breast, down the gentle curve of her belly. He wanted to brush it over her shoulder, kiss his way down her body and taste her again.

His fingers begged to touch her; his body burned for her. Forbidden fruit.

"I'll go with you."

"No." The word shot from him before he could stop it. Not that he wanted to. Kaya's eyes narrowed, and he sighed. Running a hand over his face, he gathered his clothing, forgotten in a pile at the foot of the bed.

"I don't want you in the souk." He stopped as he heard his own words, his extremely weak excuse. He knew she was about to fight him. He deserved it. He deserved a lot of things, but not that soft look she gave him. Not her trust.

"I need you safe, Kaya." The words tore from his heart.

"And you think me safe here? Alone?"

Damn her for always having a valid argument.

"All right." He snapped the vest over his shirt and glared at her. It was his only defense. "Stay close. No wandering away."

"*I* did not wander to the head of the street with

Anatoly." She spoke entirely too reasonably for an argument. When he looked at her, he realized only her tone was reasonable—face set, eyes dark with anger, she glared at him as she, too, dressed.

This was not how he wanted the aftermath of their first time—well, second time. He'd enjoyed lying with her, her warm body flush against his, the lazy intimacy of staying with his partner. Paul wanted more of that, the quiet cuddling of after, the talking, the…the intimacy, the comfort of holding her in his arms.

Not that he'd thought of that—making love to Kaya or the aftermath.

Not that he'd thought of it *often*.

Paul dropped to the bed and tiredly tugged on his boots. Nothing had gone as planned since he stepped foot in Tahir's house—all right, since he *broke* into Tahir's house. Nothing.

"I shall stay close," Kaya agreed in a tone that sounded more like she was bestowing favors than agreeing. "Then I want to further explore Damietta."

He didn't bother disagreeing. How had things changed so drastically between them in the space of a heartbeat? Maybe he should wonder why he'd made love to her in the first place.

No, he knew damn well why. She was irresistible, tempting, beautiful and smart, curious and innocent and passionate. Paul scrubbed his hands through his hair. She'd captured him from the first and hadn't let go.

And she didn't even know it.

"All right. Stay close."

With his luck, she'd sneak out of the inn and explore on her own, leading to nothing but heart failure for him. Or apoplexy.

Chapter Fifteen

Muscles loose, body still humming with unfettered energy, Kaya slipped her hand through the crook of Paul's arm and let him lead her through the winding streets of Damietta.

She had strapped her khanjar to her waist. Paul made no comment, but *Madaam* Nephthys had eyed it suspiciously.

Kaya ignored her.

This time, Kaya paid better attention and memorized the route from the inn to the souk. Paul led them in a circuitous path, down one street and up a parallel one.

"On your early-morning trip to purchase my gown and your new clothes, did you map the city?"

He shot her an amused grin. He seemed to have moved beyond whatever made him so short with her earlier. He'd been as aloof and unfriendly as he was during their nighttime desert walk. Now, relaxed as they walked the streets, he had returned to the man she knew. Her Paul. "Yes."

"I should've known."

Earlier, she'd been too enamored with the sights and scents to observe their surroundings. On their rushed return to the inn, she'd been energized by the kidnapping attempt—despite the danger—and the inherent promise in Paul's kiss, his touch.

Paul walked beside her, his gait even with hers. He stared straight ahead. Kaya knew him well enough by now to know he was assessing every person, every hidden corner, every potential threat. His awareness of their surroundings both chilled and comforted her. A tingle raced down her spine—people watched her. She felt their gaze as surely as she felt Paul's arm beneath her hand.

In the heat of the late afternoon, she shivered.

"What's wrong?" he asked. He didn't turn his gaze

from the street, but she hadn't expected him to.

"I'm not used to being in the open." Kaya licked her lips and shook her head, dispelling her lingering unease.

Even in the unlikely scenario the Ottomans found her in Cairo, even if they knew what she looked like, even if they followed her to Damietta and saw her transformation from Egyptian to wealthy Englishwoman—

No. Kaya released her breath and held her head high.

No one had ever seen her outside her home, and Kaya felt that relief move through her like a breeze.

"I love it," she rushed to clarify and realized how true those words were. "But I'm not used to so many people seeing me. Watching me."

He stopped and turned to face her. His gaze was soft, and it settled on her, his hands cupping her shoulders through her scarf.

"You can protect yourself," he whispered. "I've seen you fight, and it's amazing."

Kaya nodded, short, jerky movements. "I can, yes."

"These people, they don't really see you." He frowned and seemed to struggle for words. "They see *you*, they see *us*. They don't know who you really are. They don't know the real you, so it's impossible for them to see the real you." His fingers brushed over her cheek, a comfort she hadn't realized she needed. "I won't let anything happen to you, Kaya."

He'd promised that before, and, just like before, she believed him. Each time he said it, she believed him.

"I know. Thank you."

Paul slipped her gloved hand through the crook of his elbow. "I don't think Anatoly had anything to do with— with—" He cleared his throat, fingers clenching around hers. "Stay close."

Kaya pressed her lips together on the retort. *She* hadn't been the one to wander. All right—she hadn't been the *only one* to wander. Instead, she squeezed Paul's arm in silent assent.

Truly, she had no desire to re-create the scene from earlier.

As thrilling as the fight was, as eager as she'd been to put her skills to practical use, Kaya could still feel that man's hand clasping around her nose and mouth, cutting off her air. She swallowed hard. Best to put that behind her. To erase the sour scent of his touch, the creeping disgust even now choking her.

She'd have nightmares about it.

"I know you do not trust Anatoly." Kaya ignored Paul's mild snort of amusement. "But do you believe him?"

"I believe he fought next to me," Paul said slowly. "And I believe he was truly concerned about your welfare. Either he is a great actor, and planned to fight the men distracting us so as not to cast suspicion upon himself, or he had nothing to do with those men."

"I suppose we shall see."

They turned onto the street with Anatoly's stall. Kaya saw the tall, pale man instantly and waited as he hurried toward them. He bowed before her. "*As-salamu alaykum, Madaam* Conrad."

"*As-salamu alaykum, sade* Anatoly."

"You are well?" He eyed her carefully. "Unharmed from earlier?"

Impressed with his tactfulness, Kaya merely nodded, careful of her wide-brimmed, slightly crushed hat. "I am, thank you."

"Paul, my friend, you should not have brought her back here." Anatoly glanced around the street, an odd tension in his shoulders and voice.

"I couldn't leave her in our room," Paul shot back.

Anatoly scowled. Kaya thought he wanted to argue.

She wondered why he thought she'd be safer alone in their room, in an inn surrounded by strangers, than here with Paul. These interactions, they confused her. Or maybe these men did.

Anatoly blew out a breath that Kaya knew held annoyance and acceptance. Paul had the same reaction to much of what she said. He mumbled something in a language she didn't understand and gestured for his stall.

"I have no news on the men who tried to take *Madaam* Conrad." He looked at her, those blue eyes hard and penetrating. "They were slavers, but—" He shook his head. "Slavers rarely take women off the street. Not here in Damietta, at least."

Everything in her went cold. Her fingers tightened on Paul's arm, but she dared not look at him.

If what happened earlier wasn't the act of slavers, then who? Fear held her in its grip, unrelenting and unyielding. A bone-deep terror that Gidd's worst nightmare had come true.

Kaya swallowed around a lump of grief and terror. "That horrid man wanted to take me, either for ransom or to sell as a slave."

Fear that the sultan's guards had found her wedged deep in her soul, but she refused to show it.

"Who did they work for?" Paul demanded.

His harsh words shook her from her terror, and Kaya focused on his conversation with Anatoly. That seemed the better course than letting her thoughts whirl with no logical end.

"Who did they work for?" Paul's voice didn't rise but turned deadlier—a testament to his dangerousness. "You know everyone here," Paul hissed, fury thick on each word. "You know every smuggler and pirate along the coast, and every single person willing to skip the customs agents. *Who were they?*"

To Kaya's surprise, Anatoly didn't answer Paul. He bowed deeply to her. "*Madaam* Conrad, I vow to you on my life, on my soul, I shall find the men responsible and see they pay for what they've done to you."

"Oh." She felt as if she should say more. Part of her wanted to point out they hadn't done anything but prove to her that Gidd's training had not been in vain. That men like that were the very reason he'd trained her. Instead, Kaya nodded. "Thank you, *sade* Anatoly. I leave their fate in your hands."

Paul growled, anger stiffening the muscles beneath her hand. It wasn't the pleasant sound of earlier that shot down her spine and wrapped around her. It was tense, a strained fury pushing to be unleashed.

Kaya squeezed his arm and tilted her head to look up at him. His eyes blazed with sudden clarity, and she knew one word from her would snap his control. Swallowing her choking fear, she nodded once, a long, slow movement of her head.

"I believe *sade* Anatoly will honor his word." If Anatoly did not, they'd be long gone from this place and its dangers.

Paul's mouth tightened, but she knew he agreed. Turning to Anatoly, he said, "Good."

Anatoly bowed again and changed the subject. "My good friend, Captain George, captains *The Cyprus Rose*. He has agreed to take you as far as Cádiz."

"When?" Paul's voice hadn't lost any of its severity, its hard, vibrating fury. Anatoly didn't seem intimidated. In fact, he looked at Paul with even more respect.

Kaya added that to her list of personalities she did not understand. Angry intimidation meant Anatoly respected Paul? Men, they were most eccentric.

"Tomorrow, on the afternoon tide."

Paul nodded and stepped back, a little of the tension leaving his body. Kaya wanted to ask about the ship. She'd only ever seen them last night, when they entered Damietta. However, she didn't want to draw attention to her lack of knowledge, so she reluctantly remained silent.

Silence infuriated her; not knowing, not understanding, annoyed her. Book learning had not prepared her for life.

"Now, my friend, I don't think you should stay in the souk. Let us visit the British Quarter." Anatoly paused and looked as if he wanted to say more. His gaze rested on Kaya and, in a quiet voice that barely carried to her, he whispered, "It is dangerous for you to remain on the streets."

"I think we'll dine at the inn," Paul said in that false-easy voice.

"Let's see the rest of the city," Kaya hurried to say. She didn't want to return to the inn, no matter how pleasurable she found learning Paul's body. She wanted to explore. "We've seen so little of it, and we sail tomorrow."

Deep lines etched the sides of Paul's mouth, and he stood tense and ready at her side. He wanted to object. Kaya knew the dangers of the streets, the hidden perils of simply being here. To see Damietta, however—the city tempted her. The newness of everything tempted her.

Leaning closer, she tilted her head so her hat didn't hit him and whispered, "I promise not to wander."

She thought he'd at least attempt a grin, but his head jerked around. Paul met her gaze, his own wary, uneasy. Kaya opened her mouth to ask why he didn't want to dine in the British Quarter, but Paul straightened.

"You'll join us, Anatoly?" Paul asked, once more in that easy tone she knew to be fake. "You can tell us more of the city. I'm sure my wife is very curious as to the history of Damietta."

Well, yes, of course she wanted to know about

Damietta. Kaya suddenly had the feeling the British Quarter held more dangers than the desert and the souk combined.

Anatoly bowed. "I am honored."

He closed down his stall, pulling items inside and releasing the propped-up wooden piece with quick ease. Kaya wondered what it was called, that propped up wooden piece. Nervous energy thrummed over her skin, and she pressed her fingers into Paul's arm.

Now that they'd committed to exploring Damietta with Anatoly, she found herself uneasy. Perhaps it was anticipation. Or a combination of anticipation and unease.

"We can return to the inn," he whispered as Anatoly locked the stall.

"Do you wish to?"

Paul shook his head, a brief movement, and his lips twisted in a grimace of a smile. "I wish to keep you safe, Kaya."

"I'm safe with you." The words left her mouth before she realized their meaning.

Paul looked at her, as surprised as she, it seemed. Then his face darkened. "I'll protect you," he promised.

She couldn't help but notice he hadn't agreed with her. Then again, he hadn't contradicted her, either.

Paul's gaze shifted to just over her shoulder, but Kaya tilted her head back, doing her best to ignore her hat. His face had closed off, but it wasn't blank—his jaw was clenched, and his gaze darted from alley to alley.

"Paul?" She lowered her voice, a compassion she didn't understand winding around her heart. Kaya reached out, following the instinct that had urged her to touch him.

He jerked his head around, gaze rooted to her hand. Kaya couldn't read his expression, not because his face remained blank, but because she didn't understand the emotions there. Lips parted, she struggled for words but had none. His expression broke her heart, and she didn't understand why.

"We can't go to the British Quarter." Paul shook himself and retreated, though his hand covered hers. "I don't want anyone asking too many questions."

"Questions?" He didn't answer. Questions about what? Her? Him? Their past? A sinking sensation warned her that Paul feared for his own safety as much as her own. "All right."

Paul dropped his hand, not meeting her gaze. He seemed to brace himself, and a heartbeat later Anatoly stood beside them.

"Maybe it's best we return to the inn," Kaya began.

Anatoly waved her off. "Nonsense, *Madaam* Kaya. I promised to show you Damietta, and before you leave on the tide I shall do that."

Paul nodded, his lips pressed in a thin line and his arm stiff beneath her hand. "After you, *sade*."

They walked along a maze of streets. Their quick pace had Kaya wondering if they hurried through dangerous sections of town, or if Anatoly wished to arrive in the British Quarter in reasonable time.

"Damietta used to be under Byzantine control," Anatoly said as they exited a shaded street lined with quiet houses. "The Arabs, they took control over a thousand years ago. Many Christian armies tried to recapture it, but none have been successful."

"They wanted access to *en-Nīl*." Kaya bit her tongue and hurried to correct her language mistake. "Controlling the Nile at a tributary meant access to Cairo."

Anatoly nodded, seeming not to have noticed her slip. She doubted that very much—the man noticed quite a lot. Beside her, Paul stiffened further, if that were possible. Resting her other hand on his arm, she hoped he could feel her light caress beneath his clothing.

Anatoly had slowed in a nicer, more brightly decorated section of town, and she didn't want to draw more attention to herself than necessary.

"Foreigners aren't allowed, of course," Anatoly added. "But Damietta boasts many beautiful mosques, a testament to the great Mamluks."

He continued about the architecture and history, extolling the city's rich Islamic past.

They walked through residential streets with houses that bracketed beautiful gardens vibrant with life. Kaya wanted to stop and admire them; she hadn't seen such gardens since the previous rainy season. Slowing to study them, she turned to Anatoly to ask how these places survived.

"Wealth," Paul muttered, and she frowned up at him. "We're in the wealthy section of the city," he said. "Closer to the British Quarter."

The way he said it sounded as if the British section was the wealthy section. Kaya didn't ask. For all she knew that might have been true, but Paul made it seem dirty.

Rounding another corner, Kaya noticed Paul's hand on his dagger. She didn't understand his reluctance, his absolute refusal to enter the British Quarter, but took her cue from him. Wary, she dropped a hand from his arm and let it hover by her waist, near her khanjar.

"Have you a favored establishment?" Kaya asked Anatoly, far too on edge to notice her surroundings.

"I have several clients." He slowed more, nodding to a group of men in British army uniforms much like the one Paul wore in Cairo that first night.

Oh. Paul's behavior made sense—whatever happened in Bombay had caused him to not reenlist and instead travel to Cairo. Did they hold the same code and loyalty to the service her own grandfather had abided by?

The more she knew about Paul, the less she understood him.

"Have you a craving for a more traditional fare?" Anatoly asked as they meandered along the street. "I know an excellent British tavern at the corner."

"No." Paul forced a smile and stopped in front of what looked like a *kahwa* house. "Here is fine. We enjoy the local food."

"Yes." Kaya grinned up at Anatoly and hoped her smile looked more authentic than Paul's. From the way Anatoly looked between them, Kaya doubted her success. "I shall miss the *ful medames*."

Anatoly shrugged and ushered them inside a spacious inn that held fewer tables than *El Reyah* but far more men who looked as if they'd rather rob her than offer her a seat. Kaya tilted her chin, adjusted her hijab, and tried not to stare.

"Bloody perfect."

She looked up at Paul, concerned by the anger in his tone. "Paul?"

"It's fine." He didn't smile at her so much as bare his teeth. She did not like the look on him. "Remember, Mrs. Conrad, we're passing through on our way back to England."

"Yes," Kaya said slowly, utterly confused. "I remember. What's wrong?"

After a moment, he jerked his head in a semblance of negativity. "Nothing." He met her gaze. His own was hard, troubled. "Don't worry."

Too late for that.

Chapter Sixteen

Kaya walked beside Paul as they returned to their inn. Anatoly had left them after a pleasant afternoon exploring the city and enjoying the local fare. He'd continued to watch them, but he hadn't said a word about Paul's suspicious nature.

Now, as the two of them returned to the inn, Kaya struggled to pinpoint what had caused Paul such apprehension.

The sun dipped behind the buildings, casting the streets in shadow, but she felt no rush to hide indoors despite her experiences outside.

Between the slavers, the near-kidnapping in the souk, and Paul's strange behavior as they walked the streets of Damietta, Kaya had amazed herself with her lack of fear. No, not that—nothing so foolish as not fearing men who were attempting to harm her. She struggled to place the emotion.

She carefully chose her words, unsure of Paul's reaction or reply. "I had feared for my safety, but not to the point of being immobile." Kaya didn't know if her words helped Paul or not, but she needed to say them. "I still fear the Ottomans, no matter that them finding me here and now defies logic."

"Kaya." He stopped and turned to her, his face set. "If it lays within my power to prevent it, nothing will harm you."

"I know." Again, Kaya knew she spoke the truth.

That knowledge moved through her, a warm contentment Kaya didn't understand. Paul had entered her world such a short time ago. After all they'd been through, she didn't know what to make of him.

Or her strange feelings for him.

The trust she recognized, but a new emotion grew around her heart. One she didn't understand, had no basis to understand.

"Did you recognize any of the soldiers on the street?"

Paul stiffened beside her. Kaya tilted her head—mindful of her hat—and studied him, his clenched jaw, pursed lips, heavy breathing.

"Paul?" she asked, concerned.

"No." He continued walking for several moments, and Kaya struggled to form another question. "I didn't recognize any of them."

"You expected to—for them to recognize you, or for you to know one of them, correct?" He didn't answer immediately, and she stopped, exasperated. "Paul!"

He turned, faced her, but his eyes darted over the street. The way he watched the front of *El Reyah* and every alley surrounding it, as if he expected an attack at any moment, chilled her bones.

"Paul," she said, softer now. "What's wrong? Why do you fear the British soldiers?"

The instant the words left her mouth, Kaya knew she'd spoken the truth. Her mind had danced around the facts before, but now, standing on the semi-crowded street with a soft sea breeze, Kaya knew she was right.

He looked at her for a long, long moment. The street narrowed, and the world fell away until only the two of them stood there. The call of the birds and the shouts of people faded to nothing more than a distant buzz.

"I disagreed with them." She barely heard his words; he spoke so softly. "They—the order my commander gave, it wasn't—" Paul met her gaze, bleak and broken. "He ordered the deaths of hundreds."

"Was that why you didn't reenlist?" Kaya took his hand, stiff and tense. His fingers flinched in hers, and he dropped his gaze.

"I only want to protect you, Kaya." She didn't

understand the faint thread of—of *something* she heard beneath his honesty. "Soldiers, British or otherwise, aren't known for common decency. Or common sense."

He held her gaze again, but the shadows of before haunted him. Kaya reached out, brushed her fingers over his cheek. She wanted to feel the stubble of his beard beneath her fingers, but her gloves prevented that. Instead, she squeezed his hand.

This disagreement with his commander did not tell the entire story. Whatever happened in Bombay to cause him to agree to Gidd's letter and trek across the Sinai to marry her had been far more than a mere disagreement.

"Thank you, Paul." She meant the words and hoped he understood. Hoped her sincerity showed she trusted him, showed her desire to be trusted.

He breathed out her name and pressed his lips to her forehead. She leaned into the touch—not exactly proper—and took comfort in his arms around her.

Paul released her. He held her gaze for another long moment, then stepped forward, opening the door to the inn and ushering her inside. *Madaam* Nephthys sat at her preferred seat, and several men sat scattered through the dimly lit room. Kaya kept her gaze straight ahead, her head high.

Paul spoke to *Madaam* Nephthys and accepted their key, but Kaya didn't pay attention to the conversation. When his hand settled on her back, she turned for the stairs and climbed them, each step heavier than the last.

"Kaya!"

She blinked at Paul, frowning. "Yes?"

"Are you all right? Are you ill? Faint?" The concern in his eyes, the worry etched on his face, confused her as well.

"I am simply tired." She gazed at their open door.

His frown didn't abate, but Paul brushed his fingertips

over her cheek. "You're exhausted." He kissed her forehead, and once more that shiver of comfort wrapped around her. "Lie down, try to rest. I need to speak with *Madaam* Nephthys again, but I'll bring up supper."

She wasn't hungry, not after their meal in the British Quarter, but she accepted his offer and stepped into their room. Paul moved easily behind her, silent, but she felt his eyes on her back. He didn't divest himself of his dagger or the satchel, and a distant part of her wondered why he kept the bag on him.

"Do you—" He cleared his throat. "Do you need help undressing?"

"No." She met his gaze. Her own eyes felt huge and scratchy, but she made no move to undress.

His hand found her cheek again, and he cupped it, thumb sweeping over her skin. Kaya leaned into the touch and sighed, eyes closing.

"Undress, Kaya. Lie down. I won't be long." He hesitated. "Keep your dagger close. Just in case."

She didn't even have the strength to make a pithy reply about how she always kept her khanjar near. Kaya merely watched him, her head too heavy to keep upright.

He kissed her forehead again and left.

Kaya unlaced her bodice and sat on the bed with a tired puff of skirts. Up until Paul's arrival, the only change in her life had been Derya's death. *Derya.* Kaya sniffed back the ache and tried to remember all the joy they shared. Not this clawing, heavy grief. Closing her eyes against the tears, she fell to the bed.

The knock startled her awake. Jerking upright, she blinked in confusion. She didn't realize she'd grabbed her khanjar until the knock sounded again.

"Kaya, open the door."

Nauseous, legs weak, and not rested in the least, Kaya

stumbled to the door. She couldn't make her fingers unclench from her dagger.

Looking even more tired than when he left, Paul carried a tray of food. The smell churned her stomach.

"Did you sleep?" He entered their room and latched the door behind him.

Crossing to the table, he set down the tray and turned to her. His large, warm hands cupped her cheeks, and he looked at her as if he knew her soul. Terrified he'd read her so well, that he knew her better than she knew herself, she stumbled back.

"What's wrong?"

Kaya opened her mouth to give him a litany of *wrong*, but no words emerged. She snapped her mouth closed on her growing feelings for him. Her fear.

Paul frowned at her silence and cautiously rested his hands on her shoulders. "Let me help you undress." His words were evenly spaced, slow and gentle. "A lot's happened today."

In her mind, Kaya scoffed at his words. She wondered what her face showed.

"Maybe food will help," Paul continued.

"I'm not hungry." The words echoed strangely in her ears, and her stomach did another nauseous roll.

"Kaya—"

"Leave me alone, Paul."

She turned for the bed and let her bodice fall. The jewels clanked dully on the floor, and her numb fingers fumbled with the ties of her skirts. They, too, dropped where she stood. Staring at the bed, clad in boots, stockings, chemise, and hijab she felt Paul's gaze on her but forced her body not to react. Not to acknowledge his concern, his watchful gaze. But forcing her body not to react lay beyond her capabilities.

In a week, Kaya had grown to care for Paul far more than she'd believed possible. And she had no idea what that meant.

* * * *

Paul sat at the table, in their single chair, and listlessly stirred the soup. The flatbread tasted like ash, and the soup was thin and unappealing. Kaya might enjoy it. It had smelled appetizing when *Madaam* Nephthys offered a bowl for his wife.

Wife.

The spoon clattered against the wooden tray. Paul whipped his head around to check on Kaya, but she didn't so much as move. He breathed out a sigh of relief and silently pushed back from the table. His boots didn't echo across the floor as he crossed the room. The only sound was the faint rustle of his clothing.

Kneeling beside the bed, he brushed Kaya's hair off her cheeks, away from her neck. No breeze filtered through the small window, and the room remained closed and stuffy. Kaya sighed into his touch but didn't otherwise move.

"What are you doing here, Kaya?" Paul leaned over and kissed her softly. "Tahir made a mistake in contacting me. You deserve so much better."

She didn't respond. Just as well. He didn't want to know her answer.

He pushed off the floor and stalked to the window, as far from her as the room allowed. Before him, the night stretched out, silent and empty. He liked the night—or used to. It hid his sins, concealed his crimes. He knew nighttime Bombay better than in the daylight.

Basu's laugh echoed in his memory. His friend had shown him Bombay, taught him the language, the secrets of the city. The wine and opium, the women and gambling, the quickest way to make a rupee and the easiest way to spend it.

Paul looked over his shoulder to where Kaya blissfully slept. If Basu saw him now—hell, if John or Oliver knew how he'd changed, they wouldn't believe him. They'd want to know what he gained from this.

"Nothing." The sound of his voice shocked him.

Liar.

He eyed the bodice where it lay crumpled on the floor, Kaya's jewels hidden inside. He waited for them to tempt him. For his feet to take him across the floor and his fingers to find the jewels sewn inside the bodice.

Nothing. He didn't care. Not about the jewels or the money. A lifetime scrambling for riches, and now that they lay within his grasp…

Paul didn't care.

His gaze drifted up, rested on Kaya's face. Pale cheeks, dark bruises beneath her eyes—even in sleep, a faint line creased between her brows. Paul wanted to sooth it, ease her tension and worry.

She'd married down. Even before he knew of her royal pedigree, Paul knew Kaya was the granddaughter of a celebrated Egyptian general. It wouldn't have mattered if she'd been a peasant girl.

He was several steps down for her. She was one hell of a step up for a kid from the backstreets of London. One whose maid mother cared more for the master of the wealthy house she worked in than she did for her own son. Then again, Paul had always suspected the master of that house fathered him. In the end, it hadn't mattered. Still didn't.

The thought of telling Kaya what sort of man she'd married sickened him.

He wanted her to respect him for the man she *thought* he was. The man he showed her. The man he wanted to be for her.

Not his past, his transgressions—those stories, he

hoped she'd never learn. The one good story he had from India involved Tahir, and Paul had barely remembered the incident until Tahir's letter found him.

What would she think of him now, the man who'd seduced her? Paul frowned. He shouldn't have done that, slept with her, consummated—

His knees gave out.

Paul slid to the floor. His fingers curled through his hair, into his scalp, and he tried to forget what he'd done. Growling, he banged his head against the wall. What *had* he done?

Unsteady, Paul stood and slowly made his way to the bed. He sat on the floor, back against the mattress, and turned his head just slightly. As much as he wanted to join Kaya, find comfort in her arms, Paul stayed where he sat. Close, yet still too far.

He didn't consciously move, unaware he was holding her fingers until they curled around his. Pressing his lips to the back of them, he held her hand for a moment. Warm but not weak, capable but not hard—words that described Kaya perfectly.

The moment stretched out, both silent and cacophonously loud, soft and rushed. No matter how he tried to hold onto this moment, it flitted away.

"I'm sorry," he whispered. He gently set her hand back on the bedding, stroking the back of it. "You deserve better. I never should have touched you. Shouldn't have—"

For all his vows not to get close to her, he'd done a hell of a lot more than that. He'd developed feelings for her, grown to care for her.

Stupid fool.

He loved her.

Chapter Seventeen

"Good morning," Paul said.

The early morning sun barely dented the dim interior. The small window faced the west side of the city, and neither of them bothered lighting the single candle. The darkness added to Kaya's disorientation, the strange feeling of not being entirely awake but certain she no longer struggled in dreams.

"Morning?"

Kaya, sticky from the poorly ventilated room and still exhausted, blinked open gritty eyes and forced herself to straighten from their bed. *Their* bed? *The* bed? She wasn't entirely certain how that worked.

Her body ached, her mind refused to clear, and she desperately wanted to crawl back in bed and sleep. Dreamlessly, if possible. Her sleep had been restless, disturbed. Terrifying.

"Sleep well?" Paul's voice carried a hint of concern and something Kaya couldn't place.

"No." She didn't elaborate.

She dreamt Paul had left her, uncaring of all they shared and only concerned with himself. Alone, she stood in the middle of the vast desert as he walked away, taking the only things she claimed as hers: her khanjar, her bow and quiver, her jewels.

She cared less about the jewels than her weapons. Conversely, the jewels were the only things able to see her through such a desertion. Remembering Paul walking away from her crushed her chest and rolled her empty stomach.

"Did you?" she asked to fill the odd silence between them. It vibrated along her skin and echoed in her heart.

"No," Paul admitted in that same strange voice. He didn't elaborate, either.

Each time she'd jerked awake, Paul was sitting on the bed. Through the darkness, she knew he watched her, steady and calm in the piercing blackness. He ran his hand down her bare arms, brushed hair from her cheeks. His quiet understanding soothed her, made her—secure? content? safe?

Tired, irritable, and confused, she stretched. Then whimpered. Her entire body *hurt*. Every muscle, even those—especially those—she hadn't realized could be sore, ached.

"Stiff?" Paul's voice reached her from the window, where he once more looked out over the city.

"Even Gidd's training never hurt like this."

"You've never had sex before." His voice sounded so bland, so reasonable, she wanted to shove the words back into his mouth.

Forcibly.

Instead of snarling at him, Kaya bent forward to hide her scowl and let her hands hang down and touch the floor. She tried not to whimper at the tugging between her legs, though, honestly, she didn't care if Paul heard.

The strangled sound he made in the back of his throat told her he had. She straightened too quickly.

"Oh." Kaya shook her head, but that didn't help, either.

The jumble of emotions clashing in her heart had no point of reference. No matter how she tried shoving her feelings away, they leaped back again and again.

Kaya slowly raised her arms over her head. Wincing at the tug in her shoulders, she instantly dropped her arms. She sighed, brushing a hand through her loose hair.

"I'm sorry I don't have a warm bath for you to soak in."

His sincerity stole her breath. Paul suddenly stood before her. He'd washed, and his clean hair now curled loosely around his head.

His fingers caressed her jaw, touched her skin with the gentlest of strokes, his gaze boring into hers, so focused and determined. None of the distance shone in his gaze, only the vibrant heat of what drew her to him.

Kaya cleared her throat, or tried to. "Maybe you can massage my legs again?"

Why, why, *why* had she said that? The instant the words left her mouth, Kaya wanted to swallow them. Shove them back in and lock them there. Until she figured out her own feelings, she saw no need to lead him on with idiotic comments.

Kaya didn't remember the soothing massage from the desert; rather, the way his hands had run down her legs as he took off her stockings. How he'd kissed his way back up her inner thigh, his large, calloused hands holding her open to his touch, his mouth. His hands on her arse. The hot, coiling tension throbbing deep within her.

Her face heated with memories and embarrassment. With hot passion that even now settled low in her belly. Paul's fingers tightened on her cheek; his eyes darkened, the deepest blue. Kaya's breath caught at the look—hungry, greedy.

"Yes," he whispered.

He leaned down, and Kaya froze as his lips brushed hers once, twice. Tentative. Then he deepened the kiss. His fingers slipped from her cheek to tangle in her loose hair, and he angled his head, deepening the kiss even further.

Kaya opened to his kiss, greedy for his taste, the thrill down her spine whenever they touched.

The change in him—distant to passionate, aloof to hungry—muddled her already confused feelings. Kaya kissed him back despite her confusion. Paul cupped the back of her head, even as he pulled back with a small touch to her lips, the corner of her mouth, her cheek.

Breathing heavily, he rested his forehead against hers, his hands still tangled in her hair, his breath fanning over her cheek as quickly as her own.

"I don't understand you, Paul." Kaya pulled back just enough to meet his gaze. "You confuse me."

He laughed, an exhalation of sound, and shook his head. He still cradled her face, thumbs running over her cheeks. "Kaya—"

The knock jerked them apart. Kaya scowled at the door and grabbed her clothing from the chair, which was not where she remembered placing them. She turned her back to *Madaam* Nephthys and did up the laces on the front of her bodice as quickly as her shaking fingers allowed.

She smoothed her hands down the stiff material of the blue gown, adjusting its too-tight fit. The jewels still dug into her belly, but she accepted the slight pain.

Settling her hijab around her head, she faced the other woman, who scrutinized her as if she were a rare, fascinating specimen.

Paul took the tray of food with a charming smile and a—did he *wink* at her? *Madaam* Nephthys blushed. Kaya clenched her jaw. She did *not* like Paul dallying or flirting or—or *any* of that with the other woman.

Jealousy twisted through her, hot and sharp, pressing into her chest.

Kaya returned her gaze and kept her own feelings in check. She didn't want this woman to know anything about her.

Oh. *Oh...*

The door closed with a sharp click, startling her back to the moment.

"*Madaam* Nephthys knows what we did yesterday afternoon." Kaya met Paul's amused gaze. "I was not quiet. The entire inn must know."

Her face heated, and she crossed to the window. What little breeze made it through the small opening did nothing to ease the flush of her cheeks.

Paul cleared his throat, clearly amused. "But I like hearing you." He sounded close, but she did not turn.

One hand rested on her shoulder, and he turned her. Kaya forced herself to meet his gaze, not entirely certain how to take his declaration.

He held out a hot cup of *kahwa*. Kaya accepted the offering, ignoring the twinge of her muscles, the deeper, pleasurable one between her legs, the whirling haboob of her feelings. The ache in her heart.

It was going to be a long trip to Cádiz.

* * * *

The Cyprus Rose loomed over her, dominating its place in the harbor.

Head tilted, Kaya tried not to gape. Were all ships so large they overpowered everything around them? She never expected her first journey to be on a ship so *huge*. She'd always wanted to travel the boats on *en-Nīl*, to feel the wind on her skin, see the pristine sky overhead.

The Cyprus Rose did not look like the feluccas she envisioned. Those much smaller ships where she might enjoy the sun and open air and daydream of life outside her walls.

Standing on the docks with Anatoly while Paul spoke to the captain, Kaya played the well-traveled Englishwoman and said nothing to dissuade anyone in Damietta of that façade. She hated it.

"She's a fine ship." Anatoly stood beside her and grinned as if he captained *The Cypress Rose* instead of his "good friend George."

"Yes." Kaya, at a loss as to what to say to that odd phrase, tore her gaze from the thing. "*She* looks very…sturdy."

Kaya did not understand the use of *she* and was not entirely certain what *a fine ship* looked like. Or how sturdy it ought to be. It did not sink—surely that was a good indication of sturdiness.

Tilting her head to the other side, as if that afforded her a better look, Kaya pushed thoughts of ships and sturdiness—or seaworthiness, or whatever one called it— from her mind.

She turned to Anatoly and offered a smile. She tried not to shift uncomfortably in the open, alone with a stranger. Even one she trusted. Well, no, trust seemed too strong for what she felt for him, but Kaya believed his promise to find the men who tried to take her from the souk yesterday.

She trusted him to see to his own needs, though she felt as if Anatoly, much like Paul, was atoning for a past sin. She'd never know Anatoly's past, but she very much wanted to know Paul's.

Perhaps once they left Egypt.

Kaya turned into the wind and let the sharply scented sea breeze cool her face and dry her tears. Once they left Egypt, they left any hope of ever seeing her grandfather again. *Please let Gidd survive. Let him live years yet; let the Ottomans forget about him. Please.*

"Do you need to sit, *Madaam* Conrad?" Anatoly's voice startled her.

Shaking her head, she turned back to him and offered a small but nearly real smile. She did the best she could. Anatoly lost a bit of the alarm that was widening his eyes and bracketing his mouth, so Kaya thought she managed well enough.

"What is taking my husband and Captain George so long?" *Husband* sounded odd on her tongue. Foreign. Saying the word caused an odd fluttering in her chest and a wish for the future.

Her heart leaped at the thought.

Anatoly barked out a deep laugh and jerked his head to the buildings behind them. "He settles accounts with Captain George."

Kaya angled her head around, careful to keep a hand on her unnecessarily large hat. Scanning the crowds, she easily skimmed over the men—none of them were Paul. From here, she couldn't see inside the many windows dotting the busy office buildings, but she suspected Paul was watching her.

He rarely let her out of his sight. Yesterday's incident—and her subsequent nightmares—had caused him to remain physically close.

That Paul left her now puzzled her.

That she did not wish him to leave her side puzzled her even more.

She certainly didn't enjoy her confusion over Paul. Life was not as straightforward as she once envisioned, and the turns and twists it had taken since meeting him confused her further.

In Cairo, Kaya had sworn she wanted nothing to do with him. Here in Damietta, a week or so later, she…missed him. Missed him? Yes, she supposed that was the term. Kaya added it to the ever-growing list of things that baffled her.

"He was most reluctant, *Madaam* Conrad." Anatoly's voice drew her back to the present.

She didn't think she'd ever grow used to that salutation, or to the use of Conrad.

"However, Captain George—" He said something Kaya didn't understand.

"What does that mean, *trebuyet vzyatku*?" She carefully pronounced the words.

Anatoly shifted and refused to meet her gaze. "It means…cautious, fussy about his passengers."

A chill raced down her spine. Kaya didn't think this captain was *fussy*. Yesterday, Anatoly had mentioned nothing of that, and Paul certainly hadn't complained about Captain George's inflexibility. No. Paul needed to convince the captain to allow them onboard. He would not have left her side otherwise.

"Teach me Russian?" Kaya asked instead and remained still. From where she stood, she knew Paul watched her, and she vowed to remain clear of any obstacles that might hinder his view.

Just in case of another kidnapping attempt, or a theft, or any number of dangers she had once only heard of but now might experience firsthand. She carried her khanjar at her waist despite it not being fashionable. Or English. Or ladylike. None of which bothered Kaya.

Her satchel and bow and quiver had stayed with Paul, as did his pack. When they left the inn, Paul reasoned she'd be less of a target with no obvious bags.

Given what happened in the souk, Kaya disagreed, but she hadn't argued.

They argued over nearly everything. Her safety, her exploring and experiencing. It exhausted her.

Except sex. Kaya turned toward the building again. The way he made her feel so alive. His touch sparked her nerves and pooled heat low in her belly. The way he watched her, his yearning evident in every move. How he touched her, careful and hungry. Tasted her.

It all swirled around her like a haboob, wild and exciting and chaotic.

"In the next half hour?" Anatoly looked dubious.

Kaya scrambled to remember the question. Ah, yes, learning Russian.

"Yes." She smiled up at him, not at all put off by his reluctance.

His startling blue eyes assessed her. She wondered what he saw, *who* he saw when he looked at her. She was not certain herself anymore.

"Travel words," Kaya added. "Ship and sails, water, land, docks."

He nodded and turned his back on *The Cyprus Rose*. They spent the next little while as student and teacher. Anatoly gave her the basics in what he called *Russian Every Discerning Traveler Ought to Know*. Kaya soaked it up and felt as if she was doing something more than standing around, waiting for Paul.

"What brings you to Damietta?" Kaya asked after committing *Please show me the way to the nearest inn* to memory and Anatoly was satisfied with her pronunciation.

"My father lived in a small village by the River Volga. He left home at fourteen, traveled for adventure. Married a Turkish woman."

Kaya startled. "You are a long way from home." She stopped, swallowed hard. She did not want to ask her next question, but it must have shown on her face despite her best intentions.

"No. She was not a slave, but the youngest daughter of a fishing family near Tekeli." His voice softened; his face became pensive. "My mother's family saved him when he became lost at sea. They fell in love, and my mother joined him on his travels."

Anatoly met her gaze. Instantly, Kaya knew his mother was the reason he'd sworn to find the slavers who tried to take her yesterday. She swallowed a lump of gratitude and empathy. Perhaps Anatoly did not atone for his past, but for something else. Either way, Kaya felt sorry she had mistrusted him without truly knowing him.

"They loved each other," he added quietly.

She didn't like his use of past tense and tried to change

the subject. The weight of too many goodbyes, too many losses, pressed on her chest and squeezed her heart. "I, too, have wanted to travel."

"You're also a long way from home, *Madaam* Conrad. I think you've seen more than you realize."

Nodding in short, slow movements, Kaya offered a faint smile. "There is much to see in this world." Kaya clamped her hand on the hat and looked at Anatoly. "I shall like to see it all."

Anatoly barked out another laugh. "I have a feeling you will do just that." Then he abruptly straightened.

Without looking, Kaya knew Paul had exited the building. With one hand on the annoyance of her hat, she turned and watched him. He strode across the docks, ignoring the workers scuttling around him as they jumped out of his way. They quickly moved from the unyielding path of the wooden beam Paul once again carried across his back. A faint scowl darkened his face.

"Paul, my friend. I see you have worked everything out?"

Paul shot an angry look over his shoulder. "We can board as soon as they finish loading."

He stood so close to her she felt his body vibrate with tension. She slipped her hand down his arm and wrapped her fingers around his.

"Excellent, excellent." Anatoly bowed. "Then I shall take my leave."

He took Kaya's hand and brushed his lips over her gloved fingers. She was so shocked at his touch, she stilled.

"*Madaam* Conrad, it has truly been a pleasure." Anatoly winked up at her from where he bent over her hand. "I hope we shall meet again, though I feel this is not to be."

Return to Egypt? Kaya's heart sang with the prospect. She briefly closed her eyes and prayed for Gidd's safety and health. Swallowing a lump of grief and sorrow, she managed a smile and squeezed the hand Anatoly held.

"I, too, hope for that, *sade* Anatoly." She wasn't entirely sure how to return his rather gracious goodbye. "May you find your own adventure."

His smile softened. It looked more natural than the one he'd given her previously. Anatoly nodded again, clapped Paul on the shoulder, and disappeared into the crowd.

Chapter Eighteen

Kaya did not watch Anatoly leave.

She had said enough goodbyes; she did not wish to do so again. Instead, she wished her new friend well and turned to Paul.

"Anatoly said Captain George was fussy about his passengers. I don't believe him. What really happened?"

Paul snorted. "You're too observant by half, Kaya."

He tugged her into his embrace and hugged her tight. Her hat fell, but Paul deftly caught it. Their few items lay at their feet, waiting to be taken aboard. Kaya kicked the pack out of her way, stepped over the beam, and wrapped her arms around him.

She ignored the scandalous looks from the dockworkers.

"We don't have papers." Paul's voice barely reached her, even in their closeness. "Anatoly forged our papers, but, of course, he and Captain George are close—I had to bribe the good captain."

"Bribe?" Kaya nodded. "That makes sense. I wonder if that's what *trebuyet vzyatku* means."

Paul jerked back and blinked down at her. "Where did you learn *that*?"

"Anatoly." Kaya dismissed it and rested her head on his chest again. She quite enjoyed the comfort of him. She took her hat from Paul. Maybe if it just happened to float away on a strong breeze? "It's not important. Go on."

She felt him shake his head. He smoothed a hand down her back and kissed her forehead. "Because Captain George knew our papers were fake, he demanded a bribe."

"How does one demand a bribe?" Curious, she tilted her head but didn't move from his arms. "Does one simply say—you must pay a bribe to me?" She sniffed. "Seems rather…*bold*."

Paul laughed, one of those lighter sounds he made when he found her truly amusing. "He demanded extra payment for knowing our papers were forged."

"I don't understand." Kaya pulled back just enough to look up at him. "Papers for what?" Then she sighed. "I dislike not knowing so much of what I need to survive in this world."

Paul brushed his fingers across her cheek. "I know. I'm sorry. I wish things were different for you."

Kaya stilled beneath his touch, letting his gentle honesty wrap around her. Despite her fears and confusion, she offered him a small smile. Before he could further explain, the jovial voice of Captain George cut through the noise of the docks.

"My dear *Madaam* Conrad, I trust we have not kept you waiting?"

Well, of course he had. Was that not his intent?

"Captain George." She inclined her head. "I spent a pleasurable hour with *sade* Anatoly. I assure you, I was not bored."

"Good, good." His voice quieted, but his predatory look had not eased. She narrowed her eyes in whatever warning her narrowed eyes might convey, and he looked to Paul. "We are nearly finished, only a few minor additions. Please." He gestured to the plank leading to the ship. "We sail within the hour."

Paul picked up their things and settled his hand on the small of her back. Kaya carried her hat. Keeping her hand by her dagger—just in case—she followed the captain onto his ship.

Their cabin, below decks and down a tight, dark hallway, closed in on her. The narrow bed looked built into the wall, and a small table leaned against the opposite wall, bolted to the floor. The single chair, also bolted to the floor, looked precarious and rickety at best. A small, round opening looked out onto the water with a thick, metal-rimmed piece of glass hinged to it.

Kaya stood on her toes but couldn't quite see out.

The faint breeze had kept the cabin from growing stale, and it looked clean enough. Kaya eyed the bedding. Relatively clean. Her standards had lowered considerably since leaving Cairo.

"Please." Paul's hands curled around her upper arms to caress her shoulders. It was most distracting. "Don't leave the room without me."

Kaya tilted her head. His fingers brushed along the side of her neck, beneath her hijab, and she shivered at the intimacy of his touch Warmth bloomed in her chest. "You don't trust the captain? Or his crew?"

"Kaya," he said exasperatedly, "when will you realize I don't trust *anyone*?"

She made a noise in the back of her throat, half amusement, half disbelief. "When you realize I have been trained to take care of myself."

Paul opened his mouth—most likely to argue—then snapped it closed and kissed her. Kaya didn't object to the kiss, the way his mouth moved over hers, the way her skin tingled and her blood raced. She certainly didn't object when Paul backed her to the bed.

"Are you still sore?" He gently removed her hijab and folded it carefully. Kissing down her neck, he nipped the pounding point of her pulse.

"Not enough for you to stop." Kaya's body ached. She'd fought off an attacker yesterday and felt the glorious pleasure of Paul. Twice.

She wanted to feel that pleasure again.

"Paul." She stopped and studied him in the dim cabin light. He'd latched the door behind them, offering whatever privacy that provided, but also cutting off what little light came through.

He waited, patient and understanding.

"You haven't taught me everything." That wasn't what she'd planned to say, but when she heard the words, Kaya knew they were the right ones for the moment.

He made a noise in the back of his throat. "Kaya." The growl had such feeling behind it, such hunger, such *yearning*—it took her by surprise.

Paul unlaced her bodice, fumbling with the ties in his haste. He gave up, and unintelligible words muffled against her throat. "Damn dress. Damn skirts."

"I want to undress you." Kaya pressed her lips to his and pushed his coat off. She struggled with the buttons to his waistcoat but didn't let that stop her. "I want to see you, every inch of you. I want to know what you feel like beneath my fingers. How you taste."

He growled again but covered her hands with his own. Kaya met his gaze. His eyes were a stormy mix of blue and green and focused on her with single-minded need. Yet they were tired, and still so dark with shadows and secrets.

Kaya hated that he kept secrets from her after all they'd been through. She longed to know him completely. Wholly. To explore the world and the intimacy of sex with him.

Confused, with part of her yearning for freedom and part of her content right here in his arms, Kaya pulled back as if he'd burned her. "Paul, I—"

She shook her head, banishing her bewildering thoughts, and untied his trousers with a triumphant cry that returned them both to this instant.

"We don't have time to fully undress." His words sounded strangled, raw, and they made her shiver.

"Oh." Kaya reached for him. "You—you're—" She

shook her head in another vain attempt to clear it.

With Paul half-naked in front of her, her simmering arousal burst to life. Kaya licked her lips. She'd touched him yesterday, felt his hardness pulsing in her hand. Here and now, with him ready for her and her own body aching for his touch, lightning skimmed over her skin, the drive to touch and kiss and take.

She wrapped her hand around him and glided her fingers over his hardness. He jerked at her touch.

"Kaya," he hissed.

Her fingers clenched around him. "Show me how you like to be touched."

Paul wrapped his hand around hers. Together, they moved her fingers over his erection. She tugged, and he moaned her name. Beneath her touch, he grew harder, thicker.

"Wait."

She tilted her head up. Her fingers tightened over him, reluctant to let go. "I thought you enjoyed this?" Her voice sounded hoarse to her own ears, low and dry. Heavy.

"I do." Each word ripped from him. His hand clenched around hers. "Too much."

"I don't understand," Kaya admitted in that same gasping voice. Her fingers remained around him, glided up and down against the soft hardness of him. "Is that not the purpose? To fly without anything holding you down?"

Paul yanked her half-unlaced bodice open and cupped her breasts, rolling her nipples between his fingers. She cried out and arched into his hands. He lifted her so quickly she didn't see him move. Laying her on the bed, he knelt in front of her.

"That is exactly the purpose." He bunched her skirts around her waist and brushed his fingers over her wetness. Kaya whimpered and moved into his touch. "But a gentleman always sees to his lady's pleasure first."

"You told me you were no gentleman."

Even in the dim light of the cabin, she saw his face soften. Paul brushed his lips over hers, an oddly tender touch that made her heart flip. "Only for you, Kaya."

He gently spread her legs. Despite yesterday's pleasure, she felt wicked with him kneeling there. Unable to deny her need, the hot throbbing that begged for his touch, she rolled her hips against his fingers and moaned. Paul kissed her there, that same spot he'd worshiped yesterday.

"Oh! *Yes.*"

"You're so responsive." He slipped a finger into her, and she shuddered at the sinful feel of his touch. "I love watching you."

"I want to watch you, too." Her eyes closed, and her fingers dug into the bedding.

Pleasure built inside her. Its name eluded her, a wild and coiling ball of need. Her hips jerked into his touch, and he eased a second finger into her. She shuddered again, the strength of her need blinding, hot. The world fell away, until it was only his touch, the slow, almost lazy thrusting of his fingers. His mouth on her, his tongue tasting her so intimately.

"I'd like that." He spoke against her, lips moving over her heat, teeth scraping the spot that sent her flying upward, so free and uncontrolled. So close. Tightness wound through her. "But I like being buried in you more."

"That is a very persuasive argument." She may not have spoken that final word.

Paul tasted her again, his fingers shallow, just enough to build the exquisite pleasure. His lips moved over her, tongue pressing hard.

She shattered. Without warning, her pleasure broke, rushing through her. Kaya cried out, her heels digging into his back, her fingers scrambling for purchase. She came. Hard.

"Paul." She didn't know what she wanted, only knew she wanted more. Wanted him. "*Paul.*"

Then he was over her, his hardness between them, his face set and committed. Kaya reached for him, curled her fingers around him, rejoicing in his hardness, his obvious pleasure. He shuddered in her arms, a broken moan of need.

"Guide me into you." He spoke through clenched teeth, the words short but no less compelling. "Go gently, ease me in."

Kaya braced her booted feet on the edge of the wooden frame and lifted her hips. Slowly, she did as instructed, easing him in as she had yesterday afternoon. Her fingers brushed her own wet heat, and she shuddered. She shifted her hips, and Paul slid deeper until he filled her.

"Oh." She opened her eyes and met his. "Yes." She adjusted her hips again until she felt comfortable. Not comfortable—full and ready and— "Move, Paul. *Please.*"

Arms braced on the bed, fingers tangled in her hair, gaze steady on hers, he moved. This was not the buildup of before, but hard and fast, each thrust deeper and deeper. Kaya met his thrusts, his rhythm, dug her nails into his back and sank her teeth into his shoulder.

She broke, cried out as the storm fractured within her, and she shuddered in his arms. Paul continued to move, harder and deeper, and she held his body to hers, kept his weight against her.

She wrapped her arms and legs tighter around him. She sighed at the feel of Paul. He withdrew from her as he came, jaw clenched, hands fisted by her head.

Kaya only had the strength to let her legs fall to the sides, her arms following suit. She managed to open her eyes and watch him, trying to steady her breath. He had quite literally taken it away.

"Why do you pull out?" Kaya paused. Something

tugged her memory. "Oh. Yes. I read about this."

He shuddered, blinked open his eyes, and watched her curiously. "You *read* about it?"

"Derya, she smuggled books for me."

Paul stared at her another moment then moved off her, rummaging in her satchel. Pulling out a handkerchief, he cleaned up her belly and thighs, then tossed the soiled material to the floor. Crawling into bed, he gathered her to him. Kaya tugged her skirts down and rolled into his embrace, resting her head on his chest.

"Of course she did," he snorted, and Kaya looked up, puzzled at the humor in his voice. He met her gaze, grinning. "You've read about more things than I know."

"You know much about the world." Kaya frowned and tilted her head. "Together, we have quite the extensive knowledge."

Paul chuckled, the quietly amused sound that made her heart flip. He smoothed a hand down her arm, pressed his fingers to her scalp, and kissed the top of her head. "What did Derya show you?"

"Some of the books were quite scandalous. They talked about what happened between a man and a woman."

He reared back, and when Kaya looked up at him, she couldn't place the look on his face. Paul opened and closed his mouth several times, then settled on a huffing laugh and relaxed back on the bed.

"And Derya gave these to you?"

Kaya sniffed. "Of course, who else did you expect? Certainly not Gidd!" She shook her head and shifted on the bed to better see him in the dim cabin. "I was curious, and knowing what happens between a man and woman is important in a marriage. Derya said in the harem they had many of these books, and so many stories. I don't know where she found them."

"It's probably best you don't." He laughed again. "I can just imagine you sneaking out and searching for more."

Kaya met his gaze and grinned back. "Possibly." She hummed contentedly and lowered her head to his chest. Beneath her ear, his heart still beat fast, but his breathing had mostly evened out. "However, they were full of information."

"Such as?"

"Such as why a man pulls out of a woman." She pressed her lips together and absently toyed with the ties on his shirt. "To prevent pregnancy."

His hand tightened on her shoulder, and he stilled. Then all his breath rushed out. "Yes." He cleared his throat. "Yes."

She let that knowledge settle in and nodded. "Good. Thank you."

"I—" His hand tightened on her arm. "Yes."

Kaya thought he'd say more. She tilted her head, and he cupped her chin, kissing her slowly. Sighing into the kiss, Kaya threw her leg over his, absently hiking her skirts out of the way.

"I may never get enough of this," she admitted against his lips. "It is quite…enjoyable."

Paul choked out a laugh and tightened his fingers on her thighs. "Enjoyable. Yes. Yes, it is."

"Is it like this with everyone?" In the uncertain light of their cabin, she met his gaze. Something she didn't understand shifted in their blue-green depths.

"No." The word caught, and he cleared his throat. "No, it's not like this…with everyone."

Chapter Nineteen

"Ah, *κυρία* Conrad."

Paul barely held back a snarl at the cheating, exorbitant captain. He was certain the smile he forced looked more a baring of teeth than a friendly exchange. Good. The underhanded captain was lucky Paul hadn't given in to his far baser instincts and physically hurt him.

Only Kaya—and Paul's desperate need to keep her safe and get her out of Egypt as quickly as possible—had him paying the bribe. Seeing the grinning captain now, despite Kaya's hand on his arm, unraveled all his hard-won control.

The sun set behind Captain George, who stood at the head of the steep stairs onto the main deck. In the open air, the wind whipped harder than on the wharves and brought with it the scent of dead fish, unwashed bodies, and rubbish.

He glanced at Kaya, who didn't seem to notice.

She smiled, her head tilted up to the open sky. The wind took the ends of her hijab, and it fluttered around her. She hadn't bothered with her hat. He wanted to hear her laugh float in the wind, so alive and free.

Shaking his head at his own fancifulness, a trait he never before possessed, Paul turned back to the captain.

"I trust you have settled in?" Captain George said with a knowing smirk.

Damn. Paul stepped protectively in front of Kaya. No matter how difficult it might be, he wanted to keep her from the prying, lecherous eyes of the captain.

"The cabin is very spacious," Paul lied. "It suits our needs perfectly."

He really should warn her not to be so vocal, but Paul enjoyed hearing her when she climaxed. *Loved* hearing her. Wanted to spend hours—days, weeks, a lifetime—tasting her, learning her body, finding all the ways to make her scream his name.

His arguments against touching her vanished whenever he looked at her.

Kaya's fingers dug into his arm, and she stepped beside him. He didn't look at her. Couldn't, now, and not remember how she'd looked when she came, mouth open, back arched, so beautifully unguarded. Beautiful and sated and completely in the moment of her orgasm.

"I hope we're not intruding on the deck," Kaya said smoothly. "I wished to see us sail from Damietta."

She didn't repeat what she'd told him. That she wanted to see the first city she truly experienced as it faded into the distance from the first ship she ever set foot on. As far as the thieving captain knew, this was not their first boat trip. Paul had gone to great pains to ensure George and Anatoly—and *Madaam* Nephthys—believed her to be as English as he.

"Of course, my dear Mrs. Conrad. Please feel free to stand by the railing." Captain George walked them to the port side. "You'll be well out of the way here as we leave port, and with a good view of the docks."

"Thank you, Captain." Kaya swayed into Paul with the rocking of the boat. He easily caught her round the waist and held her tight.

Captain George gave them one last speculative look, then nodded and left them alone.

"Don't overcompensate with the movement of the ship." Paul breathed against her skin, scented with sex and the pomegranate oil she used to wash. He could easily become addicted to that scent. Maybe he was already. "You'll grow used to it soon enough."

"Really?" Kaya sounded dubious as she watched the birds squawking overhead.

"Soon enough." Paul laughed and pressed his lips to her the top of her head. "Not that Damietta is all that appealing, but take your fill."

"The city is beautiful." Kaya curled her hands around the railing and leaned her head against his chest. The position made his heart flip. Hard. Stupid, traitorous thing. How many times had he tried to ignore it since meeting Kaya?

He snorted. "Kaya, you find beauty in everything."

She tilted her head back and grinned up at him. "Everything is beautiful the first time you see it. Though"—she frowned—"I believe I shall always find your body beautiful."

He sucked in a sharp breath, then growled. Just when he thought he'd put enough distance between them, she said something or did something to make him forget their boundaries. The boundaries he'd purposely placed—or tried to, or maybe just hoped to—between them. Stepping behind her, he clenched his hands next to hers on the rough wood railing.

Mouth by her ear, he pretended to look at the docks. "Keep talking like that, and we'll never leave the cabin. Everyone will know what we've been up to in there."

"Oh." Even in the shadows of the setting sun, he saw her blush. "I—I had not realized." She shuddered in his embrace. "I supposed that was naïve on my part. Of course they knew. Could hear. I...I didn't—"

Kaya broke off and shook her head. She turned, the movement bringing her soft skin in contact with his lips. Paul didn't even pretend he was going to move. She shivered again, most definitely in arousal.

"I shall endeavor to be quiet next time we enjoy sex." She announced it so matter-of-fact, Paul snorted.

"I told you before." He laid his hand over hers. "I like hearing you."

The dress really was a perfect find. He hadn't asked Anatoly where he'd acquired such finery—a lady's trunk, stolen goods, a pirate ship. It didn't matter. The blue made her skin golden in the setting sun—and showed off her luscious curves.

Everything about her constantly tempted him. Simply listening to her laugh aroused him.

Paul pressed against her magnificent arse. He adored her body and wanted to touch it again. Kaya shivered, and her voice caught on whatever she was about to say. She elbowed him in the stomach.

"Stop that," she hissed. "I may not know all your little customs, but I do know we shouldn't do things like…like *this* on the deck of a ship." She sniffed disdainfully. "People tend to stare, even if it's none of their business."

He laughed. "Kaya, you are a world of contradictions."

She sniffed again, though the sound lost its disdain, and met his gaze over her shoulder. "I shall take that as a compliment." She spoke primly, then grinned widely, sending a sharp pang through his heart. "Now. What do we need papers for?"

Paul breathed deeply. Her pomegranate-scented skin had haunted him since they left Cairo a lifetime ago. Two. So much for keeping his distance.

"We need papers to travel between countries. We have none." He rested his chin on her shoulder. Kaya made that strangling-choking sound in the back of her throat. Paul tightened his hands on her waist, enjoying the way she remained off balance. "When I arrived in Cairo, I had Tahir's letter to gain entry. When we left, again we had Tahir's letter to grant us safe passage. Now we have nothing. I needed to find someone to forge papers so we could pass through customs."

He didn't have to see her to know she frowned. "Customs?" She tilted her head. "I have heard this word. You must pay to enter a country, yes?"

"Yes." He straightened. Not normally one to care about public displays of affection, especially if his commander frowned on it, Paul also found himself in the odd position of not wishing to disrespect his wife.

Kaya.

He meant Kaya. Who happened to be his wife. Paul stepped back from her curvaceous body and addictive taste and dropped his hands from hers. What was he *thinking*?

"*Madaam* Nephthys suggested Anatoly." He forced his voice to sound dispassionate.

Kaya stiffened and jerked her head around, narrowing her eyes. Intimately familiar with the slightly betrayed look she was giving him, Paul forced himself to ignore the stab to his heart. He hated hurting her.

Yet he seemed so very good at it.

Her censoring look didn't surprise him, given the way they'd made love an hour ago, only for him to flinch back now.

"Anatoly recommended George, who doesn't look too closely at anyone's papers so long as they have the coin to pay."

He needed to let her go, couldn't hold her to him no matter how he felt about her. The setting sun cast her in shadows, but Paul couldn't look.

"And the man from yesterday?" Kaya leaned on the railing, her back to Damietta, to Egypt, to the view she'd desperately wanted to see. "He was—what? Only a coincidence?"

"I don't believe in coincidences." Paul shook his head. Fear clogged his throat, terror at letting Kaya go, and he reached for her. She flinched at his touch, and Paul couldn't blame her. "Anatoly, he was honestly horrified at the— *attempt*."

The word soured on his tongue. It plagued him

whenever he closed his eyes, mixed with the blood on the streets.

"What do you think?"

"I think they wanted to kill me and take you." He swallowed; his hands clenched. Helpless. That's what he'd been on the street. Helpless to help her, protect her. "But I do not believe either Anatoly or George had anything to do with that."

Kaya stood silent for several moments, then pushed off the railing and closed the distance between them. "What happens after Cádiz?"

His stomach plummeted. "What do you mean?" Paul frowned. He wanted to touch her, take her hand, hold her close. "I promised to see you to England."

She scowled. "I've no wish to go to England. I wish to see the world." She stopped and frowned. "Well, the world outside the Ottoman Empire."

"Yes," he said dryly. "Outside the Empire."

"I'd have liked to see India." Kaya hesitated, then looked at him with a strange mix of curiosity and shyness.

Paul nearly laughed at the shyness—in the time he'd known her, Kaya hadn't been shy about anything. Still, the thought of returning to India grabbed him by the throat and strangled him. "No." His voice cracked, but he could do nothing about that. "Not India."

She reached for his hand, and he wondered what she knew about his time there. If Tahir had told her anything. Probably not, the wily old man. Kaya was neither blind nor purposely obtuse. What she might know chilled Paul more than he wanted to admit.

"Why did you leave?"

"Kaya—"

"Not because Gidd wrote you. You had to have a reason other than his letter."

Jewels. Money. Stealing everything in your house and escaping before I had to marry you. Paul didn't say that. Honesty twisted his heart, but he swallowed the words. If she knew the truth about him, what he'd done in Bombay, who he'd been… Tahir hadn't known. He couldn't have, if he'd truly trusted Paul with Kaya's safety.

"I promised your grandfather—"

"I know what you promised him," she snapped. "And I know what he promised you." Kaya dropped his hand, and he missed her touch. "I no longer live in that house, and Gidd no longer—"

She broke off on a choked sob. *Damn.*

"Shh," he muttered. It was hopelessly inadequate. "Kaya, I'm sorry."

He gathered her to him, trying to comfort her in whatever small way he could. The walls around his heart shattered. Paul let them. Only Kaya mattered, only her comfort. She allowed him to hold her for a bare minute, then pushed back. She sniffed back tears and tossed her head, wiping beneath her eyes.

He hated seeing her cry. Paul wanted to comfort her more than simply holding her. Ease her pain and grief, but he had no idea what to say. Trite words—remembering them, honoring them—would sound even more pedestrian than those he carelessly threw around.

Threw around in his previous life, as the man he never wanted Kaya to know.

The sun had well and truly set by now, and the half dozen or so oil lanterns hanging from various hooks lit the deck. The wind picked up and blew across the ship.

"I'm returning to the cabin."

Without another word, she spun on her heel and swept away. Paul watched her leave, torn between following and leaving her to her private grief.

"Women troubles?" Captain George appeared from nowhere. Paul knew he hadn't been lurking; he always kept an eye on their surroundings, and the thieving captain hadn't been nearby.

"We received word her family—her grandfather is ill," Paul amended, not wanting to say anything, but not seeing a choice. "They are very close."

"Ah." Captain George nodded, as if he knew Paul was only telling half the truth. Paul tried not to snap at him.

"Once we're clear, we'll have dinner." George clapped Paul on the back, much the same as Anatoly had. Paul clenched his jaw. "You can introduce your lovely wife to my cook. Jabir is a fine hand in the galley."

Captain George left, shouting orders in what Paul presumed was Greek. Whatever the language, the crew jumped to attention.

Paul turned to Damietta. The city was fading in the moonlight. Kaya should see this—add it to her growing list of experiences. He scrubbed a hand down his face and leaned against the railing she'd so recently occupied. He never should've made love to her. After the attempt on her life, he'd been so furious and scared—and thrilled she was still with him—he hadn't thought beyond the moment.

Beyond wanting her.

In the cabin, he hadn't thought at all. Stupid, stupid man.

"Keep your distance," he muttered. "Was that so difficult? All you had to do was *keep your distance*."

Now he had feelings for her. Cared for her. Wanted her. Loved her. Beyond the desire to keep her safe and show her the world. All that, the desire, the caring, the tightening fist around his heart…

It terrified him.

* * * *

Kaya didn't jerk awake so much as float to wakefulness on a tilting bed that smelled entirely too strongly of her and Paul and their very pleasurable activities for her current comfort. The scent was not what woke her. It did, however, add to the nausea.

Or maybe that was the memory of their fight afterward.

Either way, her stomach tilted.

"Kaya?" Paul's voice echoed around her, sharp and worried. It did not come from beside her.

She opened her mouth to ask why he had not slept on the floor beside her as he had other nights. Then she promptly closed it.

Her stomach very definitely did not like her.

"I'm hot." The words took all her strength to say, and she swallowed hard against the awful grasping in her throat. "And sweaty. I don't feel—I don't understand."

"Damn. Don't move."

She couldn't see in the dark cabin, but she heard him scrambling. The noise needled like an annoying squawk of birds. His leg thunked against the wooden bedframe, and he cursed. Kaya hadn't the strength to lift her head, let alone ask what happened. The bed dipped, and Paul smoothed a hand down her back.

"Here." His voice whispered over her, as soft and gentle as his touch. "The bucket's right in front of you."

"Buck—"

Oh. Oh, what was this awfulness? Disgusting. Kaya emptied her stomach of their delicious dinner and heaved in deep breaths. Unbearably hot and sweaty, she could barely move.

Her mouth tasted vile.

"What?" She barely got the word out. It took all her energy to say even that.

"I don't think it was dinner." Paul's soft whisper came from beside her. His hand continued its soothing motion up and down her spine, across the back of her neck. He moved her chemise away from her damp skin, and his touch felt wonderfully cool on her shoulders. Kaya didn't want to move.

"I'm not sick, and the fava beans tasted fresh," he added after a moment.

They were. She didn't say that aloud, merely thought the words. Oh. Oh, here it came again.

"Shh." His breath cooled her skin, and suddenly she felt a wet cloth on the back of her neck. "No, I don't think it was dinner."

Kaya heard the frown in his voice, but also the smile. It confused her, but she ignored it. Her capabilities extended to focusing on only one thing: her intense desire to curl up into a ball and whimper.

"Kaya, I'm afraid you're seasick."

In the darkness, she frowned at him. Her mind wanted to ask what he meant, but she only managed a vaguely interrogative grunt. Thankfully, Paul seemed to understand.

"You've never been on the water. Your body isn't used to it. I've seen it take over the hardiest of men. Even seasoned sailors succumb to rough waters."

Kaya wanted to rail at him—This wasn't fair! Her first sea voyage should not make her so sick that she missed—*umf.* Again? How disgusting.

Paul pressed his lips to her neck. Kaya wanted to push him away, but instead leaned into him and accepted what comfort he offered. The cool cloth returned to her neck, and she shivered. He moved it along her cheeks, over her forehead, along her hairline.

Finally, he eased the foul-smelling bucket from her clutching fingers, which only marginally helped her stomach. Her arms fell to her sides, refusing to work, and her neck felt as if it carried the weight of the world, not just her head.

"Easy," Paul whispered, his breath the gentlest of brushes over her cheek. Cupping the back of her head, he pressed his lips to her forehead. "Back into bed. Lie down, I'll grab the blanket."

He didn't jar her, but eased her onto the bed. Kaya willed her eyes to open, but they didn't obey. Just as well. The room refused to regain its former steadiness and spun around her.

"I'll see if Captain George has anything."

She felt his lips against her hair as he stood, making the room sway again. Her stomach swayed with it. The chills abruptly ended, and her skin flushed hot and dry. With the last of her strength, Kaya rolled to the side and hoped he'd return soon with a cure to this terrible affliction.

She wouldn't make it to Cádiz like this.

She must have drifted to sleep, because the next thing she knew, Paul was sitting next to her. Kaya didn't bother to talk, just blindly reached for the comfort of his touch. Even that slight movement jarred her, and she scrambled for the bucket.

Had he taken it with him? She couldn't remember.

"Here." His voice drifted over her again, quiet and understanding. "I've fresh water, and Jabir swears by his special remedy."

Anything. She'd try anything to stop her stomach from rolling. Kaya hoped her threadbare whimper conveyed as much.

Paul helped her sit and carefully moved so he could brace her from behind. Kaya gratefully leaned into his solidness, even when the room tilted again—and with it her stomach. He patiently held her, one hand over her chest, the other holding the bucket.

"Better?"

Not in the least.

"Can you drink anything?"

Her throat burned, not from thirst, though she was thirsty. Her stomach rebelled. Or maybe not. The cup pressed to her lips, and Kaya dutifully opened her mouth. Swallowing several sips of a truly abhorrent concoction she hoped she didn't ever have to taste again, she batted weakly at Paul's arm, but he didn't remove the cup.

"I know. It's disgusting, but Jabir swears it works."

Jabir lied. Kaya knew her groan conveyed *that*.

"Can you drink any more?"

No. Not one more sip. Well…with the constant tilting of the bed and the way her stomach flipped with it, maybe another sip wouldn't hurt.

"Good. A little more. That's good."

Hmph. Paul should try it, then. See how he liked it.

"Now rest. I'll clean this up and be back with more water."

Water. Yes. Water sounded good. Carob juice, even. Not that vile thing Jabir, whom she'd liked prior, insisted on foisting upon her in her weakened state.

Kaya closed her eyes and felt Paul lay her back on the bed. The stupid thing tilted again, but she was far too tired and drained to care. She thought she heard him set the bucket on the floor next to her.

She hadn't the energy to open her eyes and look, only enough strength for a faint prayer that it *did* sit by her head.

Kaya had a feeling Jabir's cure had not worked as promised.

Chapter Twenty

"What do you mean it did not work?" Jabir frowned, as if Paul had personally violated his sacred recipe. Drained, hungry, sore, worried for Kaya, and in no mood, he scowled at the cook.

In the galley, both he and Jabir swayed with the steady movements of *The Cyprus Rose* as they sailed across the Mediterranean. The seas were calm and the wind was fine, and still Kaya forced herself over the edge of the bed. Her sickness hadn't abated, and she grew weaker with every turn.

It had to be dawn now, but Paul didn't bother to look. Even with the galley portholes open and a fresh breeze slipping through, he only cared about Kaya.

"She couldn't keep it down." Paul rubbed his tired eyes.

He'd stayed up with her all night, holding her through the sickness. Wiping her face, stroking her back. Anything to comfort her, even if she hadn't been aware of his presence, his touch.

Jabir looked affronted. "My *gidda*'s *gidda* passed down that recipe!"

Paul shook his head. Even that was a little much for his aching head. He ran a hand over his face, pressed fingers to his eyes, and debated how much to tell the cook. Paul certainly couldn't say Kaya hadn't ever been on a ship before.

He decided on, "She barely has the energy to be sick. Nothing stays down."

Jabir narrowed his eyes, as if Paul lied—or didn't know the difference between seasickness and whatever else Jabir thought was happening.

Oh.

Ice settled in his stomach and rapidly spread through his veins. Pregnancy. Jabir thought Kaya *pregnant*.

Cursing his own carelessness, his thoughtlessness, Paul hastily swallowed. No. No, she couldn't be. He shook his head, a short, hard movement, both for his own state of mind and in answer to Jabir's unasked question.

No. She wasn't pregnant.

Paul sighed again and braced his hands on the thick wooden table. Digging his fingers into the rough wood, he tried to think. He needed to focus on the here and now, her seasickness, helping her get well. Not maybes and what-ifs. Insubstantial possibilities.

"She doesn't…travel well."

Not his best line ever.

Kaya traveled superbly over land—the sea defeated her.

Jabir stared at him through slightly narrowed eyes. "Ginger." He nodded decisively and turned for his stocks. "Ginger helps."

Paul watched the cook move about his space in a daze. He didn't like leaving Kaya alone for so long, but he hadn't a choice. She lay helpless in their bed, weak and sick. Defenseless.

Exhaustion tugged his limbs and closed his eyes. It did not still his thoughts of Kaya. Even if she were pregnant, it was too soon to tell. What if she were? What if—he cut that thought off.

Damn stupid fool.

The wood dug into his fingers, but Paul barely felt the pain. He used it to focus, banish those what-if thoughts and concentrate on the present. Slowly, he forced his fingers from the counter and straightened.

He needed to get her well, then he could rest. He'd barely slept since leaving Bombay, and he thought by now exhaustion would've caught up with him. He'd been wrong. As exhausted as he was, as much as he wished he could sleep, every time he closed his eyes, he saw the same blood-soaked ground.

Kaya lay among the dead, her body trampled beneath English horses. British bayonets had pierced her chest, her blood seeped into the sand. Her pale, thin hand reached for him. Her sightless brown eyes looked directly at him. Dull. Dead.

The dream haunted him. Followed him during his waking hours and kept him from sleep. Kaya's very essence mixed with the night terrors. Her scent enveloped him, lulled him with a sense of safety, of comfort. Over the last days, Paul had found himself doing or saying things to make her smile. To hear her laugh.

"Are you listening?"

Paul blinked and brought the ship's galley back into perspective. "Yes?"

Jabir scowled. "How do you intend to help your woman if you doze standing up?"

Had he dozed? Probably. Paul scrubbed a hand down his face and shook himself. When he looked back at Jabir, he nodded, more alert if not more awake. "I'm listening. What do I need to do?"

Jabir watched Paul another moment, no doubt wondering if he was about to keel over. "Ginger. I have made tea. *Madaam* Conrad should drink it as often as possible." Jabir glared at him. "Make sure she keeps it down."

Paul nodded obediently but had no idea how he was supposed to do that. Kaya hadn't kept anything down thus far. What made the cook think his ginger tea would be any different? At least there would be something in her stomach when Kaya inevitably got sick again.

"I'll send the cabin boy with a fresh pot every two hours." Jabir glared again.

Paul ignored it. "Send him with a fresh bucket." He

shuddered at the remembered stench. "And a cleaning rag and water."

Jabir snorted in what seemed to be agreement and turned back to his food preparation. Paul took the clay teapot and single cup and returned to their cabin. He opened the unlatched door to their cramped, dark room, his eyes immediately seeking out Kaya.

She hadn't moved, not that he'd expected her to. Curled on her side, half over the bed, she looked to be asleep. Paul hoped so. Hoped she slept peacefully.

"Kaya?" He closed and latched the door.

Any breeze that had filtered through the door immediately cut off, leaving the cabin stale and stilted. Despite having left the porthole open, the stench of sickness clung to the small space.

"Kaya, I brought tea." Paul crossed the narrow room and knelt by the bed.

He set the teapot on the floor and poured a cup for her. She hadn't moved. Not even a flicker of an eyelid. Paul smoothed her hair back from her clammy forehead and kissed her cheek. Her skin felt taut and dry beneath his lips.

Setting the teacup on the floor, he shifted behind her and held her up. Stretching awkwardly, Paul twisted his body around hers to reach the cup. Her head flopped against his jaw. Wincing, he quickly eased her upright. Kaya made no move, no sound to indicate she even knew he was holding her.

"You have to drink something, Kaya." Finally, he managed to reach the cup and lift it without spilling too much. Holding it in one hand, he dipped his finger into the warm tea and touched her lips. "Please," he begged.

"Hmm."

It wasn't much, but it was life. He patiently waited as she sipped the ginger tea, then waited once more while she threw it back up. Kaya whimpered again, a small, pathetic sound, and he eased her head onto his shoulder. Rubbing a hand up and down her arm, he held her as tight as he dared.

"I'll take care of you." He settled against the cabin wall, Kaya in his arms, and held her close. "I promise, Kaya." Paul kissed the top of her head and closed his eyes. "I'll take care of you."

He didn't know how much time passed before the knock startled him from a light doze. "Come in!" Scowling at the faint rattle, he glared at the door. He'd forgotten he'd latched it. Bad enough he had to leave Kaya for the galley, he absolutely was not prepared to fight off anyone who decided to take advantage of the situation.

He eased Kaya onto the bed. She didn't so much as whimper, though she instantly curled onto her side. Paul crossed the few steps to the door and unlatched it. Immediately, a slight breeze wafted into the room. Better than nothing; it eased the heavy odor of sickness. A small boy, no older than ten, stood on the other side.

"*Beyefendi* Jabir sent me," the lad said in careful English, his voice thick with a dialect Paul didn't know. "*Hanımefendi* needs tea."

It was only then Paul remembered the ginger tea. He nodded, hastily poured another cup for Kaya, and forced the boy to wait as she sipped the now-cold tea. It wouldn't stay down, Paul knew that, but at least drinking it forced liquid into her.

He held her as she vomited it back up.

"What's your name?" He turned to the boy, who looked as if he were going to be sick himself.

"Akylas." He stepped back into the hall, into whatever reprieve that narrow corridor offered. Paul didn't blame him.

"I'll need a fresh bucket every time you bring tea." Paul grimaced and tried not to breathe around the used bucket. "And any bread *sade* Jabir has."

Akylas reluctantly took the bucket, holding it as far from his tiny body as his thin arms allowed. With his other hand, he cradled the teapot. He nodded and backed away from the door.

"Wait."

Akylas stilled, his dark eyes wide.

"Is there a way to keep this door open?" Paul looked to the bed, where Kaya hadn't moved. "My wife needs fresh air."

"Yes, *beyefendi*." Akylas nodded, quick, jerky movements, and fled. Paul didn't blame him there, either.

Moments later, just as Kaya's whimper signaled a fresh wave of sickness, Akylas returned. He carried the pot of tea, a chunk of bread, and a heavy metal hook. Paul took the pot and bread and waited while Akylas latched the door open.

"There." Akylas gasped in air while Paul held Kaya, who moaned and whimpered.

Paul ran the damp linen over the back of her neck and around her mouth and cheeks. She didn't move, and he didn't think she even knew he held her. Pressing a kiss to her forehead, Paul gently laid her back on the bed and watched her another moment.

"You love her."

Paul's head whipped around to look at the boy. He'd forgotten Akylas was still in the room. "Why do you say that?"

Eyes wide, mouth open slightly, Akylas glanced from Kaya to Paul, eyes skimming over the foul-smelling bucket. He looked as if he wanted to be anywhere else but there and wished he hadn't opened his mouth. However, he bravely met Paul's gaze. His dark eyes held a sort of stunned amazement.

"You take care of her. My *baba*, he never held my *anne* like you do for *hanımefendi*."

Paul stared at the lad. He didn't know the unfamiliar words but assumed they meant *father* and *mother*, though the last word sounded more formal and clearly directed at Kaya. Paul opened his mouth but found nothing to say.

Words caught in his throat, choking him. Waiting to burst out. Crowding his tongue with things best left unsaid.

"Thank you, Akylas." His voice sounded cold even to his ears.

Akylas jerked and bowed slightly as he scurried away. Paul stared at the empty doorway as if it held answers. Questions raced round his head like monsoon winds, fast and confused. Paul couldn't grasp even one.

How long had he known Kaya? Ten days? Fifteen? Not long enough to love her. Surely not long enough for that.

The promises he'd made to her, the vows he promised to keep. They had been for him. Atonement for his past sins and promises broken.

Paul tore his gaze from the door, back to his wife. Or had they. She whimpered again, and he instantly moved. Gathering her gently in his arms, Paul held her close to him. He smoothed strands of hair off her face and held the cup of ginger tea to her lips.

The boy's words echoed in his head. In his heart. An echo of what Paul already knew.

* * * *

Paul groaned and pressed his fingers to burning, bleary eyes. "She's been ill since we sailed."

The wind blew steadily across the deck, fresh and warm. The sky stayed crystal blue above and the water calm below. The sun scorched his skin, too hot, too bright in his eyes, but the breeze and the fresh open air smelled heavenly. He breathed in greedily and vowed not to take such openness, such freshness, for granted ever again.

Paul wanted to share the view with Kaya.

She'd love everything about it. The ocean view, the openness of the sea, even the movements of the sailors as they did…whatever sailors did to the rigging and sails and whatever the hell else happened on a ship. She'd find beauty and joy in all of it.

Kaya hadn't the strength to so much as lift her head anymore.

Jabir stayed with her now, concerned for her illness and her lack of appetite. The cook tried many things to ease her seasickness, taking it as a personal affront that none of his remedies had worked. At this point, both he and Paul were reduced to coaxing her to eat the smallest bites of flatbread or take the barest sips of ginger water.

It was a testament to Paul's terrified worry for Kaya that he left her at all, that he trusted Jabir and Akylas to look after her.

"This, it happens." Captain George shrugged. "I don't know what to tell you, my friend." He sighed and leaned on the railing next to Paul. "I don't think she'll make Cádiz."

Paul growled. Captain George only voiced what Paul already knew. Kaya's illness had sapped all her energy. The vibrant, beautiful woman who walked out of Cairo, head high despite her grief, who fought off more than one attacker and opened herself to him so passionately, now looked sallow, gaunt.

Only her increasingly faint whimper clued him in to when she next needed the bucket.

"I've given her everything Jabir said to give her." Paul's voice broke. He didn't care what Captain George thought. He was beyond caring what others thought. "We've tried all his sickness cures. Nothing works."

"Was she ill on the crossing to Egypt? How did you come to Damietta?"

Paul leaned his forearms against the railing and let his

head sink into his hands. Staring at the ocean below, he tried not to think about Akylas's words.

You love her.

"We mostly traveled overland." He sighed and settled on a partial truth. "We weren't together on the trip from England to Cairo. I met her later."

Captain George nodded, but Paul had a feeling he only half believed him. It didn't matter. Only Kaya mattered.

"We come to Sicily soon." Captain George straightened and pushed off the railing. Then he met Paul's eyes and nodded decisively.

Paul already knew what Captain George meant, and he knew it was for the best.

"I can drop you off at the port of Mazzarelli. It's a small town, but I can't detour to the larger port at Reggio di Calabria. You'll have to make your way overland and"—he clapped Paul on the shoulder— "I'm afraid, my friend, you'll need to cross from Sicily to the mainland, but it is better than sailing on to Cádiz."

Anything was better than sailing on to Cádiz. "Yes, all right."

His head hurt from too little sleep. At least when he had managed a few minutes, he'd done so without nightmares.

Had to find the positive someplace.

"Go. See to your woman." Captain George walked away and called out over his shoulder, "Try to get some sleep; you look like hell!"

He felt like hell too, but he didn't foresee sleep anytime in the near future. Or the distant future, for that matter.

Traveling from Bombay to Cairo, Paul had never expected Tahir's letter to change his life so completely. Monetarily, sure. He and John had planned to rob Tahir and anyone else left in Cairo. Paul had expected the gold and jewels for seeing Kaya safely out of Egypt, but he sure as hell hadn't expected to want to see to her safety honorably. For that matter, he hadn't planned on caring for Kaya so—so—

You love her.

Paul heard those words, not in the boy's voice, but in his.

Elbows on the wooden railing, Paul pressed his fingers to his eyes again. He'd met hundreds of women since leaving England, some far more physically beautiful than Kaya, all of them far more experienced.

But Kaya took his breath away.

She amazed him. Her enthusiasm for life, for learning and exploring. Her passion, the passion between them whenever they kissed, when they made love.

Kaya, she was different in a way he still didn't know how to identify. Innocent yet passionate, curious yet knowledgeable. Smart—so damn smart. Not only intellectually, but she knew how to defend herself, how to hunt. Knew history like a stodgy professor, yet explored the city with an infectious joy.

Afraid—deathly terrified on a visceral level—of his feelings, Paul admitted they'd deepened to the point he couldn't stop them. Even worse, he didn't want to.

What a damned fool.

Paul took a final breath of fresh air and turned for below decks. He needed to get back to Kaya. He'd been gone too long already.

Yes. It was too late for him.

Jabir exited their cabin just as Paul started down the narrow hallway. The other man looked tired and concerned. Twin fists clenched his heart. Though grateful to Jabir for caring about Kaya, Paul couldn't stop the jealousy twisting his gut.

Rather than taking out his—unreasonable—jealousy on the unsuspecting cook, Paul forced himself to nod to the man.

"How is she?"

"*Madaam* fares no better." Jabir's frown deepened. "She keeps nothing down, no matter what I try."

"I'm afraid it has little to do with your cooking, excellent as it is. Or your remedies." Paul grabbed the clean bucket Akylas had set outside their cabin. "The captain has promised to drop us in Sicily."

"Good. Good." Jabir nodded, but he still looked worried. "She needs dry land."

"Thank you," Paul said sincerely. "Thank you for helping her."

Jabir bowed and turned for the bowels of the ship. "She is a rare treasure! Treat her with respect."

Paul snorted and entered their cabin. Kaya was a rare treasure, all right. Jabir didn't know the half of it.

She lay where he left her, rolled onto her side, one hand just peeked from beneath the blanket, hanging limply over the wooden frame of the bed. Even with the porthole open, no sunlight penetrated the darkness of the cabin. Very little air entered to sweep the stench of sickness out despite the open door.

In the dimness, against the dark fabric of her headscarf, she looked horribly pale. Deep circles darkened her eyes and her cheeks hollowed. Her filthy chemise clung to her, but he had no other clothing to change her into. Despite his promise of another gown, they hadn't bought anything more in Damietta.

The attack and kidnapping attempt had changed his plans.

"Kaya?" He kept his voice low, even. Quiet. She didn't move. "Kaya, sweetheart, Captain George is sailing for

Sicily."

No response. Paul crossed to the bed and set the clean bucket within easy reach. Her skin felt clammy to his touch, but she slept peacefully. Her chest rose and fell with even breaths, and when he pressed his fingers to the pulse at the base of her neck, it remained steady if slow.

"Once we're on Sicily, I'll find something to help you get well." He had no idea where to begin, but he hated seeing her ill. Weak.

Kneeling on the hard floor, he gripped the edge of the bedframe. Pressing his lips to her forehead, he closed his eyes. "I promise I'll take care of you."

He meant every word, every inherent promise, but he had no idea what to do next, where to go. How to help his wife.

Chapter Twenty-One

Paul stood on the dry, rocky shoreline, satchel full of the food Jabir had insisted Kaya needed to get well and fresh ginger root. He watched the dinghy return to *The Cyprus Rose*. Akylas turned to wave one final time. Paul nodded, though he knew the boy wouldn't be able to see from this distance.

He held Kaya securely in his arms, as he had since Captain George announced they'd arrived. Now, laden with their things, he stood on the deserted beach. No plan, no friends, only he, Kaya, the jewels and gold still sewn into her dress, and a handful of English sterling and Egyptian *akçe*.

Paul shifted her ever so slightly.

She didn't whimper or move, but her breathing remained even. He'd hated dressing her in the gown with their possessions sewn into the waist. Her poor stomach didn't need the added vice of the gown or the jewels. But he hadn't a choice. He refused to let that crew see his wife in no more than her chemise.

His pack dug into his shoulders, though Paul had left the long wooden beam onboard. He couldn't carry it and Kaya. Her satchel pulled uncomfortably on his shoulder, and her bow and quiver knocked the back of his head with every step.

"Kaya?" He looked down at her.

No acknowledgement. Her face nestled into his neck, her breathing soft puffs of steady air. Her arms hung limply, one over his shoulder, the other curled on her lap.

On solid ground, and with the food Jabir had offered, Kaya would recover. Paul closed his eyes and turned from *The Cyprus Rose*. He wasn't given to prayer, didn't believe in God or a higher power. But Kaya's illness terrified him on a level he hadn't known truly existed.

"Please be all right," he whispered. Prayed. "Please, Kaya."

His fear closed his throat and suffocated him. Left him balancing on the edge of some unknown precipice. Balancing her life. The responsibility stifled him. He'd never been responsible for another's life, hadn't ever wanted to be. Well, he supposed he was responsible for his own, but look how that had turned out.

He could not and would not turn his back on her. Not when she relied on him, when she had only him *to* rely upon.

"Tahir picked the wrong man for you, Kaya. You deserve better."

Mazzarelli looked deserted in the darkness, but Paul knew better. Docks were never deserted, no matter how small the town or how infrequent the ships in port. No one bothered him or tried to speak with—or attack—them while he held Kaya.

The streets lay in darkness, an eerie silence that followed him with each step.

"Come on." Paul pressed his lips to the top of her head. "Let's find an inn. I need rest. And maybe a drink."

Paul frowned as he slowly walked along the uneven shoreline toward a row of buildings. He hadn't thought to ask Captain George or Jabir if they had any wine. Of course they had—he saw several bottles in Jabir's galley. It hadn't even occurred to him. He spent so long taking care of Kaya—his only concern, his only focus—Paul hadn't even thought about a drink.

He sighed and walked along the beach toward town. Too late now.

A faint breeze brought the scent of life. Unfamiliar food tempted him, even as it mixed with rubbish and sewage. Not stale or old, another sign life teemed in this small town. Whether they showed themselves or not. In the distance, Paul heard a dog bark—sharp, short sounds that carried along the coast.

The villagers watched him; their gaze crept up his spine and settled on the back of his neck.

His mind raced for the easiest way to defend them. How to protect a helpless Kaya without injuring her further. Paul walked faster, eyes darting from one side of the street to the other. His hands clenched at her body, pulling her tight against him. Faster.

The row of sleepy buildings closest to the beach seemed locked tight and closed for the night. Closed to him, at least.

While he had no objection to sleeping on the beach, or inland, hidden by the trees, he preferred to lay Kaya in a bed. She needed rest and food, comfort. Not further hardship. His dagger weighed heavily at his waist; Kaya's was strapped to his opposite side. His pack bumped awkwardly against her bow and quiver, the full satchel hitting his hip with every step.

A camp follower, lugging all their possessions from one point to the other. That's what he was.

Paul strode further into town, past the deserted stone building he presumed to be customs or a port office. Past whitewashed square structures that also looked closed, locked tight against the night. Or against men like him.

Paul didn't bother knocking on any of the doors. Toward the edge of town—hamlet, more like—nearer the sparse trees, a door suddenly swung open.

Startled, suspicious, Paul paused. He growled and clenched Kaya tighter.

In the doorway, illuminated by the faint moonlight, a woman stood, back straight, hair pulled into a tight braid that fell over her shoulder. Even in the dark, her assessing gaze seared into him. He met her eyes, silent and waiting.

She barked a question at him, but he didn't understand the words. He could guess—*Who are you?* or *What's wrong with the woman?* or even *What are you doing walking by my house?*

He rapidly filtered through the languages he knew but settled on English. Paul knew nothing about Sicily or its people, let alone how they felt about Egyptians or Indians. Most places didn't like foreigners.

"I don't speak Sicilian."

"What's wrong with the woman?" Her sharply accented English carried through the night.

Narrowing his eyes, Paul gauged her. She made no move to step from the doorway, nor did she retreat. The fact she'd opened her home at all had him turning more fully toward her.

He had few choices.

"She's ill. The voyage from Beirut made her ill." Paul lied easily, choosing a city at random. He had never set one foot in Beirut and wasn't certain he knew where to find it on a map. But Beirut was not Damietta.

Paul barely saw the woman in the waning moonlit night. He knew she watched him shrewdly. As if she knew he lied. Either his lies were more careless than usual, or the exhaustion of the last days had tired him to the point he couldn't properly tell them. Jabir, Captain George, hell, even Akylas seemed to see right through his careful fabrications.

Everyone they'd met since leaving Cairo looked at him as if they knew he was lying about one thing or another.

"Bring her inside." The woman turned and disappeared into the house.

Paul stared at the empty doorway. He didn't have a choice, not really. Stay outdoors in a strange land with a sick wife, or follow the woman inside and hope for the best. Paul followed.

The small house seemed more spacious inside than he'd suspected from the exterior. On closer inspection, he saw the meager furnishings that lined the outer walls and left the interior open. A single candle lit the main room, casting the edges in shadow.

A long wooden table dominated the area. Several steps inward, a bed sat against one wall, a trunk at its foot.

"I am Letizia."

"Ah, um…Paul." He grimaced. Wonderful, not even a lie about his name. He really wasn't up to his normal standards as far as lies and scams went. Definitely slipping.

"Lay her on the bed."

Narrowing his eyes, Paul studied Letizia. He certainly didn't trust her with Kaya. He trusted no one with Kaya.

Paul swore he heard Kaya's mocking laughter. In his head, she reminded him how often he'd told her he trusted no one. Fair enough. With Kaya so ill and no real idea of how to help—

Reluctantly, Paul carefully set Kaya on a narrow cot beneath an open window. They stood in the back of the small house overlooking a copse of trees. From here, he heard the rhythmic crash of the ocean and smelled the salty and earthy air. It did nothing to ease the tension tightening his shoulders nor erase the worry sitting like lead in his stomach.

Paul kissed Kaya's forehead and stood. Still laden with their things, he turned and crossed his arms over his chest. Both daggers were within easy reach.

The woman studied him with ancient, dark eyes. Her white hair glowed yellow in the candlelight, though her face remained unlined. Her graceful movements flowed around her as she pulled items down from high shelves.

He felt silly, threatening an old woman. But he'd threaten God himself to help Kaya.

"You are both far from home."

Not the opening Paul had expected, but he nodded in response. The fact was, she spoke English to strangers clearly stranded in her little hamlet. She needn't be some sort of seer or mystic to discern that.

Paul believed in neither.

"You speak English."

She looked at him, a pitying, obvious look. "I know many languages."

Paul narrowed his eyes, preparing for a fight. His fingers reached for his dagger, ready. It'd be easy enough to cut the straps from his arms and drop the pack. The bow and quiver were another matter, but they probably wouldn't throw off his balance too badly.

Letizia didn't look as if she wanted to fight—and it seemed off that she'd do so after inviting them into her house. If she wished to rob them, however, lulling him into a sense of security was the way to do so.

Clearly, she didn't know him. He and security didn't exactly get on.

"Her soul is strong, fighting even now." Letizia turned back to her mixing.

"She's ill," Paul snapped. "Not dying. On the ship, she became seasick. All she needs is rest and food, and we'll be gone."

Letizia snorted. She flipped her braid over her shoulder and returned to the things she'd set out on a long wooden table. Mixing powders with dried herbs, she ground everything together. He eyed her distrustfully, at war with himself. Kaya desperately needed help, and any help Paul offered seemed woefully inadequate.

Nothing he'd done had worked so far.

All Paul's instincts told him he could trust Letizia— when it came to Kaya, at least. Still, he didn't like it. It felt unnatural. Odd. Wrong. He did not like all this *trusting*.

He glared at the woman for no reason other than the *wrongness* of trusting another.

"I won't hurt her." Letizia raised her eyes and looked at him squarely. "She's precious to you."

Every protest Paul might've voiced dried in his throat. He tried not to think about that. About Jabir's or Akylas's words.

"Tell me what you're making." Paul growled through his clenched jaw. His arms dropped, but his fingers brushed his dagger. "I want to know every single ingredient."

* * * *

Kaya opened her eyes. She blinked slowly and waited for the ship to move, or her stomach to move, or some other horrendous movement to upset the delicate balance she was currently floating in. Nothing. No tilting, no bobbing, no waving.

Slowly, afraid to jolt herself lest she vomit—*again*—Kaya lifted her head. Every muscle ached, and her head pounded. She swallowed against a mouth as dry as *aṣ-ṣaḥrā' al-kubrá* that surrounded her home.

Alive—yes, that was this sluggish feel of relief. Coherent, awake, *alive* in a way she hadn't been since supper with the captain.

No. Best not think on supper. Or food. Or anything to do with her stomach. Her poor stomach.

Hand curled loosely, weakly, over her tender stomach, Kaya blinked in the too-bright sunlight and instantly closed her eyes. The sunlight hurt. She no longer lay on *The Cyprus Rose*.

She lay in a house.

Frowning, she blinked again to clear her eyes, opening them only enough to see her surroundings. Sparse furnishings sat against the bare outer walls, which gleamed white in the sun streaming through the open window above her bed.

Kaya closed her eyes against the harshness. It hurt her already pounding head. She heard the crash of waves but did not feel their disorienting motion.

Curious. How had she moved from *The Cyprus Rose* to this house?

Kaya lifted a hand, which took more strength than she'd anticipated, and brushed away the hair clinging to her cheek. Her mouth tasted like week-old she didn't know what, but it disgusted her. Her skin felt dry to her touch. Every movement, no matter how small, ached.

"Paul?" Her voice sounded fragile, weak, and it took all her strength to utter that one word.

No answer. Kaya frowned again, but even that took energy. She let her head sink into the pillow. The distance felt like their entire walk from Cairo to Damietta. Unfortunately, lying down did not ease the pounding in her head.

She must've dozed again. Kaya heard voices as she struggled awake. "Paul?"

"I'm here, Kaya."

His voice whispered over her dry skin, and his rough fingers grazed along her cheek. So light and gentle, she sighed into his touch. His fingers traced her forehead, down her cheek, over her lips. Again and again, he followed the same path, as if he'd spent hours doing so.

His touch felt so soothing, Kaya closed her eyes, sleep tugging her into its embrace.

"How do you feel?" His voice sounded as soft as his hands, seductive in its gentle worry. She leaned into him.

"Hmm," she sighed. Kaya wanted to smile, assure him she was much better and he shouldn't worry. However, she struggled to open her eyes.

When she finally forced them to open, Paul's own gaze—lined, exhausted, drained—met hers. As if he'd endured all she had, yet remembered every moment of it. His beautiful blue-green eyes looked shadowed in the bright sunlight. The beard he'd carefully trimmed in Damietta looked haggard once more. Her heart twisted.

She wanted to soothe him, comfort him. Reach out and smooth the lines bracketing his mouth. Chase away the shadows haunting his gaze. But she barely had the strength to wet her lips.

"Tired." Her eyes closed of their own accord, and she sighed into his touch.

"You've been sick for days." His voice caught. It sounded rough, as if he hadn't slept in days. But he gently wet her lips with a soft cloth. When he spoke, he did so quietly, as if he didn't wish to disturb her. "Since our first night on the ship."

His voice again wavered, cracked. Kaya forced her eyes open and saw his barely concealed terror. Her heart flipped, a slow movement that stole her breath. Then it raced, too fast for words, too fast to catch her breath.

"Where are we?" She swallowed hard. She tried to move, to lift her head and look around the room.

"Shh, no. Don't move." Paul caught her face between his hands, his fingers brushing ever so lightly over her temples. The movement lulled her. Safety and comfort and warmth. He adjusted her hijab and pressed his lips to her forehead. She leaned against his touch and her eyes closed again. Kaya forced them back open. "Mazzarelli."

Paul shifted onto the bed. He moved with such ease and grace she barely felt the bed shift. Supporting her from behind, his hand warm and gentle yet so firm around her, she knew he'd not let her fall. His fingers caressed her cheeks, her neck, and he nodded out the window. "Captain George landed us in Sicily. We're in a small hamlet on the east coast of the island."

Kaya frowned again. "Sicily?" His fingers returned to

her cheeks, wonderfully cool on her skin. "I don't understand."

"You were very sick, my dear," came a woman's voice.

Kaya started to speak, then whimpered again. She looked at the woman who had suddenly appeared in the room. Tall, with long, white hair, she spoke English. The sunlight illuminated her, and the too-bright glare made Kaya's eyes ache.

Confused, but lacking the strength to ask any questions, she rolled her head to the side and silently asked Paul.

"I didn't know what else to do." Paul's voice dropped even further. Their intimacy wrapped around her, as if they once more shared a bed and he was caressing her with his words.

"Oh."

"Kaya." His voice held emotions she hadn't the strength to understand.

Kaya tried to focus on him, discern what he was feeling, what he meant. She sensed he was trying to convey something, to tell her an important fact, but she didn't understand. Exhaustion tugged her limbs and made her shake from the simple exertion of staying awake.

"Paul."

"I know." He pressed his lips to her temple. "Sleep now. We'll talk when you wake."

He wavered before her tired gaze, but her eyes refused to remain open. Unaccustomed to such sickness—actually, Kaya couldn't remember ever being sick—she let her eyes close. "You'll stay with me?"

"Always." His lips pressed to her cheek again. "Drink this before you sleep." Paul held a wooden cup to her lips, and her eyes blinked open. Kaya hesitated. "Please."

Opening her mouth, she obediently swallowed the contents. She didn't know what flavored the water, oils and herbs she was unfamiliar with, but she drank the liquid because she trusted Paul. Who, apparently, trusted the woman standing in the sunlight.

How odd. Kaya didn't have the energy to figure that one out, either. She simply swallowed the liquid and closed her eyes.

"Sleep, Kaya." Paul pressed his lips to her forehead once more. His sigh of—relief? contentment?—brushed across her skin. "I'll be here when you wake."

Eyes already closed, fingers weakly curling around his, Kaya hummed an agreement. Nausea no longer burst through her, and she had no words to adequately describe the wonderfulness of that. Paul's fingers squeezed hers. She clung to their connection, the touch of him, the knowledge he stayed. The bed shifted as he climbed in next to her and pulled her close.

Kaya couldn't be sure, she was already floating on a gentle sea of sleep, but she thought she heard him say, "I'll watch over you, Kaya. Always."

Chapter Twenty-Two

"I'm not letting her eat tomatoes." Paul folded his arms over his chest and glared at Letizia. Her dark eyes looked steadily back at him, unaffected but wary.

Growling, he stalked the few feet separating them. Whatever Letizia saw on his face made her flinch. He stopped, hand fisted, jaw clenched. She'd offered her house and her help. She'd asked no questions and, even though she offered nothing about herself, he trusted her with Kaya's care.

Which probably meant she *was* a witch.

Even now, she instructed him on which herbs he needed to nurse Kaya back to health. In the two days since arriving on Mazzarelli, Letizia had also shielded them from suspicious villagers and remnants of the Inquisition.

Well, to be fair, the local priest wanted to question them, for reasons Paul didn't understand. Letizia claimed he wanted to bless Kaya. Paul, less trustful of this mysterious priestly visit—of religious figures in general—refused.

Paul had no idea what these superstitious villagers would do to Kaya if they knew she wasn't English, let alone Christian. While the village hadn't directly threatened them, Paul refused to take any chances while she still lay so weak in bed.

There hadn't been any mention of burning at the stake. That he knew of.

"She needs meat and fresh water," Paul snapped, but he did step back. Every bit of him vibrated with the need to see Kaya healthy. He'd fight Satan himself if it meant her health and happiness. "If you wanted her dead—"

"Dead?" Letizia looked at him as if *he* were mad. "No, no." She shook her head rapidly and held up her hands, a move to placate him. Paul crossed his arms over his chest and didn't relent. Worry overrode placation. "They are very good for her and will help her recover."

He glared at her, and Letizia picked up the bowl of tomatoes, which had been chopped up in fresh yogurt with lemon juice squeezed on top.

"Tomatoes, they are very healthy," Letizia promised.

He refused the bowl.

Letizia sighed. With a sharp click, she set the wooden bowl and spoon on the counter beside her. "I do not wish harm on your woman. She needs strength. Yogurt, lemon, tomato. These help her regain strength."

Torn between the very real fear Kaya *wasn't* regaining her strength and what he knew of food, Paul argued with himself. Not only did he trust Letizia with Kaya's life, he'd been forced to trust her with their safety. If it were up to him, they'd be on the other side of the island by now, even if it meant carrying Kaya the entire way.

Since arriving in Cairo, none of his plans had gone according to, well, *plan.*

He wanted to blame Kaya. She disrupted everything the instant she set foot in his life—rather, the instant he set foot into hers and she pressed her dagger to his back. Paul blew out a breath. He'd never enjoyed a disruption as much as he did her.

Nodding once, he took the bowl and spoon from Letizia. Refusing to make eye contact with her, he turned sharply toward the bed at the other end of the house.

Fear for Kaya's life beat through him in time to his heart, choking him, terrifying him. Alive and blossoming like a living thing, it slithered along his veins. Paul didn't know what to do, how to care for her. He relied on Letizia for everything.

He hated this vulnerability. This reliance.

"I'll leave you alone." Letizia kept her voice neutral. Paul wanted to snarl at her. Behind him, she picked up her basket and left, shutting the door quietly behind her.

He heard Kaya's voice in his head, laughing at his paranoia. But paranoia had kept him alive. Helped him survive.

He'd mistrust everyone in Egypt and Sicily combined to protect Kaya.

Kneeling beside the bed, he set the bowl of food on the floor and wrung out the linen. Lavender drifted from the water basin, and his nose twitched. He rubbed away the sneeze, trying his best to ignore the scent.

"I need you to wake up, sweetheart." Paul carefully bathed Kaya's face in the warm fresh water.

As Letizia instructed, he'd washed her chemise in lemon water, and it now dried in the bright Sicilian sunshine. He'd washed his own clothes, too, grateful for the chance to brush out his coat and trousers, clean Kaya's sickness from his linen shirt. Doing so had passed the time.

Those interminable hours in which Kaya slept, and he had naught to do save worry.

"Please, Kaya."

Her skin remained dry and brittle to his touch, but her chest rose and fell evenly. She no longer woke sick, but, other than those precious few moments this morning, she hadn't woken again.

He'd never cared for another the way he did for Kaya. He certainly didn't care for himself as he did for her. It wound through him, expansive and encompassing. She'd worked her way into his heart, that cold thing he'd thought long dead.

"You are the most important person in my life." The confession hung in the air, shocking even the chirping birds into silence.

Paul glared at them. Turning that glare onto Kaya, he demanded, "What have you done to me?"

Despite his harsh words, he glided the cloth over her chest and shoulders. A smooth, even touch, so as not to harm her. "I've known you barely a month. All I want is for you to open your eyes. Smile at me. Laugh with me. Please, Kaya." He pressed his lips to her forehead. "Please open your eyes."

She didn't even shift. No flicker of her eyelids, nothing. He dropped the linen in the water, held his breath as he wrung it out. The lavender still tickled his nose, and he sneezed. He hadn't realized how much he disliked lavender until now. Still, touch gentle, he started the process over again.

Kaya didn't stir.

"I've spent my life running from people, not caring about anyone but myself. You were supposed to be an easy job, Kaya. Go to Cairo, pretend to listen to Tahir, steal whatever I could carry, and leave again."

Paul threw the linen against the wall. The wet splat did little to ease the frustration pounding through him. Digging the heels of his palms into his eyes, he tried to focus. The lavender water burned his nose, irritating him more. As suddenly as it came on, the anger drained from him, and he scraped his fingers through his hair. Blowing out a breath, his head dropped to the bed. The wooden ceiling offered no answers, only the mocking silence of his own consciousness.

"You were supposed to be a means to an end, *my* end. I never expected to care for you." Turning his head to stare at his beautiful wife, his passionate lover, he brushed his fingertips over her forehead, down her cheek. Drawn to her. "I never expected—"

Who was he to speak of feelings when he'd only ever cared about himself? Caring for friends who could look after themselves, and would no matter what, didn't compare. Caring for Kaya, this huge, devastating emotion that burned through him, changed him.

Surprised, Paul blinked as if the world had shifted. Maybe it had. Maybe he had. Kneeling beside her once more, he looked at the woman who'd changed his entire life.

"You missed the rest of our voyage, Kaya. Jabir was quite upset you could not taste the meals he planned just for you. He was thrilled to cook for you."

Paul lifted her hand and kissed her palm. It was limp and unresponsive, but he nonetheless curled his fingers around hers. "He worried about you. So did young Akylas. You would've liked him, I think. And the sunrise on the water. You missed that, Kaya. No land for miles around, only the sea. You would've loved the sunrise over the water."

She stirred, huffed out a soft breath. He waited, prayed as he never had in his life. She moved again, only to face him more fully. As if she'd heard his voice. Her fingers tightened around his. Paul squeezed them and hoped she realized he'd stay with her.

Always.

He held her hand until he thought she slept again. With a gentle kiss to the back of it, he carefully released it. Standing, he retrieved the linen and resumed wiping her face. He drew in a deep breath, sneezed at the lavender scent, and tried to shake it away.

Another argument with Letizia. Another she'd won. Lavender, Letizia insisted, soothed the skin. It made him sneeze and pounded horribly behind his eyes. But if it helped Kaya, he'd bathe her every day in the blasted scent.

Paul didn't know how long he knelt there, running the wet linen over Kaya's face, down her neck and shoulders, over her arms. He bathed the tops of her breasts, her belly and ribs, too prominent after her sickness.

The sun moved across the sky, its rays bathing Kaya's paleness in golden light. Paul tried to block the light from her face. He didn't want the light to pain her if she opened her eyes. In the distance, the hamlet buzzed with life. Paul listened to every rise and fall of noise, tense. Ready to protect her.

Kaya groaned. Paul stilled, heart thundering, and waited. Finally—finally!—her eyes struggled open.

"Kaya." More relieved than he had words for, he dropped the linen in the basin and shoved the scented water aside. "Here." He scrambled onto the bed and helped her sit. Kaya swayed against him, and Paul held her tight. "Steady. I've got you." He pressed his lips to the top of her head. "I've got you, sweetheart. I've got you."

"Paul?"

"I'm here." He wrapped his arm around her and held her close. She sighed and melted into his embrace. The vice around his heart loosened, and, for the first time since waking on *The Cyprus Rose* to Kaya's sickness, Paul breathed easy.

He kissed the side of her neck, so relieved she was conscious he almost didn't care about anything else—not even the lavender clinging to her. His nose twitched again, and he scrunched it against a sneeze.

"Are you hungry?" he whispered against her skin.

"Little."

Her voice floated to him, thready, weak, tired. Her hand tightened around his, which he took as a sign she was alert.

Lifting the bowl of yogurt from the floor, he brought it around her front. Her head rested on his shoulder, and he moved it slightly until she lifted her head.

"Tomatoes?" Her voice perked up, and he mentally forgave Letizia.

He'd probably have to apologize to her, too. Damn woman. Women.

"Yogurt, tomatoes, and lemon juice." He raised the spoon, purposely catching a diced tomato despite his original vow not to feed her any.

"Haven't eaten tomatoes in months." The words slurred with her tiredness, but Kaya chewed the bite and hummed gratefully.

"Nasty, mushy things." Resigned, he scooped another spoonful of yogurt and tomatoes.

Kaya sighed, a bare puff of air against his skin. "They're delicious. Gidd planted them in my gardens when I was young. He claimed they were not found anywhere else in Egypt." She once again rested her head on his shoulder. "I'll make you *ful medames*, real *ful medames*. The way it's meant to be eaten, tomatoes and all. Not like we had in Damietta."

"I like *ful medames*," he admitted. "I had no idea there were tomatoes in it."

"The plants all died this year. The rains never came." She turned her head and pressed her lips to the side of his neck. "You'll love it."

Frozen, the spoon halfway to her lips, Paul blinked. Her promise, the wording of it, settled in his heart. A future. She'd promised a future. The gentle press of her lips to his neck sparked over his skin. "I'm sure."

Movements jerky, he fed her another spoonful, then carefully moved around her to place the bowl on the floor. "I'll love anything you cook."

She hummed, but he knew she was sleeping again.

He leaned against the wall, still holding her blanket-covered body. Kaya hadn't even noticed she was no longer wearing her chemise.

Combing his fingers through her hair, Paul leaned against the wall and adjusted Kaya in his arms. He held her for a long, long time.

* * * *

Kaya opened her eyes to darkness. Still disoriented, she remained motionless as she tried to take in her surroundings, the soft scent of salty air, the unfamiliar rhythmic echo of water. Though she heard no other sounds, nothing from the village or household, her world still tilted wildly around her.

Confused, she tried to roll over. Caught tight, her heart skipped a beat. During that beat, her hands flailed for her khanjar, her body tense.

Paul's hands tightened around her, and only then did she realize she was sitting upright, her back against his chest.

Peace. Contentment. His arms wrapped around her as surely as the scent of lavender clung to her skin. Breathing deeply of the scent, she sighed and let her eyes drift closed. The steady rise and fall of his breathing eased through her.

Exhaustion blurred her mind, but Kaya knew he'd stayed with her. Taken care of her when she could do none of that herself.

All her fears of his desertion vanished. How ridiculous they sounded now. With his arms so tight around her, the even fall of his chest against her, a strange feeling of contentment heated her veins.

She wanted to be here.

That knowledge bloomed warmly through her, tingling along her fingers. It grew and grew, a pleasant pressure in her chest she had no precedence for. It threatened to burst along her nerves. She embraced it, held it close to her heart.

Shifting slightly, Kaya felt a rough scratch of material against her skin. Though her arm trembled with the effort, she lifted it and let her fingers fall to her chest. Naked. Her mind might have been hazy, but she did not recall undressing.

A question for another time.

Returning her head to Paul's shoulder, she closed her eyes and let his breathing lull her once again. Kaya was glad Paul slept. In the days since leaving Cairo and truly getting to know him, she'd worried about his lack of rest. His nightmares. His evasiveness when it came to them.

Something happened in his past that still haunted Paul—and worried Kaya.

Mayhap now that they were on Sicily, away from Cairo and off that wretched ship, he'd relax and trust in her to keep him safe, as he had her. She cared deeply for Paul and wanted him to sleep, wanted to soothe away the terrors that gripped him whenever he closed his eyes.

She wanted to do that for him, the man who didn't hold her back. He embraced her exploration—of herself, her passion, this world.

"Kaya?" Paul sounded alert and awake.

Disappointed she'd somehow woke him, she relaxed further into his embrace. Licking dry, cracked lips, she swallowed past the lump in her throat. "I'm here."

"You're awake." The relief in his voice twisted through her. He sniffed, his voice blocked, and she frowned. "Are you hungry?"

"Thirsty," she whispered.

"Good." Paul jostled her a little but never released her. "Good. I have juice."

He held a smooth wooden cup to her lips, and Kaya drank the warm liquid. She managed two sips then pulled back. Her stomach protested again.

"How do you feel?" His hand brushed her forehead, his arm around her chest both a comfort and a prison. She didn't know how to separate anything, even though she knew Paul would never hurt her or trap her. "You sure you don't want to try a bite of food?"

Her throat closed at the thought. "No." She swallowed and squeezed her eyes shut against tears, glad for the darkness. "Not now."

He sighed, a warm puff of air against the back of her neck. "All right.

Paul's fingers combed through her hair, and he sneezed. She jerked at the sudden sound, the jostling movement. Rolling her head, she tried to look at him.

"Are you ill?"

He cleared his throat. "No." She heard the humor in that single word. "Just a stuffy nose."

"I don't understand." Kaya frowned and struggled to sit. Paul's arms tightened around her. Just as well, as she had no energy for such movement, however she wished otherwise.

"It's the lavender," he admitted. "Makes me sneeze."

"Lavender? I did not know it made people sneeze."

"Maybe only Englishmen." He chuckled, and Kaya relaxed.

"Why am I bathed in it? Why stay with me if it makes you sneeze?" She shook her head and instantly regretted it. Maybe she did need food. Or maybe rejecting it had been a good idea. Kaya really didn't know anymore.

"You were sick." Paul said it as if it were the most natural thing in the entire world.

His voice lowered, intimate in the night, a stroke along her skin. His thumb moved in small, sweeping motions over her bare belly, and she shivered at the touch. Kaya's heart raced, her body finally waking. His touch sent lightning along her nerves, a craving for more. She licked her lips again and grasped for words.

"You stayed." She'd meant to ask it as a question, but the words sounded more like a statement. Fact, not query.

"Of course."

She felt his lips against her temple, his fingers press to her skin. Each patch of skin he touched tingled with awareness. She tried not to shiver in his embrace. Not to let him see how he affected her, even when she lay so weak in his arms.

Kaya did not understand the swirl of emotions battling for her attention. The simple joy in his arms, the drowsy satisfaction. He'd stayed with her. She didn't know why when he could have easily left her.

He could've continued on the ship where she was far too ill to survive. Abandoned her on the island. Who would have known? She had long assumed he'd do so. Only now did she realize how on guard she'd remained since stepping foot outside her home's front door.

Anticipating just that.

Paul had protected her, fought to keep her safe. Threatened those who would see her harmed.

The man who taught her such pleasure that, even now, sick, tired, and weak, Kaya felt his touch keenly. The lightning press of his fingers, the restrained power of each stroke of his thumb.

This same man who'd taken care of her, who now held her gently. He held her naked body and didn't need to pretend he did so for her comfort. He simply did. Paul asked nothing in return, no favor. He simply…held her.

"Where are we?" she asked, though she had a vague memory he'd already told her. She wanted to ask the myriad questions about what had shifted between them. When it had done so. Uneasy feelings waited to fall from her tongue.

She swallowed them all.

"Mazzarelli. Little nowhere village in Sicily. Captain George dropped us off when even Jabir's grandmother's recipe didn't help your sickness."

"Sicily?" Kaya hesitated. "Miles from Cairo."

"Yes." He stilled for a moment. "An island between Cairo and the mainland. But"—his tone lightened, and he resumed his caress— "I told Letizia we sailed from Beirut."

"Letizia? Who is *Letizia*?" she demanded, far more shocked at this new name than at the idea Paul had lied about their port of origin.

Of course he had. In the days since meeting him, she'd come to realize he didn't lie so much as misdirect. To protect himself and now her.

Letizia. Kaya had a vague memory of a tall woman standing in the bright sunlight like an apparition.

"She offered us shelter."

Kaya struggled to sit up. Paul grunted and helped her turn. She caught his gaze in the dark cottage. "The voice sounds like the Paul I know, but I don't understand." She was trying to joke, to lighten the uncertainty and the churning anxiety in her belly. But Kaya suspected her humor fell flat. "You trusted another?"

Even in the darkness, she saw his frown. "You—no matter what I tried, you didn't respond." The torment in his voice hollowed her heart. His fingers clenched around her arms, only to loosen so as not to hurt her. "You were constantly sick, refused to eat or drink anything. Barely woke."

His fingers brushed her skin again, but this time Kaya suspected it was more because he needed to touch her than anything. His lips pressed hard to her forehead, and he made a sound in the back of his throat she had never heard from another.

"I recall the sickness." Again she tried for humor, and again she fell short.

Paul made a choked sound and turned her around again, settling her back against his chest. His fingers stilled on her skin but pressed tight.

"I carried you from the boat. Letizia opened her door and offered help."

"Oh." Kaya raised her heavy hands from where they lay limply on her lap. She maneuvered them beneath the blanket and covered Paul's hands with hers. "Thank you."

She struggled for more, but their position, the intimacy of it, the comfort, seemed too easy, too private. Kaya didn't know how to feel or what these feelings for Paul even were.

Paul sneezed and cleared his throat. He jostled her again, then blew his nose.

She waited while he repositioned himself and held her close once more. Her head rested on his shoulder, and she closed her eyes, physically content to be in his arms. Emotionally was an entirely different matter.

Finally, *finally*, she'd escaped Cairo. Finally, she stood on foreign soil, no longer hidden from the world. What now?

"She showed me which herbs you needed," Paul said. Kaya snapped back to their conversation. His voice sounded somewhat lighter. Clearer, at least. "Which food strengthened you and why you needed to be bathed in lavender."

He sniffed and, unable not to, she grinned. Kaya turned her head into his neck and kissed the skin there. Tears blurred her vision—or maybe exhaustion did.

"Thank you," she repeated. "I—" Words closed her throat, thanks and warmth and understanding and this ever-growing expanse she didn't understand. "I didn't know you spoke Sicilian," she said instead.

She didn't know much about Paul. Part of her wished to know everything. The other part didn't want any more temptation to stay. A third part, whose voice grew increasingly louder, wondered if it wasn't already too late.

"I don't." He snorted and jerked. She felt him turn his head before he sneezed again. "Damn lavender."

"You don't?" Kaya frowned, and her eyes drifted closed again. "I'm tired, my mind is foggy, but I don't understand. If you don't speak Sicilian, how did you speak with Letizia?"

He stilled, hesitated. Paul was an excellent liar. To Kaya, at least, who had never lied to anyone and had never known anyone to lie to her. Well, not directly—she now knew Gidd had spent her life keeping secrets. Had he ever outright lied to her?

It wasn't important. Not now. Not any longer.

"Paul?"

"She speaks English," Paul admitted.

Kaya frowned again. "I'm not well enough for this," she admitted. "How is that a problem?"

"What makes you think it's a problem?"

She snorted. It took too much effort for the weak sound she made. "You clearly think it is."

He stilled, and Kaya wondered why. Honestly, she needed more rest before she could deal with the constant mountains and valleys of their relationship. Not that they had a relationship. Well, sex, which was very, very nice but—

"Paul?"

"A little nowhere village like Mazzarelli?" She felt him shake his head. His hands never left her skin, fingers continuing to stroke lightly over her. "One, maybe two hundred people here." Again he shook his head. "Maybe. It's a port town. I don't know, maybe that's all. But she speaks very good English." His cheek rested against the top of her head. "Almost as well as you."

"You trust her." Amazed, Kaya blinked in the darkness. She didn't turn to look at him, not sure what she'd see. Hoped to see. Kaya didn't know. "You trusted her to help me." She closed her eyes. A smile played around her lips. She refused to acknowledge it. "That's not necessarily a bad reason, Paul."

He hummed, fingers gliding over her arm. She huffed slightly and settled more comfortably into his embrace. Paul didn't answer, and Kaya drifted in that soft in-between of waking and sleeping, perfectly content. Her hands fell from his, and he caught them, held them tight.

She shifted a little to rest her head more comfortably against his shoulder.

"It's a problem when your life is on the line, Kaya."

Chapter Twenty-Three

He shaved.

Kaya reached out to touch his bare face but snatched her hand back. How odd to feel an aching sense of loss over facial hair.

Of all the things she wanted to say, the confused emotions racing through her, noticing Paul had bathed and shaved ranked low. It distracted her. Now all Kaya could do was focus on his clean-shaven cheeks.

"I miss your beard."

"Forget what I looked like already?" Paul grinned at her, his cheeks paler than the rest of his face.

"It's strange." Kaya gently tilted her head, mindful of her continued weakness. "It seems so long since we left Cairo."

Paul's grin widened. He crossed the room in long strides and leaned down. His lips were warm on her forehead, his hand firm on the back of her head. "A lifetime."

Kaya remembered falling asleep in his arms, the heavy warmth of his body pressed tight against hers. Holding her steady throughout the night. Last night, with the small house dark and Letizia elsewhere, Kaya closed her eyes and tried not to pretend the soft scratch of his cheek against hers was as natural as breathing.

Liar.

A lifetime since Cairo.

She frowned and met his gaze. "How long have we been here?"

"Five days." His face darkened, his gaze intent on hers. His fingers clenched on his dagger, knuckles white. "You've been recovering for five days."

"Oh." Kaya looked out the window instead of at him. She didn't know what else to say and couldn't look at him.

Not with the way he watched her. As if his fear of losing her still tightened his heart. Clearly Paul remembered every moment of her illness.

Kaya licked her lips and tried not to give in to the draw between them. Her near physical need to stand and wrap her arms around him. Hold him close. Comfort him.

What happened after? What came next?

She had no wish to live in England. Not with an entire world to explore.

An entire world minus the Ottoman Empire. France and Prussia, Russia and India and China. Not to mention the Americas—though she'd have to travel across the vast ocean. With her seasickness, that might not be as feasible as she'd originally believed.

"Thank you, Paul." Kaya sat straighter though her legs shook, and it took most of her strength to remain upright. At least her head no longer swam, and her stomach had settled.

She appreciated the small things.

Paul eyed her suspiciously and handed her the wooden bowl full of yogurt, tomatoes, and lemon juice. Kaya remained as impassive as possible and accepted the bowl with a nod.

Her impassivity didn't convince either of them.

She didn't know how to accept her conflicting feelings for Paul. Their escape from Cairo—which sounded far more treacherous and exciting than it had been—brought them together in ways Kaya had never imagined. She had envisioned the bare conversation of that first night. Polite civilities.

Never the shared intimacies of the cave.

The thought of him simply leaving, tossing her out as Gidd had when he'd married her to Paul, terrified her. Fear settled in her stomach, a rolling, choking, clawing nausea. Would he leave her now that they'd left Cairo? Even with them so far from England, they were away from Gidd and Egypt and any threat the Ottomans may have posed.

Kaya swallowed the yogurt, which tasted like ash in her mouth.

She couldn't— Kaya didn't know how to feel, what to do. Everything changed so fast, and now—

Loneliness loomed, as imposing now as it had been when she'd lived in the Cairo house.

Rather than the lovely, warm burst of feeling, she felt only cold, numb. Alone.

Her fingers fumbled on the spoon.

"All right?" Paul knelt before her in an instant.

Kaya shivered and forced herself to meet his gaze. "Yes." She scooped a spoonful and purposefully ate it. "Regaining my strength."

Paul didn't look convinced. He watched her a moment, then stood and resumed his activities. He checked their bags, rerolled the bedroll, tested the edge of her khanjar. Where had their tent beam gone?

Looking out the window, as if that would somehow offer an answer, all Kaya saw was trees. Openness. Deliverance.

Once more on solid land, even if that land was an island, the temptation of her freedom dangled before Kaya like the most precious of jewels.

Jewels.

She hadn't even *thought* about their jewels! Her jewels. *The* jewels. Kaya sighed. Even simple pronouns troubled her.

They were her only means of surviving. Especially if Paul abandoned her, left her.

Panicked, Kaya looked around the room. The blue dress lay neatly folded on a chair beside the bed. It looked clean and untouched, and her heart slowed.

Kaya pressed her fingers to her temples, rubbing short circles over the sensitive skin to ease the ache. First that wretched vomiting; now her head ached. She did not enjoy sickness.

"It's a sunny day." Paul stood at the window, his back to her and his arms folded over his chest. His stance reminded her so much of their room in Damietta, when he'd distanced himself from her. Kaya's heart clenched.

Or maybe it ached with such uncertainty.

Did she want that distance? No. Yes. She didn't know. She ought to. It was for the best, but the thought sent a bolt of fear through her. All her breath rushed out, and she wanted to grab on to Paul and hold him tight instead.

Hold him so he didn't leave?

Or leave him before he left her?

He turned to look at her. "If you're up to it, we can walk in the wood."

Swallowing hard, Kaya slid her gaze from his piercing one to the view beyond the window. Her fingers smoothed the linen of her chemise while she sorted her reply. So much for a simple yes or no. Her life had never been complicated before she met Paul.

Liar.

That was unfair to him and his place—wherever that may be—in her life. Unable to meet his gaze, Kaya stared out the window. The sunlight beckoned her, and the scent of the sea added another layer to the temptation.

"I'd like to explore," she finally admitted. "I missed our voyage." She grimaced at the memory and hastily ate another spoonful of yogurt.

"Finish your yogurt." Paul turned from the window. "Then rest. We'll go as soon as you wake."

Kaya obediently finished the bowl of yogurt and lay down. She tried to sleep. Physically exhausted, her mind whirled from topic to topic. She dozed, her memory wandering along their trek from Cairo to Damietta, from the souk and the press of Paul's lips on hers.

Where did they go from here?

She missed Derya and Gidd. As much as she rebelled against the shackles keeping her hidden, her anger over Derya's death, over Gidd's abandonment, she missed her family.

Paul had promised to see her to England, but now?

Now they had months, years maybe, of travel overland. What happened next?

Kaya curled onto her side and hugged the thin pillow to her chest. Unable to hold back her sobs, she cried quietly into the pillow, afraid and ashamed and alone.

* * * *

Something bothered her.

Kaya refused to meet his gaze, which was so unlike her Paul almost thought her possessed by the Marathi spirits Basu had enjoyed telling him about in Bombay.

He dismissed that thought almost instantly.

Basu was a good one for spirit stories. His Marathi friend often regaled him, John, Oliver, and Harry with stories about ghosts and demigods and demons. Paul missed Basu; it caught him tight, like a punch to the gut.

Paul tightened his hold on Kaya and willed away the memory of Basu's dead eyes staring up at him. His friend's haunting accusations from the bloodied street.

He didn't even want to think about John—Paul had abandoned him in Cairo without so much as a note. Paul shoved all thoughts of his friends aside. That was his past, a previous life.

Kaya was his present. His future.

He didn't like her evasiveness. The standoffish way she treated him, the short sentences and awkward silences.

Steadying her around the waist, they strolled out of Letizia's cottage and into the warm afternoon sunshine. She sighed and leaned into him.

Maybe she still felt unwell; the seasickness had taken much out of her. He preferred cuddly, sleepy Kaya who laughed in his arms to this version of his wife. The woman who averted her gaze, who coldly answered his questions without the normal inflection of wonder.

Paul growled. Kaya glanced up at him. Just as he met her gaze, she looked straight ahead.

He scrubbed his free hand over his face and pinched the bridge of his nose.

He loved Kaya.

Paul had no idea how or when it happened. One minute they were walking out of Cairo as strangers, the next he stumbled at her feet, ready to offer her his body, heart, and soul. Or what little remained of his soul.

She deserved more.

The breeze curled around them, salt water and greenery on its tendrils. Paul looked down at her, fully dressed in her gown and headscarf. He tightened his arm around her waist. She'd insisted on walking barefoot. The simple fact she was moving about on her own thrilled him.

"I've never seen so many trees."

Kaya stopped and stared at the line of fig and olive trees. She craned her neck and looked at the boughs in awe. Watching her discover new things was a sight more beautiful than anything he'd ever seen. Except possibly her face when they made love.

"I've eaten figs all my life." She met his gaze, the dark brown of her eyes bright in the sunlight. "I've grown a fig tree in my garden, but only the one. I've never—"

Kaya shook her head and looked to the trees again. A row of lemon trees grew several paces to the right of them.

She stepped forward, and Paul instantly grabbed her around the waist.

"I can walk on my own," she snapped.

"This is your first day out of bed." He spoke evenly. His heart clenched in remembered fear.

"We are gone from Cairo." She didn't look at him but walked ahead, her body stiff. Each cautious step seemed to take much out of her. While she didn't shrug off his touch, she no longer leaned into him, either. "You have kept your promise to my grandfather."

Paul stopped dead.

Seabirds called out above. The wind rustled through the trees, bringing with it the scents of figs and olives and lemons. Behind him, the Mediterranean continued its gentle crash along the shoreline.

The sounds roared in his head, a cacophony of noise that nearly blocked out everything else. Everything but Kaya's defiant eyes. Her set mouth. The stubborn tilt of her head.

"I have." He straightened, shoulders rigid. Paul's voice slipped into the easy dismissiveness he'd often favored—before her. "But I promised Tahir I'd see you to England."

Her head whipped around, and her eyes blazed with passion, anger, rebelliousness. The stubbornness he both adored and abhorred. Christ, he wanted to kiss her, touch her skin, comb his fingers through her long hair and taste that lush mouth.

"And I have told *you* time and again I've no wish to settle in England," she shot back. "I shall see the world on my own terms."

Damn if he didn't agree to that. Damn him for wanting to give her everything.

"On your terms?" he sneered. "Yes, I'm sure you'll survive well *on your terms*."

He needed to cut his tongue out.

Kaya stood straight, head tilted, eyes ablaze. "I admit," she said coldly, "that first night outside of Cairo, I knew very little about surviving on my own." Kaya's lip curled. It should not have been so sexy. "However, you are a very competent teacher."

Her gaze deliberately ran over his body, and, before she uttered the words, Paul knew what she was going to say. Damn her for knowing the exact point in which to hit him.

"In all things," Kaya added.

His grinned coldly at her. "Pretty quick learner, you." Paul nodded and crossed his arms over his chest. He rocked back on his heels and cast her the same deliberate look. "For someone so sheltered, I'd say you're a *very* fast learner."

The jabs hurt him as much as Paul knew they hurt her. They were designed to, after all. His heart ached at his barbs, and he watched Kaya with a steadiness he didn't feel.

Amazing how one realization in the middle of the night had changed things. Changed him.

"I release you from whatever promise you made to my grandfather." Her cold, regal voice cut through him, sharp as a lance through his heart. "He could not and should not have expected you to remain with me."

"Oh, Tahir paid me well to keep you safe, Kaya." His words dripped with contempt, and Paul didn't know who he was angrier with: himself or her. Kaya's eyes narrowed, and he wondered if she'd hit him. "But I swore on my honor I'd see you safely to England."

"I'm not traveling to England." She snorted. "You haven't listened to me since the first time we met. I refuse to travel to England and *settle* there," she spat. "I'm finally free from that house and those rules. I shall see as much of the world as I wish."

Paul didn't know when he'd stalked forward or when

he'd taken her arms. He only realized he was holding her, his fingers curled into her muscles, when she pushed him back. Horrified at his actions, Paul dropped his hands and clenched his fists.

Forcing his jaw to relax, he fought for words that wouldn't damage. Even as he opened his mouth, Paul knew he'd failed.

"A woman alone? One who can barely see to herself?" He laughed. Fear gave it a mocking tone. Fear for her safety, her life. Fear she was about to desert him. "Best of luck there, sweetheart."

Kaya reared back as if he'd smacked her. She looked at him in wide-eyed shock. Jerking an unsteady step back, she glared at him with all the disdain he no doubt deserved.

"Yes," she said coldly, nobly. "You have taught me well, *Sergeant*. I have learned much about how men truly act in this world. Much about their *honor*. You are also correct in that I now know the value of mistrust."

Paul watched her turn, a little unsteadily, and walk back to the cottage. Christ, he hadn't meant—the words had fallen from his lips. Fallen so easily. He'd slipped into his former self with barely a thought. Maybe that former him wasn't as former as he liked to think. As he hoped.

How he handled it, what he said—that was the man who hid from the world behind quick smiles and quicker words.

Not the man who loved Kaya.

Roaring, he turned and slammed his fist into the nearest fig tree. The leaves shook violently, and several pieces of fruit fell around him. His fist throbbed, and his knuckles bled, but he didn't feel better.

He needed a drink.

Chapter Twenty-Four

Sweetheart.

Paul's mocking voice stabbed her painfully. Her heart beat hard in her chest, and her throat closed. She refused to cry.

The only other time he'd used that term, it had been wrapped in soothing concern, in calm comfort. With his arms around her and his breath brushing her skin, he'd held her to him as if he never wanted to let go. Back then, he'd said the word as if it meant everything.

Now, his contemptuous voice echoed with ridicule, scorn. Not the caring compassion she had come to expect. Instead, the word fell between them like broken promises. Condescending and disdainful.

Eyes hot but dry, Kaya lay in bed, head pillowed in her arms. She refused to cry.

She thought she'd released all her anger and hurt earlier. Distanced herself before being cut. Kaya closed her eyes, but it didn't banish her whirling thoughts or help her organize them.

She wanted to ask Paul how he felt about this consummation of their marriage or his beliefs on divorce. She had no idea if he would still be willing to forget this marriage ever existed. She doubted he had strong feelings in favor of marriage, but she knew so little about him.

Kaya also didn't know how she felt about it.

So much of the world lay shrouded in mystery to her, and *she didn't know*. Instead of asking him, of speaking rationally and calmly, she'd snapped. Poured all her fear and grief into harsh, terrible words aimed directly at him.

Each arrow had hit its mark.

Her bruised heart thudded hollowly in her chest, a cold, empty reminder of all she grasped. All she lost.

She and Derya had had arguments before, of course. But they had never felt as final as her argument with Paul. Never as heartrending. Derya would always return to the house and Kaya would never leave it. It was different with Paul. Everything was different with him.

Kaya sniffed back tears.

With Paul gone and her in the cottage because her legs had refused to carry her farther, Kaya realized what knowing others also brought: joy and happiness, conversation and knowledge, yes.

Heartbreak, anger, sorrow. Tears.

Her control shattered.

Kaya tried not to make a sound, but then she was so very good at hiding her feelings and emotions. Even in this currently empty home, she kept silent. Maybe she didn't want to hear herself cry, either. Hear her own desolate loneliness and isolation.

Arms shaking, she wiped her cheeks and searched for a handkerchief. Blowing her nose, Kaya pushed herself to a sitting position and waited while her breath steadied. She hated being weak. If the last hours had taught her anything about her body, however, she needed to be at her best, in peak condition, to leave this place.

Leave on her own, by herself.

The thought made her ill. It no longer brought joy, as it had when she left Cairo.

Before she knew Paul. Or thought she knew him.

She suspected Paul fought better than he negotiated. How had such a man caught General Tahir's attention? Gidd, who excelled at both tactical advancement and negotiation.

Kaya knew Paul had grown up in England, but she knew nothing of his family—mother, father, siblings. Friends. He'd spent most of his life in Bombay with the East India Company Army, but Kaya didn't know what job he held there. Or why he left.

No, she didn't know him. Not really—not at all.

He wielded a dagger with deadly accuracy and had no qualms in killing. He'd done so to protect her. Paul was a passionate lover—not that she had any basis for comparison. He'd taken care of her when she was quite unable to take care of herself.

She knew he had promised to see her safely from Cairo to England.

When she stripped everything else away, she knew she'd grown to care for him. Possibly love him—though again Kaya had no basis for comparison.

How did one know if they were in love?

Freedom lay within her reach now. Finally. She needed to grasp it. The freedom to choose her own path, her own destination, be it physical or spiritual.

It tasted like ash and emptied her.

Sitting on the bed, eyes closed, she tried to relax and focus on her inner self. Her argument with Paul circled round and round her head. Words she wished to say, and those she wished to pull back and hide forever.

She heard Letizia enter the cottage and hastily lay down, shut her eyes, and pretended sleep. Kaya knew she hadn't fooled the other woman. No matter how she craved it, she didn't look forward to conversation with Letizia.

The irony did not escape her.

* * * *

Paul sat beneath a fig tree, knees bent, head in hands. His fingers dug into his scalp. He hoped the pressure might ease the voice condemning him for his cruelty, for hurting Kaya. Beside him, the bottle of wine he'd bought at the local tavern tempted him.

As yet untouched, the wine taunted him as much as Kaya's words had. For the first time in his life, Paul regretted the things he'd said.

A fool in love.

Pathetic.

He grabbed the bottle and stared at it. The wine called to him, its scent a familiar lover. Paul all too easily felt the wine slide down his throat, its heavy taste a balm to his nightmares. His first drink in weeks—since their wine had run out somewhere in the Sinai.

Paul didn't drink.

With enough wine in him, he could be poetic, foolish. Passed out drunk. That potential tempted him. Beckoned him. Called to him like a siren of old. Torn between sitting right there and drinking or hitting something to expend this energy winding through him and wanting to explode, Paul sat. He probably made the wrong choice.

Always the wrong choice.

He did not drink, however, and that had to be something. Right?

He heard Kaya's slow, uneven gait, and his head whirled to find her. He wanted to stand and help her, but he doubted she'd welcome his help. He stumbled to his feet, the wine bottle clenched in his fist.

Head held high, she walked barefoot across the sandy terrain. Each step was a slow, careful movement over the uneven ground littered with figs, olive pits, shells, and who knew what all else. The ends of her headscarf fluttered in the wind.

Her eyes caught his, unreadable in the setting sun.

Words crowded his tongue. She shouldn't be out of bed, or walking around alone. She needed rest after the sea voyage ordeal.

I'm sorry.

Once upon a time, Paul prided himself on his way with words, but that was before meeting a woman as unusual and enticing as Kaya. A woman who pulled truths from where he'd buried them. A woman who made him want to be a better man.

Kaya hadn't mentioned their marriage, and Paul could only be grateful he hadn't blurted anything out. Another sentence he couldn't take back. Another piece of him laid at her feet.

That dark pit of need closed around him—Paul wanted to be the one to show her the world. Wanted to see her face alight with pleasure—not only in bed, but at the simplest sights. Those sights he'd previously ignored or hadn't cared about.

The everyday life that faded into the background.

Kaya brought light to his life. He hadn't realized such light, such joy, existed. Not for him. He still didn't deserve her. Never would. Not the happiness she brought to his shallow, pathetic existence. Not her innocence, not her passion.

He'd only extinguish it.

Paul licked his lips, thought he tasted wine but knew he hadn't a drink. He glanced at the bottle and set it by the tree, afraid of his weakness. He only had eyes for Kaya.

"You shouldn't be up." The instant the words left his mouth, Paul knew he deserved the angry glare she shot him.

"I wish to apologize."

"What?"

"To you," Kaya clarified, as if the object of her apology needed clarification.

"What?" Paul glanced at the wine bottle, now several arms' lengths away. "Why?"

Kaya stood before him, her hands folded carefully in front of her. He hadn't seen her so still, so poised, since acquiescing to Tahir's marriage proclamation. The weeks had changed her. Not, he feared, for the better. She shouldn't have seen the death and ugliness of the slavers, of the man who tried to take her in the souk.

He blamed himself for that. For all of it.

"You promised Gidd to see me safe. It was your vow to him, on your honor. I understand that, and I apologize." She eyed the wine bottle. When she met his gaze again, her face remained impassive.

"I failed." Judging by the way her eyebrows shot up and her head tilted, his words had surprised Kaya more than him. "I didn't keep you safe."

"I don't understand. I am gone from Cairo, from Egypt."

It choked him, the revulsion, the anger, the *fear* for her life. Rose up and cut off his air, a vise around his throat until he saw Kaya, bloodied, broken, and lying on a dirty, horse-trampled road.

Kaya swayed, and Paul caught her. Somehow, he'd kicked the wine. Its deep red contents spilled into the land.

"I am fine," Kaya said stiffly.

He slipped one hand around her back. Paul didn't release her, had no intentions of doing so no matter her insistence. He'd be damned if his anger and her stubbornness caused her more harm.

"I'm responsible for you, and I failed to protect you."

She batted his hand away and stepped to the side, out of his reach. Once again she swayed, and once again he reached for her. Kaya flinched. Paul jerked back, his hands curled at his sides. Her face paled in the golden-red rays of the setting sun. He needed to help her. Redeem himself in her eyes, even if he didn't deserve it. Even if he could never redeem himself in his own.

She deserved better.

"You have protected me," she told him, but it didn't sound conciliatory. "You do not trust me. That is the problem."

"I do." He wondered how she'd heard his whispered words, but Kaya closed her mouth on whatever she was going to say next. "I *do* trust you."

Himself, his friends, the army—no, he did not trust them. Especially himself. Kaya? Yes. He trusted her far more than he'd thought himself capable.

"Do you?" Again she looked at him, head tilted, eyes assessing, as if he were a specimen to be studied.

"Kaya, I trust you more than I trust myself."

"Oh." She paused. "You have a very strange way of showing this trust."

Paul snorted. "Trust—trust is not an easy thing to show. It's not—I don't trust many."

"I hadn't noticed," she said, in what had to be the driest tone he'd ever heard.

He snorted out a short laugh. "Yes, well…yes." Paul ran a hand down his face and sighed. "I do trust you, Kaya. More than—you're the only one I trust. The only one I want to."

"Then we are at odds in the execution of your vow to Gidd." She tilted her head again, that inquisitive little movement that drove him crazy. "And to me. You promised we'd figure things out. What things did you mean?"

"At the time, I meant our arranged marriage."

"Ah. Yes." She turned away.

Paul frowned. Her coldness he understood. Her anger he accepted. This strange shyness baffled him. Did she blush? Confused, Paul glanced at the wine staining the ground.

"I understand." She sniffed and straightened, feet braced, hands curling into fists.

Bewildered, he shook his head. *What the hell?*

"I am a foolish woman." Kaya cleared her throat but held his gaze. "I foolishly believed that chasing my desires, seeking only what I wanted to learn, exempted me from repercussions. It does not."

"Kaya, I don't know what you're talking about."

She pressed her lips together, but her eyes remained uncertain. Definitely not the Kaya he knew. Completely lost, Paul opened his mouth, then snapped it shut. Motioning in a way he hoped encouraged her, he waited.

She cleared her throat again and dropped her gaze, but only for a heartbeat. "I didn't—when you signed the marriage document, and you promised to protect me, I didn't believe it."

"I'll always protect you." The words slipped out before he thought to stop them.

"I know." Kaya closed her eyes, and for a heartbeat Paul thought she might cry.

Panicked, he stepped closer, reached out to touch her, hold her. He stopped himself, uncertain as to how she would receive him. His hands hovered over hers, desperate to feel her beneath his fingertips. Swallowing hard, against his better judgment, he dropped his arms.

"I didn't believe it then. I didn't know you." She swayed, and Paul caught her.

Kaya didn't try to jerk away, which worried him.

"I've got you. Come on, Kaya." Easing her to the ground beneath the fig tree, Paul kicked the wine bottle away. He didn't mourn it. "Close your eyes and breathe in. That's it, just rest."

He brushed her cheek. Paul cradled the back of her head, simply holding her. Protecting her. They sat like that for a while, the breeze gentle over them, the sun a slow slide along the horizon.

"Thank you."

"You shouldn't be up." Paul pressed his lips to her forehead.

She sighed into his touch, and a piece of the wall he'd hastily built around his heart cracked. He sat beside her, drawing Kaya into his arms.

"I needed to speak with you." She sighed. "Apologize."

"You don't need to apologize," he insisted.

"I do. I am not as honorable as you. You vowed to protect me, swore to my grandfather to honor me. I had no intentions of ever keeping those marriage promises." She lifted her head from his chest and met his gaze. "But we consummated our marriage."

"Ah." Paul cleared his throat. He shifted uncomfortably, hand tightening around her shoulder. "Yes."

"You realized."

"I did."

"Why did you not say anything?" Kaya pulled from his embrace.

"You mean stop you?" He scowled, offended. "I don't know if you noticed, but I wanted you, too, Kaya."

"No. No, I don't mean why didn't you stop me from having sex with you." Her hand drifted down his chest and took his. "That was my choice; I chose to go forward with it." She smiled, a coy turn of her lips. "I wanted to. Want you."

Once more, he floundered. Huffing an amused breath, Paul combed his fingers through his hair. "You continue to surprise me, Kaya."

"Why did you not say anything about our marriage?"

Leaning his head against the tree, Paul closed his eyes. He heard every breath Kaya took, felt the slight movement of her leg against his. Her hand held his tightly, as if anchoring them together.

"I didn't want to trap you." Opening his eyes, Paul met her curious brown gaze. "I didn't want you to stay with me because I forced you to. If you wanted to leave, I didn't—I won't force you to stay because we consummated vows you never wanted to make."

"Oh."

"Aye," he sighed. "Oh."

Chapter Twenty-Five

"And now?"

Now, he didn't know. Hell, he'd planned to—what?

"I hadn't thought that far ahead," he admitted. "I hadn't thought any farther than smuggling you out of Cairo, hopping a ship to England and—and…hell." He sighed and shrugged helplessly. "I never planned to stay in England."

She jerked back, dropped his hand. "You were going to drop me off at port and leave again?"

"You don't sound surprised." Paul eyed her and wondered if she might hit him. She looked furious enough to.

"I—I am." She pressed her lips together. "And I am not."

She pulled away. Damn him and his honesty.

In the sea breeze, her scarf floated around her. For a vulnerable moment, she toyed with the ends of it, a nervous move he hadn't ever seen before.

It broke something inside him—he'd made his strong, proud Kaya so defenseless.

"I was afraid you might, but also you had promised." She broke off, struggling. "I don't know. At first, I thought you might kill me and toss me in *en-Nīl*, yes. Steal the jewels and leave my body in the desert, yes. Abandon?" She shook her head.

"You—" He cut off, incredulous. "You thought I'd kill you and *throw you in the river*?"

Kaya cleared her throat and had the decency to look abashed. "I didn't know why Gidd trusted you. Derya"—her voice broke— "she told me stories of unwary travelers."

She swayed again. Despite her obvious reluctance for his touch, Paul gathered her to him and tried not to think about how this might be the last time he held her. The thought carved a hole in his chest.

Kaya didn't shrug off his hands, which only showed him the depth of her exhaustion. It twisted through him, her weakness, her illness.

"Why have you no wish to return to England?"

Christ. He didn't want to tell her. Didn't want her to know what happened in Bombay. Certainly didn't want to relive the blood and pain and death of his last days there. Paul leaned back and let his head hit the fig tree. He deserved that pain.

"You promised to see me to England as Gidd wished. I have no desire to settle in England. Clearly, I can't travel the world by ship. However, I am perfectly capable of walking."

Paul snorted and rolled his head to the side, looking down at her. So determined, so fierce, so very Kaya. Feet crossed at the ankles, fingers brushing down her arm, he continued to stare at her. She watched him with a still steadiness that made him want to shake her. Want to see the Kaya he knew instead of the woman who'd witnessed so little in her life.

"Well, I've no desire to see England, either."

Kaya frowned, shoulders jerking. Sitting had not helped. She breathed harder. Every breath was a struggle, and simply sitting upright required all her energy. Shifting, he made room against the tree so she could lean there and steady herself.

Paul pressed the fingers of his free hand into his thigh, a futile attempt not to reach for her. He wanted to carry her back to Letizia's cottage and hold her in bed, make her rest.

At least keep her close.

"I do not understand." Kaya's fingers pressed into her own legs, and her head leaned against the tree. However, she made no move to leave neither the grove nor their conversation. "Why agree? Why promise to see me there if you have no wish to return to England?"

He ran a hand down his face and grasped for words. Not the truth, never that. Paul dropped his hand and once more looked into Kaya's dark, serious eyes. She didn't look away, didn't impatiently rush him along. As always, she waited for him to speak. To talk to her.

"Don't lie to me, Paul." Her lips pressed together for a quick moment then softened. "Please."

Trust her.

"I've broken every promise I've ever made, Kaya." The words started slow, quiet. When she waited for him to continue, Paul did so with a confidence he never expected to feel for the truth.

"Every single one. My promise to the Army, to the Company, to John and Oliver. To whomever had the misfortune to make me promise anything. I've broken them all. Oh, I don't necessarily care about my promise to the Company, those—" He clenched his jaw, teeth grinding painfully, and eyed the spilled wine.

Murdering bastards. No, he didn't regret breaking that promise. They didn't deserve his loyalty.

"I do regret breaking my promise to John." Paul scrubbed his hands through his hair and looked to the shoreline, the empty docks, the endless blue of sky and sea. Instead of the vast expanse, the calm waters and the cloudless sky, Paul saw John, that last day in Cairo, the day of his marriage to Kaya. "Maybe I'll forgive myself for that one someday. But my promise to Tahir…"

He pushed off the tree and hunched over, unable to look at her. No. He'd be honest, and he could at least look at her while offering that honesty. Paul shifted until he was kneeling in front of her, open and bare and naked.

All he was, all his secrets, spilled before her. For the first time in his life, he spoke candidly. Laid everything at her feet, his past, his hopes. His love.

"One, just one promise I thought I managed to keep."

"The one to Gidd," Kaya whispered.

"My promise to you." Paul reached out and cradled her hands. He didn't have the right to touch her, but he so desperately needed to. She grounded him. Kaya didn't pull back as he expected her to, but leaned in, her gaze steady.

"Do you remember when I told you I wasn't a good man?"

She nodded, the barest movement.

"I've done things…lied, stole. Cheated men I called friends." He paused but forced the word out. He never wanted her to know the sort of man he'd been. Before. Now, he could no longer hide from her. "Killed. Mostly because I was drunk on wine or opium." He dropped his hand but didn't move back, unable to break from her steady gaze. "I joined the Company to escape England and never looked back."

"Do you not believe your goodwill outweighs your sins?"

"I haven't enough good to outweigh the bad."

"Do you wish to?" she asked softly.

"For you? Yes." He hoped she heard the sincerity, the truth in those words. "I arrived in Cairo wanting only to rob Tahir and leave with whatever I could carry." He snorted at his naïvety. "As much gold as I could carry. That's why I snuck into your house. To rob it before Tahir arrived and signed the marriage contract."

"Oh." Kaya cleared her throat. "Why did you stay?"

"Hadn't expected to see you. Didn't think the house was occupied." He shrugged. It seemed a lifetime ago. "Seeing you there, with your knife at my back, threw me off. Then Tahir arrived, and it was too late."

"You could've said no. Refused the marriage."

Paul opened his mouth then snapped it closed. He shrugged. "I supposed I could have, but I saw you. Spoke with you. By then it was already too late."

"Oh," she whispered again.

"I had hoped keeping my promise to Tahir, keeping you safe, might balance the scales."

"Why did you leave India?" Instead of demanding an answer, her question drifted quietly between them.

Paul closed his eyes against the images of horses trampling the bodies of innocent Indians. Redcoats splattered in darker blood. Men running the hard steel of their bayonets through soft bellies.

"The Company—they ordered a massacre." Paul stopped, but it didn't dispel the images. Kaya's hand curled around his, lending him her strength. "They suspected an uprising; there'd been rumblings in the streets. They wanted more money, more food, better housing against the monsoons, better protection against French attacks."

Paul stared at their joined hands. "I didn't care about any of that. It didn't matter to me what they wanted or what the Company did or did not promise."

"You must've cared a little," she whispered. "If this haunts you."

He violently shook his head, but it dispelled nothing. A shiver raced along his skin, and Paul tightened his hand around Kaya's.

"The people, the Indians, didn't want the British there. The Company didn't care what they wanted. There *were* rumors of rebellion. But the Indians, the ones on the street that day…they only wanted food. They were starving in the streets. The Company didn't care. It—"

His voice broke. The images stayed with him. Haunted him. Taunted him.

He focused on Kaya, thin, weak, but alive. So alive. He wanted to gather her to him and hold her close, if only to block out the screams, the pleas, the terror. The crying children, the sobbing women and dead men. The blood he still smelled.

"The officers trampled their bodies in the street and *laughed*." He snarled the words, all the anger he'd felt that day finally breaking free. "They rode their horses right over them, then laughed as they butchered those people. Because they were English, and the dead were mere Indians. Not *worthy* of walking the same street as English soldiers. Eating the same food."

"Could you have stopped it?" Kaya whispered.

"What?" Paul snorted. "No. When the Company speaks, their army jumps. And oh, did they jump."

"Did you?"

"No. Yes." Paul sat on the ground, defeated. "At first, it was just another order to follow. But Basu—I saw him there. Right in front."

"Basu—this is a friend?"

"No. Yes. Well…yes." Paul tore his gaze from their hands and met hers. "Until that day, I considered him more an acquaintance. He showed me Bombay. We gambled together, visited the dens and drank together." *Whored together.* Despite his honesty, he didn't want Kaya to know that part. "Friend?" Paul moved his shoulders restlessly. "Yes."

Kaya frowned and opened her mouth, but then snapped it closed. "Continue, please."

Paul wondered if she wanted to ask about the dens or what they bet on. In fact, he'd bet every jewel in her bodice she'd been about to ask those questions. Part of him wanted the segue, wanted to tell her about the card games and dice they'd played, the *pehlwani* matches, *pulu* horse games, and cricket matches they'd won and lost money on.

He didn't give into temptation. Well, that was a first.

"I don't know what made him join the crowd. Basu— he'd never been interested in anything outside of making money and enjoying any pleasure he could find." Paul snorted. "Well matched, we were, when it came to that."

"And your other friends? John? Oliver?"

"They—we enjoyed the same things." That admission hurt. Paul hated reliving his past.

Kaya tilted her head. "I see. Basu?"

"I don't know how it started. Someone threw rotten vegetables at the major. Don't blame them there, right bastard, he was. People shouted, I'm not—I don't remember all they said." He sucked in a deep breath. The Sicilian breeze carried the memories of blood and sand and death. "We readied our guns. The officers sat on their horses. Something broke. I don't know what, the crowd, the men, I don't know."

"The army attacked."

Paul choked out a sound he couldn't identify. "They massacred them. Killed everyone. Ordered us to shoot, then laughed and trampled their dead bodies with their horses."

Bile rose in his throat, and he pressed the heels of his hands into his eyes. Basu's sightless gaze continued to taunt him. "I didn't fire, but I don't think that makes me a better person for it."

"I'm sorry."

She took his hands and held them as fiercely as she'd fought in the souk. Her eyes blazed, but her hands gentled around his. Soothing. Understanding.

"You could not file a formal complaint, follow the chain of command? Report the incident to your superiors in England?"

He frowned at her but in the next second realized how much Tahir had taught her about military tactics and organization. An amazing woman, his Kaya. "No. The Company is its own entity."

"So you left." Kaya nodded. "You may not believe it, Paul, but leaving an institution you could not keep your fealty to is the honorable thing to do."

"I deserted. There's a difference."

"Yes." She looked stricken for a moment, sick. Licking her lips, she slowly nodded. "You did. I allow, there is no honor in desertion."

Paul felt as sick as Kaya looked. Honesty was shit.

"I also admit I'm unsure how to feel about that." Kaya sighed. "My grandfather taught me many things: honor, loyalty, keeping one's word. But Derya, she taught me the difference between obeying and listening to one's heart. You chose to desert, yes, but you did not do so for frivolous reasons."

Paul opened his mouth to refute that, then stopped. "No, I suppose not. Never occurred to me to leave before then." He looked into the wood, shook his head, then met Kaya's gaze again. "Thought I'd die in Bombay. Either the drink would kill me, the dens, the disease, or I'd finally be too slow in a fight."

Kaya sucked in a breath and looked horrified. Paul wanted to ease her concerns, reassure her, but he didn't know what to say. This honesty was *hard*.

"I'm glad you left when you did," she whispered.

His lips twitched, and he kissed the backs of her hands. "Me too."

Her absolution lifted a weight he'd carried for a thousand miles. She wrapped both of her hands around his and tugged him forward.

"That's what your nightmares are about?"

The words caught, trapped behind screams and death. Broken, bleak, he met her gaze. Kaya understood. He saw it in the softening of her gaze, felt it in the squeeze of her hands around his.

"I'm sorry." She cupped his shaven cheek. "I'm so sorry, Paul."

How had they even gotten on the topic of what happened in Bombay? "Do you see, Kaya? Do you see why I'm so determined to see you to England? Tahir offered me a second chance, he offered atonement. Protect you. It was the one promise I've been determined to keep."

"Yes." She released his hand, a gentle discharge. "I respect your promise to Gidd, Paul, as I respect your need to atone for actions not your own. It is easy to follow the lead, do what others do. Not so much in going against them."

He opened his mouth to object, but she cut him off.

"I—I've come to care for you," she admitted, haltingly. "Deeply."

Was that a blush staining her cheeks? Or a fever? No, it was a blush. Paul stared, dumbfounded, at the sight. Never—not once, not even when he tasted her sex and brought her to orgasm—had he seen Kaya blush.

"You are correct in that I know very little of the world outside the walls of my home."

He had to blink several times to bring the current image of Kaya back into focus. The image of her spread out on their bed, open and passionate for him, refused to dislodge.

"What are you saying?" he demanded, annoyed he had no idea what she was talking about.

"I spoke hastily when I said that, now that we're gone from Cairo, we should part ways."

Paul's eyebrow raised, and he tried his best to hide his smirk. Probably failed in that. "You think we should continue traveling together?"

Kaya nodded, short, jerky movements. She lifted her face to the breeze and closed her eyes. Sighing, she smiled and met his gaze.

"I've—as I said, Paul…" She tried for prim and proper and failed miserably. If there was one thing Kaya was not, it was prim and proper. "I've come to care for you deeply."

"Have you now?" His grin broke free, and his heart felt the same.

Kaya scowled at him. She sniffed in disdain and tilted that pert chin of hers. "Yes."

"I'm glad to hear that." He held her face in his hands, not quite sure whether to believe this was real or a drunken—and poetic—dream.

"Why?" she challenged.

Paul pressed his lips to hers. "Because I happen to be in love with you, Kaya."

Her breath left her in a rush, her fingers clenching around his wrists. One promise he vowed never, ever, to break was to not forget her look of wide-eyed astonishment.

"I've never been in love," she whispered. "I don't know what that feels like. What I feel for you is different than what I feel for Gidd or Derya. It's a warm expanse inside me. I don't know how to describe it. I've nothing else in my life to compare it to."

"That's all right." Paul kissed her again, a soft, lazy kiss. He brushed his nose against hers, drew her close. Kaya's arms wound around his neck, and she returned the kiss.

The passion, always a burning ember between them, flared to brilliant life, but he resisted. She was still recovering from her illness. As much as he wanted to make love to her right now, beneath this tree he'd found refuge under, Paul sat beside her instead.

This wasn't about his own needs, nor even about her passion. For the first time in his life, it was about the long term. Not an elaborate ruse, but an actual relationship.

It terrified him.

Paul wrapped his arm about her shoulders and held her close. He tilted her chin up and kissed her again, deepening the kiss until nothing else mattered. It terrified him, oh yes. It made him feel more alive than he ever remembered feeling.

"Where do we go from here?" she asked.

"We'll figure it out," he promised.

Kaya nodded, her lips swollen from his, her eyes dazed. She blinked and pulled away just enough to look up at him. "You promised that before."

"And I promise to keep that promise. No matter what."

She was quiet for so long, Paul wondered if she regretted telling him of her feelings. "I believe you. I trust you. I—I love you."

"Normally I'd say you shouldn't." He rested his forehead against hers, eyes closed.

"What I feel for you—" She shook her head. "I can't explain it, but it threatens to consume me."

Paul kissed her forehead. He wrapped his arm around her shoulders. Kaya rested her head on his arm and sighed, her body relaxing against his.

"I promise not to let you down. Ever."

"You won't." She lifted his hand and kissed his fingertips. "I know you won't."

"We'll travel wherever you want. I'll show you the world."

Kaya and Paul's adventures will be continued in *Sins of a Rogue*, available January 2022. And in February 2022 look for *Smuggler's Captain*…

Nadia Koltsova escaped St. Petersburg in the dead of night, young, injured, and terrified. Ten years later, she's determined to protect the family that saved her. Even if it means sneaking into a human smuggler's warehouse in the middle of the night with only a dagger for protection.

Captain James St. Clair is searching for the same group of smugglers. They've killed one of his men and he's determined to bring the murderers to justice. He does not expect the witty, capable woman with the wicked dagger who insists she's more than capable of taking care of herself. He also doesn't expect to want her as fiercely as he does.

They both need help discovering where the missing people are located. Just perhaps not each other's help.

Sign up to my VIP list to learn more! https://bit.ly/3kSzMjI

Get a free short story!

I occasionally send newsletters with things like new releases, special offers, pictures of my dog, recipes, and other exciting news about my stories I hope you'll enjoy as much as I do.

If you sign up for my VIP list, I'll send you a free copy of my short story, *One Day with You*. This story, along with more short stories about Louise and Malcolm, are only available to my list.

https://bit.ly/3kSzMjI

Escorting a widow and her six children away from London and her husband's shady activities didn't fit Lieutenant Malcolm Sawyer's plan of infiltrating the seedier side of Dover. Tea with the lovely Lady Hélène, did. However, it was only a brief stop on his way to find proof of a suspected French invasion.

He had not imagined the lovely Louise Ardenne opening the door with a modified walking stick, ready to bludgeon him.

Louise had no time for dashing English officers. A refugee from France who traded all her possessions for safe passage across the Channel, she owed her life to Lady Hélène and had more serious business than blushing at pretty compliments. The tall, sapphire-eyed officer posed an intriguing mix of threat from arrest and an opportunity for help finding her missing father. If she didn't melt at his searing looks first.

Revolution had burned her world to the ground. Malcolm, with his honor and kisses that stole her breath, may finish the job. She's not a French spy. He doesn't trust her. An alliance is built not on trust but need, for the heat building between them and the answers they both seek amidst a world in chaos where even the closest friend could be an enemy.

Will their tentative alliance in the face of intrigue and spies be enough to convince him she is who she says? Or will her questions lead to her own death?

If you enjoyed this book...

If you enjoyed this book, I'd really appreciate it if you helped others enjoy it, too. Reviews are precious and help persuade other readers to give my romances a try. More readers equals more incentive for me to write! And so many more stories for you to read!

About the Author

C.K. Mackenzie is the author of a series of Georgian and Regency Romances following a family as they navigate life, love, and war. Find out more at her blog: ckmackenzie.blogspot.com. Connect with her on Twitter @CK_Mackenzie. If you want to email her, please do so at ckmackenzieauthor@gmail.com.

www.ingramcontent.com/pod-product-compliance
Lightning Source LLC
Chambersburg PA
CBHW031141160726
47991CB00004B/1517